Grizzly Killer
The Making of a Mountain Man

by

Lane R Warenski

Print Edition

Wolfpack Publishing
6032 Wheat Penny Avenue
Las Vegas, 89122

ISBN: 978-1-62918-636-8

Dedicated to Michael Gibson, a friend of nearly forty years, whose simple question years ago, "Have you ever thought about writing a book?" started me on this journey.

Note from the Author

This book is a work of fiction. Any resemblance to any actual person is coincidental. The town of Pottersville, Kentucky, is a product of my imagination. Any similarities with the history of an actual place were not intended. The places that Zach Connors, the main character of the book, travels are real, and the dates of the events that take place are as correct as my research can place them. There is some controversy of the exact location of the Rendezvous of 1826 held in Willow Valley, now called Cache Valley, Utah. Some historians believe it was held near the town of Cove, Utah, very near the Utah–Idaho border, while others believe it to have been held where I have placed it in the south end of Cache Valley, near the town of Hyrum, Utah. Some of the characters that attended the rendezvous in this book are real and, I believe, in attendance during the time frame that I have placed them there, but most are fictional.

The lands that this novel covers are all in Northern and Northeastern Utah, Southwestern Wyoming, and Southeastern Idaho. I have traveled all these areas throughout my life. My college days were spent at Utah State University in Cache Valley, Utah. I have tried to describe the land the characters travel through as accurately as possible.

I was born and raised in Utah and have a great love of the Intermountain West and the history of the area. I live with my wife in Duchesne County, Utah, and my home is virtually surrounded by the Ute Indian Reservation. Sitting on my front porch, I have an unrestricted view of the Uinta Mountains and the highest peaks in Utah. I have been an outdoorsman my whole life, hunting, camping, and fishing in the Uinta

Mountains that is the heart of this book. The rivers and streams were the pathways of the early trappers and explorers, and I have camped on and fished most all the streams covered in this book. I have tried to impart my love of the mountains and the history of the opening of the West into the characters and hope the reader can appreciate the strength, both physical and mental, that those we call mountain men had to possess to survive and thrive in a wilderness so far from civilization.

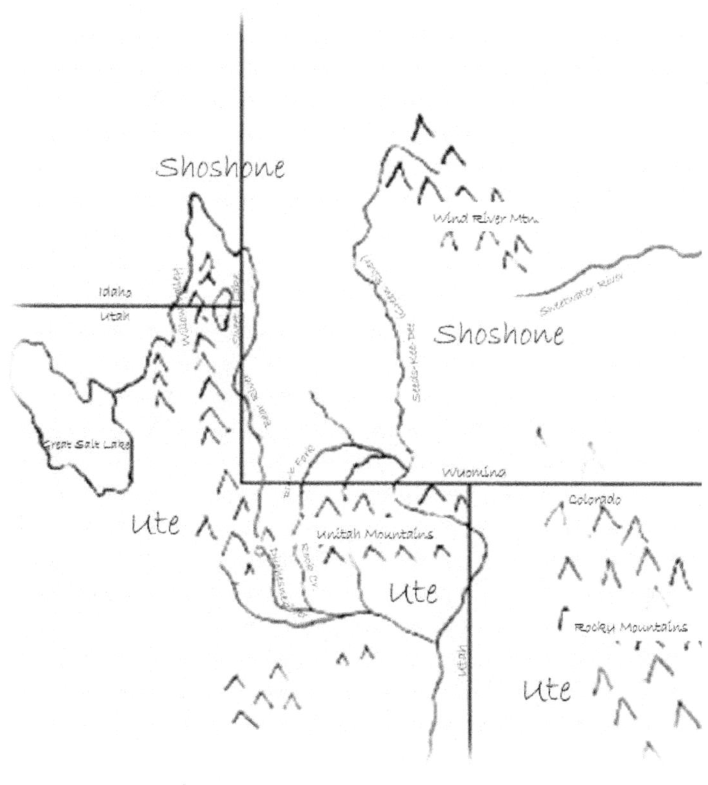
Shoshone
Idaho
Utah
Great Salt Lake
Wind River Mtn.
Sweetwater River
Shoshone
Seeds-Kee-Dee
Wyoming
Colorado
Ute
Unitah Mountains
Ute
Rocky Mountains
Utah
Ute
Piute

Chapter I

Under the Spruce

I OPENED MY EYES and lay there just listenin', not movin' a muscle. Pa had always taught me to make sure nothin' was around before I moved after I'd been asleep, so I just lay there listenin'. It was just gettin' light, and I didn't know what had woken me up. There should have been a few birds singin', but I couldn't hear a thing. I listened, and I couldn't hear Ol' Red or the horses munchin' grass either. Then I realized Jimbo wasn't lyin' by my side, but that wasn't unusual as that ol' mangy mutt liked to go out huntin' for a rabbit or squirrel this time of day for his breakfast. But not hearin' Red and no birds, I knew something was around that wasn't supposed to be.

I very slowly moved my hand and made sure my Hawken rifle was right handy and then very, very slowly slid out from under my bedroll. Now I had bedded down under the low branches of a big ol' spruce on a thick bed of pine needles that was up the hill a bit above the creek so I could move without makin' hardly a sound and almost without my movement bein' seen. But I was bein' almighty careful just the same. I had picketed Red and the horses on a nice patch of grass just across the creek. Once I got my head up, I could see Ol' Red, his ears straight ahead and his nostrils flared. He was starin' out into the meadow that was just through the willows on the other side of the creek. I couldn't see the horses as they had moved into the willows a bit. Then I heard Jimbo's low throaty growl that told me there was trouble very close by. Makin' sure my knife was still in its sheath and pickin' up my tomahawk and rifle, I started out. Stayin' in the forest where I could walk without a sound, I edged up the hill and circled around upstream from where I figured Jimbo was with his low growl. I stepped through the creek and edged through the willows, bein' real careful not to make a sound. I brought my rifle up and looked 'round the brush where I could see Jimbo standin' there with his hackles up.

Just a few feet in front of him was an Injun lyin' in the grass. He was up on one elbow with a knife in one hand and an arrow in the other. His eyes were wide, starin' right at Jimbo. Jimbo could be a mighty fearsome sight. He was big, well near two hundred pounds. He was bigger than any wolf I'd ever seen, and I think he might be part wolf, though no one will ever know for sure. He had that wild look that had come from bein' in the wilderness his whole life.

I waited there, just lookin' around that brush for a while, makin' real sure that he was alone. That Injun never moved, and neither did Jimbo. When I figured it was safe, I stepped out from behind that brush, and that Injun shifted his eyes to me but never moved a muscle, figurin' Jimbo would attack at the slightest movement. I walked up and patted Jimbo on the back and told him to stay. I could see right off that Injun was in a bad way. His right leg was black and blue from ankle to knee and was swollen to twice the size of the other. Now I figured he couldn't understand me, but I spoke anyway. And he just stared at me with a grip on that knife so tight his knuckles were white. I figured he must be in his late teens, maybe a year or two younger than me.

Now back home in Kentucky, we'd lived near a Cherokee village, and I grew up with my friends bein' from that village. I had learned a lot of sign language and picked up a lot more as me and Pa had come across the plains. So I made the sign for *friend* and laid down my rifle and told Jimbo to go lie down, and that young Injun seemed to relax, but he wasn't ready to put the knife down yet.

I walked back and got my water pouch from my pack and filled it with freshwater from the creek. I went back and set the water pouch down for his easy reach and then went out and gathered some good, dry tinder and small branches for a fire. I set up that fire where he could get some warmth from it and struck a spark into the dry tinder. Within just a while, I had an almost-smokeless fire started. Now he had been crawlin' an' draggin' that leg down through this meadow and, the way he looked, must have been movin' like that most of the night. When he could feel the warmth from the fire, he relaxed even more, and after a little while, he dropped his hand holdin' his knife. I picked up the water pouch and offered it to him, and he set down the knife, took the pouch, and drank. When he had drunk his fill, he handed the pouch back to me and picked up his knife and put it in its sheath. I noticed then that the sheath was a work of art, decorated with quills and braided horse hair. He brought his quiver, with eight or ten arrows still in it, over his shoulder and put the arrow he had been holdin' in the other hand back in it, and I noticed the quiver was decorated with the same pattern as his sheath. This was a young man that took pride in his work.

Jimbo was just lyin' there at the other side of the fire but not lettin' that Injun out of his sight, and I could tell that was makin' him plumb nervous. I told Jimbo with a hand signal to go scout the area, and he took off, silent as a ghost, and I figured he would be gone awhile.

Ol' Red had gone back to grazin', and I walked back over to my pack and brought it over by the fire and got out the makin's for breakfast. I still had some flour, salt, coffee beans, and a little salt pork left. So I put some coffee beans in a tin cup and set it on the edge of the fire to roast. I filled the coffee pot with water and set it on the coals, and in my one fry pan, I started some pan biscuits. When the water was ready, I crushed the coffee beans with the back of my tomahawk and put them in the pot.

This young Injun was watchin' me like I was crazy, but he never made a sound. When the biscuits were done, I sliced some of the salt pork into the pan and fried it. I poured a cup and handed it to the Injun and set two biscuits and a couple of slices of the pork on a tin plate and set it down right by him and then did the same for myself. He picked up the plate and sniffed the pork. I started eatin', and after he watched me for a minute, he did the same. Now I don't know just what he thought of the grub, but he ate it all, and I cleaned up and put it all back in the pack. I hoped he was startin' to trust me just a little by now.

I pointed to myself and said, "Zach." I repeated this several times until I knew he understood my name. Then I asked his. I had to ask several times, but then in passable English, he said his name was Running Wolf and he was a Ute warrior.

I got down by his leg and asked if I could look at it, and with a very worried look on his face, he slowly nodded. I very carefully slid off his moccasin and ran my hand up over the swollen leg and could feel the break in the bone under my fingers. Now I'm no doctor, but I had helped Pa set an arm bone on a neighbor back home and helped him again set a broken leg on a calf, and both had healed up just fine. So I went to lookin' for some good, straight sticks and some thick bark I could strip off. I had a couple of deer hides in my pack and got one of those out and cut it into strips. I carefully slid him over to a tree and had him hold on to a low branch while I made him understand I had to pull his leg out straight. I offered him a stick to put between his teeth, but he refused. I set the bark and splint sticks beside his leg, and putting one hand on his heel and one on the top of his foot, I looked into his eyes and nodded. He was goin' pale, but he nodded, and I pulled. I felt the bone go into place, and although he was the color of a cloud on a bright, sunny day, he never made a sound. He was breathin' very heavy as I wrapped his leg with the bark and wrapped the splints on the outside of the bark with the deer hide. He laid his head back onto the ground, closed his eyes, and tried to control his breathin'. That he was in extreme pain, I had no doubt.

Jimbo had been gone quite awhile, and I was ponderin' on just what he had found. I wondered just what had happened to Runnin' Wolf as well. But with the pain, I knew he must be in. I figured talkin' could wait a bit. I was mighty curious how he knew English as well.

Ol' Red was a big red Kentucky mule that could work a plow, carry a pack or saddle, and be a mighty, fearsome fighter whether fightin' Injuns or wolves, and he had done both and had come out ahead each time. For bein' a mule, he wasn't too hardheaded either, as long as he knew and liked you. But he was quite particular who rode and who packed him, but a surer-footed animal was never born.

While Runnin' Wolf was tryin' to relax after his ordeal, I saddled Ol' Red and started down Runnin' Wolf's back trail. Three or four miles down the trail, I found his horse, and when I saw the arrows sticking out of his side and the tumble Runnin' Wolf had taken, I had a hard time figurin' just how he had dragged himself that far. When I saw the broken bow, I wondered why these other warriors hadn't moved in and finished the job and just where they were now. Just then, Jimbo come paddin' up the trail. It was clear he had found something he didn't like, and I decided we'd best haul our hides out of there. I broke off one of those arrows that were stickin' out of that Injun pony and jumped up on Red, and we struck a lope back up the trail.

Runnin' Wolf heard us comin' as I was hurryin', not at all tryin' for quiet, and he had his knife in hand and a very determined look on his face as I approached. I threw the broken arrow down at him as I wasn't at all happy 'bout his leadin' several warriors out for blood right to me. He picked it up and made the sign for *snake*. So here I was, bein' a nursemaid to a Ute and now bein' followed by God only knows how many Snake Warriors. I figured now was time for some explainin'.

I asked how he learned to speak English. He told me that last year, a group of trappers had come into his village and stayed a few days and had bought some horses from them, and when they left, he went with them to care for their horses and to show them where there were beaver. He stayed with them for six moons, and he learned their talk. When the leaves turned, he went back to his village to help with the fall hunt and get ready for winter. He said his sister was alone, and he had to provide for her, since her man was killed.

Now if I had any sense at all, I would just load up and hit the trail just as fast as I could go, but I just couldn't make myself do it. I hadn't had much real schoolin', but Ma had taught me to read and write, and most of those lessons were right out of the Bible. Ma had been a real God-fearin' woman, and I was raised my whole life with the Bible stories. Pa wasn't near the prayin'-type Ma was, but he believed in God. To Pa, a man's word was his bond. I remembered the last words Pa had said to me: "Son, always treat people the way you want to be treated. Remember who you are, and be proud of your name. Never do anything that won't make yourself proud. Be kind to all until you have to fight, then fight to win. In a fight, you must always win to survive in this wild and harsh land." Now I know there're some who don't consider Injuns people, but I'm not one of them. Growin' up with my friend's bein' Cherokee, I knew they were no different than us. They just have different ways and beliefs.

Chapter II

The Grizzly

I HAD LOST Pa last fall on a creek above Black's Fork on the north slope of these Bear River Mountains. We were out checkin' our traps. He went down from camp, and I went up. I was maybe a mile above camp, just entering a long meadow. The sun was just hittin' the grass from over the ridge when I got there, and I was really lookin' forward to the warmth that late-fall sun would provide, as it was gettin' real cold in the mornin's, and we had been breakin' ice on the edges of the beaver ponds.

When I heard the shot, I figured that Pa could have just taken a deer or elk, but I didn't think so as we had plenty of meat in camp to last us for a while. I hightailed it back down the trail, goin' right through camp without even slowin' down. I made sure I had fresh powder in my pan, and 'bout a half mile below camp, I slowed right down. I didn't want to go runnin' right into an ambush or whatever other trouble Pa had come upon. I came around a bend in the trail, and I could see this huge ol' grizzly lyin' right in the trail. My heart fell as I saw Pa's upper half sticking out from under that big ol' bear. I approached real careful and could see Pa's eyes were open, and the bear wasn't movin' at all. I could see Pa was in a lot of pain, but when he saw me, he smiled and, through gritted teeth, said, "Get this smelly beast off me."

It took some considerable doin' as this ol' grizzly was what I figured to be near eight hundred pounds. But when I got him rolled off Pa and I could see all the blood, my heart just fell. Pa's left arm was near ripped off.

I took off my capote and used it to stop the bleeding the best I could, but I was hurtin' him something awful. He said he was gettin' lightheaded and he didn't have much time left, said it was all right, that he was goin' to see Ma, and then he kind of faded off. A little while later, his eyes opened, and he said the pain had gone. Then he told me that I was a grown man and he was mighty proud to be my pa. He said, "I fought that ol' grizz with gun and knife, but we both lost that fight." I could tell he was gettin' weaker by the minute, and his eyes were gettin' heavy. Then he told me what he did 'bout bein' proud and 'bout fightin' to win. Then he gripped my hand, closed his eyes, and just faded off to sleep. Only I could tell this sleep he wouldn't wake from.

I just sat there, tears runnin' down my face for the longest time. I watched the pink fade from the high fluffy clouds as they moved slowly across the bluest sky I had ever seen. A doe with twin fawns came out of the willows along the creek and started to graze. I watched a pair of marmots crawl out on the sunny side of a rock outcroppin' so they could soak up the warmth of the mornin' sun. I heard geese and looked up to see several flocks headin' south in their familiar V-shaped flight. I could smell the pine on the hills around me, and I watched the birds flutter through the willow branches and a red-tailed hawk survey the world from above. I watched a gray fox sneak down the far side of the creek and get a quick drink then disappear just as quickly as he had appeared. I thought of all the life around me and just how fast it could be taken away. I thought of Pa and me sittin' around the fire this mornin', havin' coffee, and how we had planned out our day. Before I realized how long it had been, the sun was well past center sky, and I knew I had a lot of work to do.

The hardest thing I'd ever done was bury Pa that afternoon. I found a spot on the western edge of a meadow that the creek ran through just below camp, where the mornin' sun would hit first thing and he had a good view of the mountains and this little valley the creek ran through. This was the prettiest spot I could find. He could see the snowcapped peaks way up above the timberline, the dark green of the pines, and the golden yellow of the quakies. He would be able to see the wildflowers across the meadow in the spring and could hear the gentle rush of the creek as it cascaded down toward Black's Fork and eventually to the Seeds-Kee-Dee.

Some of the trappers at Rendezvous were callin' the Seeds-Kee-Dee the Green River, but most still called it by its Injun name. It was well after dark when I finished, but I just sat there next to his grave. I couldn't bring myself to leave. Pa wasn't only my pa; he was my friend. We had been close my whole life. The only thing that made it easier at all was the thought of him bein' with Ma again.

The moon was just startin' to peak over the ridge, when I realized how late it was gettin', and I figured the horses and mules would be gettin' mighty thirsty by now. I went back to camp and took the mules and horses to water then hobbled them out on the meadow where there was enough graze for a large herd. I was tired, bone-tired, and didn't feel hungry though I hadn't eaten since early morn. I realized then I was mighty cold, just wearin' my buckskins, but I didn't feel like buildin' a fire, so I just crawled into my bedroll and lay there, thinkin' till I finally drifted off to sleep.

Next mornin' I woke just as the sky was turnin' light gray along the eastern ridge, and I just lay there, listenin', makin' sure everything sounded normal before I moved. I realized then how much I had depended on Pa's ears and eyes and just how much he had taught me. I hoped I had learned well enough.

Since I could hear the stock munchin' grass and some birds singin' along the creek, I knew all was well.

I made coffee, and when I poured a cup, tears came to my eyes again as I remembered Pa always sayin' how good the coffee smelled in the mornin's. As I sat there, sippin' that coffee, I planned out my day just like me and Pa had always done, and I realized I had the work of two to do. I had to get to my traps and find all of Pa's. I had a big ol' grizzly to skin, and now his body had cooled. That would be a tough job. But I could use that hide and the grease that bear would provide. I didn't feel like trappin' on this creek anymore, so I needed to move camp back down to our dugout on Black's Fork where me and Pa were plannin' on spendin' the winter. With only me doin' the work, it would take twice as long.

By the time I had gathered my ten traps, I had two beaver to skin. I got that out of way as quickly as I could and started downstream where Pa had set his traps. It took me the better part of the afternoon to find all of Pa's traps, and then I had three more beaver to skin and all five of them to stretch on the willow frames. Pa would have been mighty pleased we already had two packs bundled and in the cache and had twenty more dryin' on willow frames in camp. It was late in the day when I had these other three skinned, so I figured that grizzly could wait till mornin'.

Back in camp, I stretched those beaver skins—or plews, as they were known to the trappers—on new willow frames we had made a couple of days before and set them on the rack to dry with the others. I checked on the stock and took them to water. Then realizin' I hadn't eaten in two days, I decided I was hungry. I cut a good chunk off a deer haunch we had hangin' way up off the ground from a tree branch a ways from camp to keep bears or other critters from it, and I set it over the coals on a green willow branch stuck in the ground. I set coffee on and made some biscuits in our fry pan. Biscuits made with bear grease are kind of different, but once you get used to them, they're pretty good. I'd done most of the cookin' once we left home, and by now, I thought I was gettin' pretty good at it, though it probably didn't take much to please just me and Pa.

Next mornin', after coffee, leftover deer, and a biscuit, I headed down to start on that bear. When I got there, the tears came back, and I got all choked up, but I knew the best way to honor Pa was to get on with what had to be done. That bear had five-inch claws, and he was big. It took all day long to skin that beast and scrape the hide, and I made sure I got all the claws. That hide was huge and must have weighed over a hundred pounds by itself.

Next mornin', I went down to the meadow where Pa's grave was, and in a big ol' quakie that was right behind the grave, I carved him sort of a head stone.

Pa had been called Captain Jack by everyone that knew him since his days of leadin' emigrant trains from the east over the mountains to the western frontier in Kentucky and Tennessee. He had always been called Jack 'cause he had the same name as his pa, and he told me they called him Jack as long as he could remember. I thought 'bout home and smiled inside with all those folks back there thinkin' they was livin' on the western frontier and they had crossed mountains to get there. If they could see these shinin' mountains reachin' for the sky and just how big this western frontier really was, they would know they had just crossed some hills and got just to the edge of the wilderness.

I went back and broke camp, brought up Red and Jenny, the mules, and got them and then the horses packed. Pa's horse, Buck, was a big ol' buckskin gelding, a full sixteen hands high and was broke to the saddle but had never had a pack on before and didn't seem very happy 'bout all those plews still dryin' in their frames, bouncin' along his sides. But after a little friendly persuasion, he must have decided it was in his best interest to behave, 'cause he settled down. He still didn't seem happy, but he went along without too much more fuss. Bell was mine. She was just fifteen hands and was as good a mountain horse as you will find. She was a right pretty strawberry roan and had a gait that was like sittin' in a rockin' chair and could stay with a lope 'bout all day. I figured we were 'bout twenty-five miles from the dugout and hoped to make it 'fore nightfall.

It was just after dark when we got there, and I didn't waste any time unloadin' the stock and turnin' them out into the pole corral me and Pa had put up. There was still plenty of grass for them, and they all just went to rollin' in the dust. I went in the dugout and got a fire started and just looked around a minute. I was still fightin' that low-down feelin', and my eyes would get misty every time I thought of Pa not bein' here anymore.

It didn't take long for that dugout to warm up. We had dug out a good bit of dirt from the hillside where it came down fairly close to the stream and had stacked logs out 'bout another ten feet. There was a lot of down timber on that hillside, and we just dragged it down and had a roof of solid logs as well. We covered the roof with pine boughs real thick and shoveled dirt over it all. We used mud from along the stream and chinked them between the logs on the sides. It sure didn't look like much, but it would keep out the wind and stay warm. There were miles of meadow grass along the stream, and we figured we couldn't find a better spot to spend the winter.

Chapter III

Jimbo

IT WAS GETTIN' to be close to the middle of November, and I hadn't seen a livin' soul since we left Rendezvous down on Burnt Fork in July. The year was 1825 and I, at twenty years old, had been in the mountains just a little over a year, and I was alone, lookin' at spendin' a mighty cold, long winter by myself. Pa had been an explorer, mountain man, and trapper most of his life, and I sure hoped I learned all his lessons well enough. We had been preparin' ever since we found this spot. The dugout was finished, and we had the pole corral to hold the stock close by. We had dug a cache down a ways from the dugout to hold the plews till next rendezvous and had built a very strong small smokehouse out of solid logs that we figured would keep a bear out of our stored meat.

We had been outfitted mighty well by General Ashley at the Rendezvous as payment for helpin' him bring all his supplies from St. Louis. He had tried to get us to sign on with his Rocky Mountain Fur Company and spend the next couple of years with his brigades, but Pa told him we would rather go it on our own. I had been huntin' all fall, along with the trappin', and I had enough dried and smoked meat to get the two of us through the winter, and we had picked berries that grew in abundance along the creeks. I hated taking the time to pick berries. It seemed to me the time it took to get a hat full just wasn't worth it, but Pa insisted, sayin' we couldn't survive on meat alone. We would spread the berries out on a hide to dry in the sun. And I had to admit they were pretty good.

I had a large bag of salt, a couple of bags of cornmeal, a couple of bags of flour, a small bag of bakin' powder, and a small one of sugar, along with several pounds of coffee beans. I had no idea how long they would last 'cause the pack rats and mice became a lot more troublesome than bears. So I shoveled dirt high up around the dugout to keep them from diggin' under the logs, and I made overlapping rawhide strips around the door to try to keep 'em out. I sewed together rawhide bags for the cornmeal, flour, and sugar and hung them from rawhide strips from the roof logs to make it harder for them critters to get to.

The mornin' after I got back to the dugout, I staked out that bear hide and got set to workin' on gettin' it tanned. I stripped that grizzly skull clean and set it on a pole by the side of the dugout door. Then I took a good look around and could see right off I needed a lot more firewood. I'd also seen where some critter had been tryin' to get into the smokehouse, but I didn't recognize the tracks. He had sprayed a scent like an ol' tomcat all around the smokehouse, and it wasn't a pleasant smell. So I grabbed four traps and set them up around where the tracks were the thickest, thinkin' if he came back, I'd find out just what it was. Then I saddled Ol' Red and spent the rest of that and the next two days draggin' deadfall logs off the hill to add to my firewood supply and workin' that bear skin. It was a mighty thick skin and was gonna take some time.

I didn't have a stone wheel to keep my ax sharp like we had back home, so I looked along the stream till I found a stone with a texture I thought would work and brought it back and built a little stand for it, then went to work tryin' to put an edge on the ax. I stacked my cut firewood out a ways from the dugout. Pa had said he'd seen many a cabin back home burned by the Shawnee by settin' fire to the woodpile that was stacked right up against the cabin. He said walkin' a few extra steps for wood beat loosin' your home and maybe your hair.

A fortnight or so after I had returned, I had the plews all buried in the cache with the rest of them. I had what I hoped was enough firewood, but if I started to run low, there was enough deadfall close enough I figured me and Ol' Red could drag more down even if the snow got bad. I had my grub supplies stored as good as I could think how to store them and had that grizzly hide startin' to get right soft. It made a right warm coverin' over my bedroll.

That critter had been back to the smokehouse two more times, and each time, he had set every one of my traps off without gettin' caught. I was gettin' real tired of bein' outsmarted by some four-legged critter from the wild. So I took all twenty traps—Pa and me each had ten—and set them all the way around the little smokehouse, and then I built a couple of snares like the Cherokee used back home. Two of the traps I set on the trail I figured he was usin' and then built a snare on each side of it, right off the side of the traps.

Two nights later, I heard an awful commotion. The moon was up, so I could see pretty good, and I grabbed my rifle and headed out there. He had his head in a snare, and when that snare sprung, he must have been dancin' around, tryin' to get free, and stepped into the trap in the trail. By the time I got there, the snare had choked the life right out of him, and although I'd heard stories 'bout them, this was the first wolverine I had ever seen. That hide was gonna make me the finest-lookin' hat in the mountains.

It was gettin' on to the end of November, and I was thinkin' a lot 'bout Ma and Pa and home and 'bout the Thanksgiving turkeys we always had. Now I had brought home the turkey every year since I was 'bout ten years old. But there were no turkeys in this country, so I figured a prairie chicken would have to do. I saddled Bell and, with my squirrel gun in hand, went huntin' a prairie chicken.

Now off many miles to the north, there were miles upon endless miles of sagebrush, and I headed there, for we hardly ever went through that area without jumping those big prairie chickens. They were two or three times bigger than the pine hens in the forest above the dugout. I was out on these sage flats several miles, when I came upon a wide, shallow draw. I tied Bell to a bush and had walked but a quarter mile when I saw some chickens strutin' through the sage just ahead of me. I sat down and took a good rest on my knee and shot the head off the one closest to me. I could have never made a shot like that with Pa's Harpers Ferry rifle. It just wasn't that accurate. It hit a lot harder, but this .36-caliber squirrel gun was the best-shootin' rifle I'd ever seen. Maybe the Hawken could have done it, but I didn't have the experience with it yet. I had just won it in a shootin' match at the Rendezvous, and I had been shootin' this squirrel gun since I was big enough to hold it.

I started back to the dugout and hadn't traveled far when I saw smoke off to the east. I had no idea who might be out there, so I was a might worried. Had they heard my shot? Not wantin' to be seen but really wantin' to know who was in the area, I headed for the smoke. I stopped Bell a mile or so from where I thought it was comin' from and, on foot, very carefully moved up the ridge above them. They were camped in some cottonwoods along what I figured was Ham's Fork. It looked to be a huntin' party of what I figured were Snake Injuns. They had some game hangin' and weren't wearin' paint. But I figured any Injuns could turn into a war party mighty quick if they found a white man alone in their lands. I backed off that ridge, and when I got back to Bell, I headed due west at a good lope, hopin' to make them think I was headin' for the Bear River.

I loped Bell west for a good five or six miles then turned south up over a rocky ridge where I figured it would be pretty hard to follow my tracks. All the way back, I made the trail as hard to follow as I could, back trackin', stayin' to rocky ground where I could, and walkin' in the stream where possible. But what worried me most were the tracks I had made leavin' the dugout; they lead straight back. I wouldn't make that mistake again.

I never heard or seen a thing all the way back, but I knew that didn't mean I was in the clear, for those tracks of Bell's would be there till the next storm. Two days later, when I thought I was maybe in the clear, I was sittin' out front, peelin' some cattail roots I was goin' to use for potatoes, when an arrow stuck in the log I was sittin' on. My knife and the cattail root went flyin' as I went over the log backward. I had a rifle in hand and was tryin' to find a target, when two more arrows came in. One nicked the fur of my wolverine cap, which was way too close for comfort. I fired the Hawken at the bush the arrow had come from and heard the solid wump of a hit. I rolled to the door and slipped inside just as an arrow hit the door. I had the squirrel gun and Pa's Harper Ferry rifle both loaded and by the door. I saw one Injun tryin' to crawl up 'tween a rock and willow on this side of the stream, and I let go with Pa's rifle. I heard a muffled cry, but I knew it wasn't a solid hit. Now I had the squirrel gun, and I guess they had had enough. As one thought he was out of range, he just stood up, raised his bow, and yelled a taunting curse. He was out 'bout 150 yards, and I fired. His taunting yell was cut right off as he doubled over and fell to the ground. I was lookin' mighty hard as I reloaded the three rifles, but I never saw another one. I didn't step out for a long time, just makin' sure they were gone. I had fired three shots and had hit three Injuns, two of whom, I figured, were either dead or dyin', and the other I thought I had just winged, but it had cost them dearly to attack Zach Connors.

When I stepped out of the dugout to look around, my heart just 'bout stopped, for then I could see their plan. While the three had come at me head-on, others had sneaked around the side and had taken the stock, all four of them. I was afoot and more than a thousand miles from any civilized settlement. I knew there was no way I could catch a well-mounted huntin' or war party on foot, and I figured they would take their dead and wounded back to their village as fast as they could. I just stood there and stared off into the horizon and wondered just what would become of me. Then I saw where that arrow had struck the log I was sittin' on, and a chill went through me when I saw that if that arrow had been just an inch or so higher, I would have lost my manhood.

It was still a couple of hours till dark, and I had completely lost my hunger. Pa had always said, "It doesn't matter what happens. What matters is how you handle it." Well, I had no idea how to handle this. But I did know feelin' sorry for myself wasn't the answer. So I had to make a plan . . . a plan . . . maybe tomorrow I would think of something.

Then just before dark, I heard the bray of a mule, and when I looked out, Ol' Red was crossin' the stream, headed right for me. I don't know when I'd seen a better sight. I had said before he was right particular who rode or packed him, and those Snake Warriors must have found that out. We had us a right happy reunion, Ol' Red and me.

I picketed Red right by the door of the dugout that night, and early the next day, I saddled up, takin' all three rifles and Pa's horse pistol. We headed out followin' those Injuns. The trail led right back to their camp on Ham's Fork. I thought they were gone, and bein' mighty careful, I rode down into their camp. I could see by the tracks where they had tried to load Red. The ground, with a couple of inches of snow on it, was churned up something awful, and there was blood all around. The way it looked, Red had bloodied one of them up pretty good with his hooves then broke loose and ran straight back to the dugout.

I heard something behind me and jumped around with rifle up, only to see a half-starved half-grown pup lookin' at me. I took a step toward him, and he just cowered down like he was gonna get beat and whimpered. I pulled a piece of jerky out of my pocket, broke off a piece, and threw it to him. He wolfed it right down and took a step toward me, and I saw the limp. Talkin' real soft and with a piece of jerky in hand, I slowly approached the pup and let him sniff the back of my hand and gave him another piece of the jerky. I reached down and rubbed his ears, talkin' all the time, and when he figured I wasn't gonna hurt him, I moved my hand down his sore leg. It didn't feel broke, more like he had been kicked and had a severe bruise. I gave him another piece of jerky and figured the Injuns had left him 'cause he couldn't keep up, and they had left in a hurry. Lookin' at the tracks, it looked like there were three on their feet, one they had on a travois, and two or three others were slung over the backs of horses. I had to smile, thinkin' of them tryin' to throw a dead Injun on the back of Ol' Red. I didn't know for sure, but I thought I had killed two of them, and Red had taken out another one. They got two horses and a mule out of it, but it had cost them mighty dearly.

Now they knew where my dugout sat, but at the high cost they had paid, I didn't think they would be back. Injuns put a mighty high value on good or bad medicine, and mine was mighty good in their eyes right now. I had the sign of the grizzly by the door of the dugout, and I wore a necklace of grizzly claws. Six or seven Snake Warriors had attacked one man and stole the stock, but only three had ridden away. I surely had powerful medicine in the eyes of the Snake people.

By this time, that pup was followin' me around, and I reached down and picked him up. It was real clear he was just a pup, but when I picked him up, he must have weighed fifty pounds. I got him settled across my knees and started Red back to the dugout. Red was pretty nervous at first, but as I talked, he seemed to accept the pup up on his back. As we headed back to the dugout, I followed an indirect route as I didn't want to make a plain trail, although with the wind pickin' up out of the north and it lookin' like it would snow before long, any sign of the trail would soon be gone. I talked to the pup and Red all along the way, and by the time we got back, I figured we were all friends.

When I rode up to the dugout, I set the pup down and got a good chunk of elk I had roasted a couple of days earlier and gave it to him then pulled the saddle off Red and rubbed him down with some dry grass. I picked up the Hawken and led him out to the meadow so he could graze awhile, but I was standin' guard while he was grazin'. It would be a long time before I felt things were back to normal, and I was gonna watch over him any time he wasn't right by the dugout. The snow wasn't deep yet, and the grass was still sticking through it, so he wasn't havin' a tough time gettin' plenty to eat. But I knew it wouldn't be too long before he would really have to work to paw down through the snow to the grass.

While Red was grazin', that pup limped out to where I was standin', and we just stood there together, watchin' the clouds lower up against the high peaks until they couldn't be seen, and although it was already cold, the temperature just kept droppin'. The dark pine timber up on the ridges was slowly fadin' out of sight, and the wind was gettin' downright fearsome. There was a norther blowin' in, and I figured this was gonna to be the real start of winter. I let Red graze until I was froze to the bone, and Red didn't seem to mind at all when I led him back to the dugout. And that pup stayed right with me the whole time. I tied Red on the side on the dugout, out of the wind, as I didn't trust the corral any longer, and went in to start a fire and get my own supper. It was real plain that pup hadn't ever been allowed inside a lodge before, and it took some coaxin' to get him to come in. I got a fire started and coffee on then went to fixin' some grub. I had a couple of hard biscuits left, and I cut some slices off a smoked deer haunch and started fryin' them in some bear grease. When they were done enough, I threw a small handful of flour in the pan, stirred it up, and added water and had a nice, thick gravy. I set one of the strip steaks on a tin plate and poured gravy over it and set it down for the pup. The way he went after that, I think I had made a friend for life. After the minute or so it took him to lick the plate clean, he just curled up in front of the fireplace and slept.

The wind howled throughout the night, and I kept a little wood fed into the fire to keep the worst of the chill out. When we got up the next mornin', there were two feet of fresh snow with drifts four and five feet deep, and it was bitter cold, a cold that made your breath freeze as soon as it hit the air, a cold that burned your skin. I bundled up and went out and checked on Red. He had stomped a good-sized spot clear of the snow and seemed to be all right. I knew then it was gonna be a mighty rough winter. I had what I thought was enough grub, dependin' on how much I had to feed that pup, and plenty of furs for warm clothing. Me and Pa had had a great fall trappin' season. I still had my wool capote and Pa's and my bedrolls. I felt I was prepared for winter, but I knew it would still be mighty hard. With the pup here now, I wasn't all alone, and that made me feel better.

With all that had happened over the last two days, I had fairly forgot 'bout my Thanksgiving dinner I had planned, but that prairie chicken was hung outside the dugout and was frozen solid. I brought it in to thaw then bundled up as best I could, and me and the pup took Red out to graze. I had the rifle in one hand and the spade in the other and led Red a couple of hundred yards from the dugout to where the snow had blown off some to drift up against the willows along the stream. Red went to scapin' at the ground with his hooves, and I went at it with the spade, and before long, we had a pretty good patch of grass uncovered. By the time Red had eaten enough, my toes were so cold they hurt, and I knew then I had to make much warmer moccasins.

After we got back inside and my feet were thawed again, I made up some cornbread and put a little extra sugar and some of the dried berries in it. I put that prairie chicken on a spit over the fire and would turn it every few minutes, and 'bout the time it was gettin' done, I put coffee to boilin'. Well, this sure wasn't like our dinners had been back home, but it tasted mighty good to me. But it brought back a lot of memories, and I started to get to that low-down alone feelin' again. So to shake that feelin', I started to play with the pup. His sore leg was gettin' much better, and the limp was 'bout gone, and I decided he had to have a name. Well, I talked it over with him for quite a while, askin' him what name he liked best, tryin' all sorts of names on him to see what seemed to fit. He seemed to raise his ears some when I said Jimbo, so that was what we settled on.

Chapter IV

The Wolves

AS THE NEXT few weeks went by, winter settled in, and the dugout, bein' dark and glum inside, became like a jail to me and Jimbo. We looked forward to our daily tromps out through the meadow, takin' Ol' Red to graze. The stream had frozen over, and I had to chop through the ice to get water for us all to drink. I cleared an area in front of the dugout of snow and built a fire pit. I banked rocks up a foot and a half high on the outside edge so it would reflect heat back to the logs of the dugout, and Jimbo and me would set out there while it was light, and I worked on makin' buckskins and keepin' what I had repaired. I made several pairs of moccasins and rubbed them down with bear grease to help keep the water and snow from soakin' in so fast. I found I needed several pairs, so when one got wet, I had a dry pair to change into. I had made some of them with the fur side in and three layers thick on the bottom, and just by tryin' different things, I came up with a pattern that kept my feet warm. I had learned to make moccasins back home from the Cherokees, but they didn't need to make them as warm as they needed to be out here in these high western mountains.

The days grew mighty short, and I figured it must be near Christmas, so I went out and cut down a small pine and bought it down and set it up just outside the door. I had no poppin' corn to put on a string like we did back home, or any candles but, I had the tree, and that made me feel better. I made a collar for Jimbo and a new halter for Red out of elk hide.

I sure wished I still had some of the buffalo hide from those ol' shaggy beasts we shot comin' across the plains from St. Louis. If I had only known then just how useful they would be, I sure would have kept some. But they were so full of ticks and gray backs we cut out the best meat and the tongues and just let the rest lie.

Jimbo was growin' so much, and he was gettin' so big I doubled the elk hide for his collar and stitched along the edges with rawhide. I took three of the grizzly claws off my necklace and put them on the collar. I figured it wouldn't be much of a surprise for either of them 'cause they had watched me make them, but they wasn't gonna get them till Christmas mornin' anyhow.

By now I was gettin' a might tired of eatin' just smoked and dried meat and biscuits. I wanted some fresh meat, slow roasted over the fire for Christmas. So I saddled Ol' Red and tied the two older rifles to the saddle, along with the horse pistol, and with the Hawken across my knees, we started down along the stream just to see what we could see. Goin' through some of those drifts was pretty tough, but Ol' Red must have been as tired of bein' cooped up as me and Jimbo, 'cause he just plowed on through them and even acted like he was enjoyin' it.

It was a bright, sunny day, and the temperature had mellowed out a bit. The air was so clear you could see mountain peaks that must be a hundred miles away. You could see snow driftin' off the high peaks of the Bear River Mountains behind us and dark bands of pines standin' out against the stark white of the snow. We jumped a pair of bald eagles from the cottonwoods along the stream just below the dugout, and Jimbo scared out several snowshoe hares from the thickets over on the edge of the hill. The last one he caught and brought it back just as proud as he could be. I hurried and stripped the hide off it and gave it back to him to show him he could get his own food, and he wolfed it right down. He was learnin' mighty fast.

After a while, that bright sun got my eyes burnin', and I pulled that wolverine cap down halfway over my eyes, and that seemed to help. We were maybe four or five miles downstream from the dugout, when I saw a spot of black in the snow, just out from a patch of willows. I stopped and just let Red stand next to a cottonwood and told Jimbo to stay. We had been workin' on that ever since I'd found him. I crossed over to the other side of the stream, keepin' the trees and willows between me and that spot. I started toward it, movin' real slow and quiet. The snow was soft, so bein' quiet was easy. When I was down far enough that I figured I was 'bout across from it, I started sneakin' down through the willows and found a trail that was packed down with moose tracks. Movin' ever so slowly, I eventually got to the edge, and maybe seventy yards up the hill was lyin' a big ol' bull moose. His horns must have been four feet across. Movin' just as slow and careful as I could, I brought the Hawken up to my shoulder and eased back the hammer. I took a good aim and, just then, remembered I hadn't checked the powder in the pan. I always kept the pans primed with frizzen cover in place, but I had been taught my whole life to check the pan before I make that shot. That moose was lookin' right at me, and I didn't dare move. Then he stood and I squeezed the trigger, and that Hawken jumped back against my shoulder, and that moose took three or four bounds through the snow and went down to his knees. It took me under a minute to reload, and I fired again, and he just laid his big ol' head down and didn't move again. I reloaded again just as fast as I could and just waited there a few minutes to make sure he was down for good.

I approached him real careful and used the end of the Hawken to poke his hind end a couple of times just to make sure he was dead, stayin' as far away from his head gear as possible. When he didn't move, I whistled real loud and went to work dressin' him out. Besides the meat, I needed that good, thick hide, so I just started to skin him at the same time. In just a minute, Jimbo was with me, and Red came up just a few minutes later. I used Red to help pull the hide off, then with it laid on the snow, I went to cuttin' the meat off the bones. When I had as much of it on the hide as I thought Red could pull, I tied it up, and we headed back to the dugout. I had left over half of the meat back there on the carcass, so I planned on a return trip just as soon as I could. I got the meat hangin' back in camp and headed back for the rest of it. Draggin' that hide was just like pullin' a sled on the snow.

Before we got in sight of the moose carcass, Jimbo started to growl, and Red was gettin' real nervous. I slowed down and kept the Hawken ready as we moved ahead. When we rounded the last bend, all the hair on Jimbo's back was sticking up, and he had a real soft, low growl just rollin' out from way down in his throat, and Ol' Red was tense, with eyes and ears straight ahead. Then I could see four wolves feeding on the carcass. Jimbo was gettin' mighty big, but he was no way a match for four wolves. But I figured my rifles were, so I told Jimbo to stay, and I just charged right at 'em, screamin' like a banshee. When they saw me and that ol' mule chargin' right at them, they scattered out of the way, but they didn't go far, and two of them circled around to get behind Ol' Red. I jumped off and fired, takin' out the closest one, and as I reached for another rifle from the saddle, the two had come in from behind Red. He kicked with both hind hooves, and as he did, it knocked me off my feet and I was down in the snow. Both hooves caught one of those wolves just as he was goin' for Red's hamstring, and I caught just a glimpse of that critter flyin' through the air, but then another one was comin' at me. I had that horse pistol and my knife, and as he lunged, I fired that pistol, and it just clicked, a misfire. I put my forearm up in front of me, and as the wolf bit down on my arm, I brought up my other hand with the knife and drove that blade deep between his ribs. He yelped and jumped and then staggered off to the side and fell, took a couple of gasps, and then lay still. Then I heard a terrible dogfight goin' on behind us, and I realized Jimbo had come up and attacked that last wolf. That wolf must have been just a young one too, 'cause they were pretty evenly matched. But Ol' Red just charged right in there with his hooves flyin' and brayin' to the heavens. He must have scared that wolf something fierce, 'cause he just broke off and ran for the timber.

I had a mighty sore arm, but he hadn't broken through the leather and wool. Jimbo had a nasty gash just below his one ear and another on his shoulder, but I could sew them up, and I couldn't see a thing hurt on Ol' Red. That was one tough mule.

The wolf that Ol' Red had kicked was lyin' right where he landed. When I got over there to gather him up, I could see the side of his head was caved in from one of Red's hooves. I went right to work, skinnin' those three wolves, then had to walk back a ways to get the moose skin that had broke off durin' our mad charge at those wolves. When I got to the moose, there wasn't a whole lot left. I was amazed how much meat four hungry wolves could devour in just a couple of hours. But I loaded the head and what little meat was left, along with the wolf skins, and we headed back to the dugout.

After carin' for Red, I got a fresh piece of sinew I'd pulled off the moose and my sewin' needle and sat down by the fire with Jimbo. I tried my best not to hurt him too much, and he just sat there by the fire and let me sew up those two gashes the wolf had left him with. I stretched the wolf hides on the sides of the dugout where I could work them up off the ground and then staked out the moose hide on the ground. By the time I had those hides scraped, it was well after dark, and I was dead tired and hungry. I sliced off a few pieces of moose meat and threw them in the pan. I didn't even make coffee, just ate a couple and threw Jimbo a couple and called it a day.

Next mornin' my arm was swollen and pretty sore, and I figured this was the day for Christmas. Since I didn't have a calendar, this was as close as I could guess. So I built up the fire and brought Red and Jimbo around and gave them their presents. Now Jimbo seemed right proud of his collar, but Ol' Red seemed much more interested in goin' out to the meadow and graze. So I grabbed the Hawken and put the lead rope on Red's new halter, and off to the meadow we went. It was another right pretty midwinter day, and I could see those two eagles soaring in the heights, and then one just folded its wings in and, like a bullet, streaked down from the sky onto an unsuspecting snowshoe rabbit. It seems like you can see forever in this clear mountain air.

We got back, and I put a big ol' hunk of moose on the spit over the fire and made another pan of sweetened cornbread with berries in it, then me and Jimbo had our Christmas dinner. I even took a piece of the cornbread out and gave it to Red. He wolfed it right down and was rubbin' my hand for more.

Chapter V

The Snakes Return

THE NEW YEAR CAME, and a few weeks into the New Year, I could tell the days were startin' to get a little longer. We had settled into a daily routine. Storms would come, and we would be cooped up inside, which both me and Jimbo hated. But after the storms, the sun would come out again, and we would spend our days outside. Many hours every day, I worked with Jimbo, teachin' him hand signals and voice commands. He was learnin' real fast, and I figured I had never seen a dog with more smarts. Ol' Red's coat had grown long and shaggy, and I could tell he had lost weight not gettin' all the grass he wanted, and I made up my mind to let him graze longer each day and I would have to shovel more. When the storms would come in and we couldn't go out to the meadow, I had taken to peelin' the bark from cottonwoods along the stream to feed him. Whatever weight Red had lost, Jimbo had gained. He was growin' mighty fast and was gettin' huge.

I had seen cat tracks up and down the stream and had run a trapline a few miles upstream and had started to get a few bobtailed cats. I wasn't sure what they would bring at

Rendezvous, but I could get them, and it kept me busy. I figured it was gonna be a few weeks still before the streams started to open up for the spring trappin' season to really start.

I had that moose and those wolf hides tanned now, and the thick hide from the moose's neck and chest made real tough soles for my moccasins. I had made a coat of the wolves usin' my capote for an inner lining, and it was right warm, and I was right proud of the way it looked. I had an awl from Pa's harness repair kit, but with as much sewin' as I had been doin', I had it ground down to just a stub, keepin' the point sharp, and was goin' to need another one come rendezvous.

I was alone, but I'd grown to love this country and had started to think of it as home. I had never had better friends than Jimbo and Red. I kept workin' with Jimbo every day, teachin' him to obey my every command. We worked on hand signals more than voice commands, and I swear that dog could read my thoughts. I never saw a dog of his size or his smarts before. Sometimes I think he knew what I was thinkin' 'fore I did. I guess he wasn't satisfied with just what I was givin' him to eat, 'cause he got in the habit of goin' out just before light and catchin' a rabbit or two, sometimes squirrels, and he would have them for his breakfast. But he never turned down any food I gave him either. I believe he could eat a whole deer haunch at one time if I'd let him.

He got so he could smell the trail of a cat and followed it until he treed him. So I brought in the ten traps I had out and would saddle Ol' Red, and we'd all go huntin' those cats. That was a lot more fun than just settin' traps. I had made rifle scabbards, one for each side of the saddle, so's I could carry all three rifles, one on each side of Red so's both was easy to reach, and I always carried one across the saddle. I still had in the back of my mind them Snakes comin' back for some revenge when spring came around.

One mornin' in late winter—late February, I figured, 'cause I had started to mark off the days on a quakie branch in the dugout at Christmas—I was just gettin' dressed, and I heard

Jimbo get on the trail of a cat up the stream a ways. So I threw the saddle on Red, and off we went. I had gotten in the habit of carryin' my .36-caliber squirrel gun after these cats, so I didn't damage the hide as much by just shootin' them at the base of the ear, so that was what I had across the saddle. When I got maybe a mile or so above the dugout, I could hear one heck of a ruckus way up ahead. I urged Red a little faster, when out of the willows along the creek up ahead of me, I saw Jimbo come hightailin' it right toward me and then a grizzly right behind him. Now Jimbo could outrun anything I had seen up to now but an antelope, but that grizzly was stayin' right with him. I gave Jimbo a hand signal to go off the other side of the creek, but he must have thought that grizzly was more important than mindin' me, 'cause he just kept comin' right down the trail toward me. Ol' Red must have figured the fix we was gonna be in mighty quick, 'cause when I jerked the reins around, he spun on his hind legs and took off like he was shot out of a cannon. I just 'bout come out of the saddle and was holdin' on for dear life as we went tearin' down that narrow trail through the snow. After a quarter mile, that bear must have figured he had showed us who was boss, 'cause he stopped his charge, turned off, and headed up the hill.

We kept up a pretty good pace all the way back, and I think all three of us was a might shook up. I respected Pa as a mountain man more that anyone I ever met, and I'd seen what that devil grizzly had done to him. I knew we had us a real troublesome thing, with a grizzly livin' that close. I knew the black bears back home were mighty hungry and cantankerous when they first came out of their dens in the spring, and it appeared these big ol' grizzlies were the same, only they would make three or four of the black bears. This grizzly had come out of his den a few weeks early, and food was gonna be mighty scarce.

I kept a real close watch for the next couple of weeks by ridin' circles around the dugout out a mile or two, lookin' for tracks. The snow was meltin' off pretty quick, with days gettin' so much warmer. I was startin' to see the game come back as well after they had spent the winter downstream on the flats closer to Smith's Fork and the Seeds-Kee-Dee.

Then one day toward the middle of March, I saw tracks of six or seven horses just over the ridge to the west, maybe five miles from the dugout. As Jimbo sniffed around, he had a real low growl comin' from down in his chest. Since I had no desire to go up against that many Injuns and figurin' how they was probably Snakes maybe lookin' for revenge, I backed off the trail and covered our tracks the best I could and went off back to the east. Then comin' down the ridge above the dugout, I saw the track of that grizzly. I checked the prime in the pan of the Hawken and started to follow his tracks. I found where he had stood 'bout a quarter mile from the dugout and watched just that mornin'. The hair was up all along Jimbo's back, and he was payin' real close attention. I knew then I had to do something to get rid of this ol' bear.

That night Ol' Red started to kick up a fuss. I grabbed the Hawken and set Pa's rifle on the outside of the dugout and built up the fire outside. Jimbo just paced and growled, and Red would snort, and that went on most of the night.

Just 'fore light, I saddled Red, and we headed for a ridge across the valley where I had been seein' a few elk come out and graze the past few mornin's and set up behind some rocks and waited till light. Just at the crack of dawn, I could see three of them start grazin', workin' their way from the trees along the ridge to the flat just below me. When they got in range, I fired, and a yearlin' cow dropped. I got Red, and we dragged that elk back across the valley, and I set her just off the stream where there was still a good-sized patch of snow under an outcroppin' of rock that I figured would make a good spot to ambush that bear. I sliced her open and spread her guts around some. I figured I would get set up just before dark and wait.

Since none of us had slept all night, we went back to the dugout and tried to get some sleep. I was some worried 'bout the horse tracks we'd seen, but I knew Jimbo and Red would alert me if anyone came near. Knowin' I may be awake all night again, I went right to sleep. I was up a few hours 'fore dark and took Red out to the meadow to graze. The grass was poor. There were new shoots just startin' to grow, but it would still be a few weeks before the grass was good again. But since that was all there was, Ol' Red just munched away. I knew it was a risk, but I decided to leave Red out there on the meadow free tonight so he could run if need be. By now I figured he wouldn't go far from home. The Injuns were a worry, but they had already felt his rage once, and for just one mule, I didn't think they would be ready to try again.

Me and Jimbo ate and got ready for the night. I carried all three rifles and the pistol. After the misfire on the wolves, I put a new flint in the pistol and had cleaned out the flash hole and had test fired it several times into a log so I could dig the lead out of the log and cast it again. It was still an hour or so 'fore dark when we got set up atop those rocks and found as good a place as I could find to shoot from. Jimbo just lay down by my side and didn't move. I watched the Big Dipper move around the North Star ever so slowly. 'Bout midnight a pack of coyotes showed up and started in on the carcass, and 'bout an hour after that, three wolves came and drove off the coyotes. Jimbo just watched and never moved or made a sound. When I figured it should be gettin' light and the wolves had left after eatin' there fill, Jimbo just nudged my hand with his nose. He was starin' right at the willows by the stream, with his ears straight ahead, and in a couple of minutes, I saw movement. That grizzly came out of the willows, swingin' his big ol' head back and forth, and just charged right up to that elk like he was darin' anything to try to stop him.

By now the moon had gone down, and I was havin' a mighty hard time seein' him in my sights, and I wanted a good shoulder shot. I had put an extra charge of powder in the Hawken, and by now, I knew it was an accurate-enough rifle. So I just waited, figurin' it would be light enough in just a little while. Then that grizzly started to pull that carcass toward the willows, and I knew I could wait no longer. I sighted down along that barrel and squeezed off. The rifle bucked hard against my shoulder with that extra load of powder, and with the pan flash right in front of my eyes, I couldn't see in the dark for a minute. I heard that bear roar and knew I had hit. I picked up the other rifle and noticed Jimbo was gone. Well, I could hear the bear and then Jimbo down there fightin' him. When I could see good enough again, I fired Pa's old rifle and went to reloadin' the Hawken. I could see Jimbo was just keepin' that bear from crawlin' off toward the willows. That bear had a broke shoulder and couldn't keep Jimbo off. I had the Hawken ready to fire again and yelled at Jimbo to back off. I fired again and knew I hit again. I loaded and fired as fast as I could five more times before that bear stopped movin'. Jimbo was there, just standin' back, growlin' when I got down there. It was just light enough now to see a good bit, and that bear was still breathin', so I fired one more time right down between his shoulders, and the breath slowly eased out of him, and he moved no more.

This grizzly wasn't quite as big as the one that had killed Pa, but he was still a mighty big beast. I had him 'bout halfway skinned when Jimbo started to growl. I picked up the Hawken as I looked up, and there were seven Snake braves walkin' their horses right toward us. They stopped out there quite a ways, and one of them raised his hand up in the sign of peace. I was standin', and I raised my hand with the peace sign. Then I started to walk toward them to see just what they wanted. I had my rifle cocked and ready, 'cause I wasn't really trustin' of them after our last run-in. But as I moved toward them, they backed off, and I could see they didn't want to get very close. I thought 'bout Red bein' out in the meadow and wondered if they were just tryin' to distract me like they'd done before.

Then one of the braves very slowly started to walk his horse toward me. I could tell he was real nervous, and I wasn't quite sure why they were since there were seven of them and only one of me. But he stopped his horse 'bout twenty-five yards out and yelled something. And I raised my hand in the peace sign again. He made the sign for *grizzly* and *killer* and pointed at me and yelled again. Then he made the *big medicine* sign and pointed at me. And I figured he was callin' me Grizzly Killer and I had big medicine and they were afraid of me.

I noticed then Jimbo had taken off, and he came sneakin' up behind the others and just stopped there, lyin' in the grass, waitin' to see if I was gonna need help. I asked him if they wanted some meat and pointed to the bear. Then I walked back and started to slice off a haunch then thought maybe I could make peace with the skin. He got off his horse and slowly walked toward me and the bear. I asked for his help skinnin' the rest of him, and then he waved to the others. As they approached, Jimbo came up from behind them, and I'd never seen a bunch of more nervous and surprised men.

Jimbo came right up beside me, and I patted him on the head, and those seven braves just stood there in amazement. I asked again for help with the skinnin', and they very slowly came over and started to help. I then gave Jimbo the hand sign to go fetch Red, and he took off on a dead run. Those braves looked back and forth at one another then at me. With the help, it didn't take long to get the skinnin' done, and when Red and Jimbo came runnin' up, those braves were fallin' all over one another, tryin' to get away from Red. I walked over and rubbed Ol' Red's nose. When those Snake braves calmed down, I gave them the hide and more than half the meat off that grizzly. I made sure I kept the claws. When they were ready to leave, I made the sign for *peace* again. They made the sign for *peace* then *big medicine*. Then pointin' to Jimbo and Red, they made the *big medicine* sign again. They then rode off. And I hoped I had no more trouble with the Snakes.

Two days later, when I went out at first light, there were three horses in the corral, and the sign of the Snakes was painted on the corral gate post. Red or Jimbo had never made a sound all night.

Chapter VI

Bear River

BY NOW THE STREAMS were openin' up, and I decided it was time to get a little trappin' done 'fore I headed to Rendezvous. Rendezvous this year was gonna be in Willow Valley over on the Bear River. Me and Pa got the directions from other trappers before we left Rendezvous last summer. But I didn't know for sure how long it would take to get there. So I figured to be on my way 'round the first of June.

I spent the next few days gettin' to know the horses those Snakes left me and teachin' 'em to carry a pack saddle. There was a right pretty chestnut, a sorrel with three white socks, and a blue roan. Ol' Red and me had made a mighty fine pair all winter, and I figured to just keep on with ridin' him. I made up a third pack I could tie to Pa's ridin' saddle since I had only two packs. Then I dug another small cache up in the timber a ways above the dugout to store the items I didn't need with me, like Pa's traps, his bedroll, and the extra keg of powder. I packed what little flour and the last bit of salt pork I had left. I made sure my possibles bag was supplied and I had plenty of powder and lead. I was gettin' short on patch cloth, so I couldn't spare any to make up some charred cloth for my fire kit. I'd just have to keep some good, dry tinder with me instead.

Next mornin' I headed west toward the Bear River, figurin' there would be plenty of trappin' streams, and I wanted to get to know this country better. The country west of Black's Fork was the foothills of the Bear River Mountains, and there were large areas of sage-covered hills with cottonwoods in the bottoms and patches of quakin' aspen and pine. There were deer and elk out along the edges of trees at dawn and again in the evenin', but they sure could disappear into the trees durin' the day.

I figured it to be around the first of April and, lookin' up at those high peaks to the south still covered with snow, I knew it would still be a while 'fore the high country opened up. Jimbo would range way out in front, scoutin' for trouble. I wondered at times if he did that for me or if he was just that curious. I camped the first night in a grove of cottonwoods down between two hills where a fire couldn't be seen far off. I built a small fire up under the branches of a cottonwood so the branches would break up the smoke. I knew a man travelin' alone in the wilds wasn't real safe, but with Red and Jimbo there, I really didn't feel alone. Lyin' there in my bedroll that night, I was right glad I'd brought the grizzly robe. It was still gettin' mighty cold at night. As the stars came out, I could hear a wolf howlin' way up the ridge, and a little later, a pack of coyotes started their high-pitch yippin' on a flat just below. All seemed right with the world as I went to sleep.

I woke the next mornin' just as the night sky was startin' to gray along the eastern horizon. Jimbo had been out and had brought in a rabbit for his breakfast. Ol' Red and the horses had been grazin' most of the night, so I just packed up and chewed on some jerky as we headed out. I was just followin' where the country led, goin' around the hills and stayin' off the skyline as much as possible. Just as the sun was gettin' low enough in the sky and I was thinkin' 'bout stoppin' for the day, I topped a ridge, stayin' in the trees. When I came out, I could see a good-sized stream just a few miles to the west and figured that was the Bear. I camped that night at the base of the ridge I'd first seen the Bear River, from where there was just a trickle of a stream. There was a warm breeze pickin' up from the south, and I figured a storm would be comin' in the next day or so. I roasted a pine hen that night that was just sittin' on a branch right where I'd picked to camp, and I was able to get close enough I clubbed it with a stick.

We moved out the next mornin' just as the sun was appearing over the eastern ridge. The Injun ponies were gettin' used to the routine and seemed to like goin' just as much as the rest of us. Their packs were 'bout empty for now. I had the grub and camp supplies spread between them, giving them a good chance to get used to packin' before we headed to Rendezvous with all the plews. In the night, Jimbo pushed on my cheek with his wet nose, and I came awake instantly. I could hear the horses movin' around some, and then Red snorted, and I heard Jimbo start after something. I wasn't goin' to start after anything in the dark, so I just waited, and an hour or so later, Jimbo came back and just lay down by me like nothin' had happened.

Next mornin' I walked out of camp the way Jimbo had gone in the night, and 'bout sixty yards out, I saw a set of cat tracks that was as big as a horse's hoof print. Now that the mountain lion found out Jimbo was on guard, I wasn't at all worried 'bout him comin' back after the stock.

'Bout midday, we reached the Bear River, and I just turned and started followin' it upstream. That warm south wind was comin' down the canyon right in our faces, so at the first smaller stream that branched off, I turned up it, headin' west. We followed it up a ways and made camp on the north side of a high pine-covered ridge where we were out of the wind. There was still snow on this shady side, but I picketed the stock on some dry grass by the creek and made me a bed under the heavy branches where two pines had grown close enough together to form a natural roof. The pine needles were thick enough for a nice, soft bed.

The storm I was expectin' came in that night, and it snowed, but it was breakin' up by daylight, and it appeared today wouldn't be too bad. Although a couple of inches fell in the night, I stayed dry and warm under those pines.

I took my time this mornin' and fixed up a good breakfast. The wind had stopped, and even though this creek I was on looked to be promisin' for beaver, I wanted to look around this country some and get to know it better. 'Bout midmornin', I packed up and went back down to the Bear. The sun was ridin' higher in the sky this time of year, and I could feel its warmth. I spooked a couple of deer off the creek and watched them bound away along the willows. There were the ever-present marmots playin' on an outcroppin' of rocks out in the meadow. This was country rich in wildlife and as pretty as I'd ever seen. Out in the meadow, there was an abundance of short-tailed ground squirrels that reminded me of the prairie dogs we'd seen crossin' the plains, only not nearly so big.

With the warm sun meltin' off the snow on the mountaintops, the Bear and creeks feedin' it were runnin' mighty full. Crossin' the Bear was a fearful thing, and I had to make my way three or four miles upstream 'fore I found a place I could make it. Once I was on the east side again, the country opened up into a large sage-covered flat. As I made my way, the scent of the sage and pine of the hills made me think I could stay in this country forever. I continued followin' the Bear until I came to a good-sized creek flowing into it from the southeast and decided to follow it a ways and see just where it came from.

Just a few miles up, I came out of the trees into what had to be the most beautiful valley I'd ever seen. It was still early spring, but the grass was tall. It was still lyin' over from the snows, but there was an abundance of new green comin' up at the bottom of the clumps, and there were beavers. The bottom of this valley was an open meadow several miles long and maybe a half mile wide, and there were beaver ponds along its full length. The ridges on the east and west were high and steep, and I could see the peaks just to the south way up above the timberline. I decided right then I would stay and trap here for a while.

I set up a simple little camp on the edge of the pines where I put together a lean-to and covered the top with pine boughs. I hobbled the horses but let Red go, and they went right to munchin' on those new shoots of grass. Jimbo took off to scout the area and returned just as I was gettin' some supper ready.

Next mornin', I took my ten traps and pack and set a trapline on the beaver slides up through the meadow. I hadn't set traps for beaver since last fall, and I found my castor had dried up, so I had no scent to put above the traps. I just had to place them where I hoped one would step into a trap. The water in those ponds was mighty cold, bein' just melted snow, and when I got the last trap set, I changed to a dry pair of moccasins. I shot a yearlin' buck on my way back to camp, and while I was dressin' it out, Jimbo went down and led Red back to me. That dog continued to amaze me even though I worked with him every day and knew how quick he learned. It was almost like he knew what I was thinkin'.

Next day I rode Red up along the trapline and could see nothin' was in the traps. I knew, without scent, this might take a while. Jimbo had done a lot of scoutin' around and hadn't shown any sign that trouble was near, but I spent this day goin' back several miles along our back trail just to make sure no one was followin' our tracks.

It took a few days, but I finally trapped a beaver and got the castor from his glands and then over the next ten days caught a beaver each day.

This country was really comin' to life now. The days were gettin' longer and warmer, the meadow was green, and the first of the wildflowers was showin'. I had 'bout all the plews and furs I figured I could carry to Rendezvous with those back in the cache, so I packed up and decided to see some more of this country.

I went back down to the Bear and headed upstream. There was mile after mile of meadow with grass greenin' up, and I just followed the river up. By now it was just the size of a creek. That night I found a nice spot for a fire and picketed the stock on some good grass just across the creek. And I bedded down just above the creek, under the branches of a big ol' spruce. Well, this was the spruce I was sleepin' under when I woke and found Runnin' Wolf with his busted leg.

Chapter VII

The Fight

I KNEW RUNNIN' WOLF couldn't set a horse with his leg the way it was, and I didn't think we had a lot of time. I sent Jimbo back down our back trail and ask Runnin' Wolf how many Snake warriors there were. He held up the fingers of one hand. I can't say I liked the idea of four to one, but I just couldn't leave Runnin' Wolf there to be killed either. I checked the prime on all three rifles and Pa's pistol. I helped Runnin' Wolf sit up and handed him Pa's ol' rifle and showed him how to shoot it. I didn't think he would hit anything, but these Snakes wouldn't know that. I just stood in the middle of the trail with the Hawken in hand and the squirrel gun leanin' against a tree in easy reach. I had the pistol, tomahawk, and knife tucked into my belt. Ol' Red was standin' just off the trail by me, and I had decorated his bridle with some of the claws off the second grizzly and had added a couple more to Jimbo's collar.

It was just a couple of minutes, and Jimbo came up the trail, and I moved him off into the trees and told him to stay. It wasn't long before four Snake warriors rode into sight. They were spread out some, and when the leader saw me in the trail, he stopped, and the others rode up alongside him. They were all painted up and were a mighty fearsome sight. I raised my hand in the peace sign, and the leader just pointed at Runnin' Wolf and signed he belonged to them. I shook my head and signed back *my friend*. One of the other braves noticed Red and said something to the leader, and they all looked a might nervous as they looked around. The one in front then signed *grizzly killer* and pointed at me. I smiled and shook the claw necklace. Then he asked where the big dog was, and I pointed behind them. Two of them turned around, and I could tell now they were gettin' mighty jumpy. The leader signed again, pointin' at Runnin' Wolf, that they wanted him, and I simply shook my head no. I could tell they were mighty nervous, but they were painted warriors and were ready for a fight. I whistled once, and Jimbo jumped out on the trail behind them with a loud, mean growl, and their horses started to buck and run. One of those braves was thrown off, and his horse came runnin' toward me, gettin' away from Jimbo, then turned off the trail and went out to the center of the meadow. The others got their horses under control, and I signed for them all to leave. I signed for them to go get their horse and go.

There leader was angry, real angry, and I figured we would have a fight yet. But after a minute or two, he told the other two to go get the horse. While they were out roundin' up the horse, I called Jimbo to come up by my side. He sat down right beside me, and his head was above my waist, the grizzly claws in plain view. As the others came back, I again made the sign for *peace*, but the leader raised his bow in the air and yelled something, then they turned and headed back down the trail. I watched for a few minutes and then turned and looked at Runnin' Wolf, and he said, "They will be back." Then he got a big ol' grin on his face and pointed to Jimbo and said, "Big Medicine Dog."

I went right to work cuttin' some pine poles and lashed together a travois. I packed the horses and tied the travois onto the chestnut and then helped Runnin' Wolf onto it. I could tell that leg was hurtin' him something awful. I knew, when those Snake warriors came back, we could never outrun them, so I looked for a place we could fort up.

Just a few miles up, the creek made a bend toward the ridge where there was a rock face with an overhang, and I figured this was as good of a spot as we would find. Here we had the cliff to our backs and an open view to a meadow. There was a break in the willows right in front of the cliff, and I figured they would have a hard time sneakin' in on us.

I helped Runnin' Wolf off the travois and unloaded the stock, hobbled the horses in the open where we could see them, and then finished settin' up camp. I figured on stayin' here for a few days while Runnin' Wolf's leg started to heal. So I got Red, and we dragged a bunch of deadfall up for firewood and to make a sort of a breastwork for protection.

In the short time me and Runnin' Wolf had been together, I felt I could trust him. I know I don't have much knowin' of people, but I know when I feel safe and when I don't, and I felt safe around him. I'd seen him watchin' me with, a wonderin' look on his face, I'm sure tryin' to figure out why I was helpin' him. I didn't know why myself, except that was the way Ma and Pa had always been, tryin' their best to help someone in need. It didn't matter whether they was friend or stranger. If someone needed help, it was always our way to pitch in and help. Or maybe I was lonely and wanted someone to talk to that could talk back. Although up to now, Runnin' Wolf hadn't said much. Jimbo and Red were pretty good listeners and had helped me through the long, hard winter, bein' right good company. But I found myself wantin' Runnin' Wolf to talk. It had been a long time since I'd heard a voice besides my own.

I had 'bout enough salt pork for one more meal and not all that much jerky left, so I knew I needed to make meat. But I didn't want to leave Runnin' Wolf until I knew what those Snake warriors were doin'. I sent Jimbo down our back trail while I finished settin' up camp. I banked a fire pit so the heat would shine off the cliff for added warmth. I had my bedroll and the grizzly skin, but Runnin' Wolf had lost everything to those Snakes. So I rolled out that ol' grizzly's hide and told Runnin' Wolf that he could use it. I figured my bedroll was enough, for the days and nights were gettin' warmer.

Since we still had a couple of hours of daylight, I wanted to get Runnin' Wolf able to use a gun, since his bow was broke when his horse went down. I knew a few shots weren't gonna make him good, but I was sure it would help, since I didn't think he had shot one before. I figured the shots would tell them Snakes right where we were, but I knew they were gonna find us anyhow, and I figured him knowin' how to shoot was more important. So I got the squirrel gun and set up a bit of a stump on its end 'bout twenty yards out and had him set up. Then showin' him how to do it, I fired and knocked the stump over. Then very slowly showin' him every step, I reloaded and handed him the gun, and I set up the stump again. Tryin' to tell him how to line up the sights was mighty hard, but he seemed to catch on. I nodded, and he put the rifle up and was doin' what looked like a good job of sightin' in on that stump and then closed his eyes and jerked the trigger so hard he missed the stump by two feet. I went through the motions of showin' him how to squeeze the trigger and not close his eyes. He seemed eager to learn, but I sure wished he had his bow. I showed him again very slowly how to reload and then let him try again. This time he seemed more comfortable with it, and when he fired, he only missed by a few inches. We kept that up for another half dozen shots before he finally hit the stump. I had him reload himself the last couple and felt by now he knew what to expect when he had to shoot, but I knew he wouldn't be accurate without a bunch more practice.

I made up a pan of biscuits, and we had that and some jerky for supper. Runnin' Wolf could speak passable English, but there were lots of words I was usin' that he just didn't seem to understand, so I sat down by the fire and started to teach him some more English. I started by pointin' at something and sayin' it in English so he would know what I was meanin'. I would say it a few times then ask him to say it. I knew it would take a long while, but I didn't know any other way. Again he was eager to learn.

As the sun dropped behind the ridge to the west, I went out and brought Ol' Red and the horses up right close to camp and picketed them good and solid. Jimbo had gone lookin' for his supper, and I decided we better keep a watch all night. I explained that to Runnin' Wolf. He nodded and said "First," pointin' at hisself. I rechecked the load in the squirrel gun and gave it to him and climbed into my bedroll. Jimbo hadn't come back yet.

I had learned by now to sleep when I could and went right out. A couple of hours later, I felt Jimbo's wet tongue on my cheek and opened my eyes. Runnin' Wolf was wide awake and starin' out over the breastwork, and Jimbo made a very low, quiet growl. I rolled out from my bedroll and made a sign to Runnin' Wolf I was goin' out. He nodded, and Jimbo led the way. We walked under the pines off the trail. By stayin' under all those pines, we were walkin' on a bed of pine needles and could move without makin' hardly a sound. We walked what I figured was 'bout a mile, when Jimbo stopped and got down on his belly and made that soft growl again. We were maybe a hundred yards above the trail. I slipped behind a tree and waited. There was a half-moon, out but in the trees, it was mighty dark. There were patches of moonlight here and there, and pretty soon I saw the shadows of them Snakes makin' their way up the trail through a patch of light. I headed up away from the trail and started back to camp. I was movin' a lot faster than those Injuns 'cause I knew where I was goin'.

I made a low whistle to let Runnin' Wolf know I was comin' in. When there, I told him the Snakes were comin', and we needed to move. I bunched some wood under my bedroll and the bear skin, and takin' all three rifles and the pistol, I moved out of camp just a little ways, then went back, and mostly carryin' Runnin' Wolf, helped him get behind a big ol' downed pine. He had a pretty good view of camp from there, with the moonlight and stars, but it was almighty dark where he was. I handed him the squirrel gun and my extra powder horn and a handful of balls. Then I went out into the meadow and lay down in the grass with both rifles and pistol right beside me. I hadn't seen Jimbo since I left him in the forest a mile from camp.

We waited for what seemed like forever, and it was gettin' mighty cold lyin' there in the damp grass. The sky was startin' to turn gray above the ridge to the east and the moon was gettin' mighty low in the west, when I saw a movement along the willows just fifty or so yards from me. It was still too dark to see my sights well. Then I heard a terrible scream and the vicious growl of Jimbo, and then all was quiet again. Then the squirrel gun went off, and I saw the shadow again along the willows, and I fired. A minute later, Jimbo was by my side and lyin' in the grass right by me. I couldn't hear or see anything, so we stayed there in the grass and waited as the light started to replace the darkness across the meadow. I knew this could be a waitin' game and didn't move at all.

As the sun was risin' behind the eastern ridge, it was shinin' on the tops of the pines to the west, and that sunshine was movin' down the western ridge. I couldn't hear or see a thing over where Runnin' Wolf was hidin', and I was really hopin' he was all right. The sun finally hit the meadow and slowly moved across it until it was shinin' on me and Jimbo. Red and the horses was standin' quiet on their picket line, and I could hear birds along the creek, and a deer came out into the meadow over on the far side. I figured those Snakes had left but knew they could be waitin' just like we were. I waited until the sun was well above the eastern ridge then sent Jimbo out through the trees to come up the trail below camp.

When he moved out, I jumped up and ran to the willows over by Runnin' Wolf. I moved through the willows toward him and 'bout stumbled over a warrior with a hole right in his chest. He was lyin' only ten feet from where Runnin' Wolf still set with that squirrel gun over the log. He nodded, and I went out through the willows to where I had shot. I found a few drops of blood, but that was all. I slowly moved in and out through the willows until I came out on the trail well below camp. Then I saw another of the warriors lyin' half in the creek with the side of his throat ripped out. His buckskins were covered with blood. I pulled him up out of the water and laid him in the grass by the side of the trail. Jimbo came up the trail, waggin' his tail, lettin' me know all was clear. It had been a long night, and Runnin' Wolf had not slept at all.

After I had Runnin' Wolf back in camp, I went back to the Injun Runnin' Wolf had shot and found the Snake's bow just a few feet from his body. Then I dragged that Injun's body down and laid him out by the one Jimbo had killed then went back and picked up that Snake's bow and took it back to camp. Runnin' Wolf didn't much like the ideal of usin' another warrior's weapon, but he said it was good until he could make his own. I fried up the last of the salt pork and made coffee. We had a couple of biscuits left from dinner, so we made do with them. I had Runnin' Wolf get some sleep, and I hobbled the horses out in the meadow to graze and threw Jimbo a couple of pieces of jerky. He went over and curled up by Runnin' Wolf. I motioned for Jimbo to stay, and I went out down the trail, followin' the tracks to see if I could tell what was happenin' with those other Snakes.

It was plain one was hurt and was bein' helped by the other one who seemed to be movin' just fine. I figured they wouldn't come back for us unless there was another raidin' party somewhere near. But I wanted to move out just in case there was. I also figured they would want to take care of their dead.

I let Runnin' Wolf sleep for a couple of hours then brought in Red and the horses. I got the horses packed and brought up the travois. Runnin' Wolf made it real clear he did not want to ride on the travois again; he wanted to ride a horse. I reckoned it wouldn't do a lot of good to argue with the determined look he had, so I just checked and made sure the splint was still solid. I had to retighten the rawhide strips, and I added a couple more and then led the chestnut up and boosted him up by his good leg. He swung the broke leg up over the saddle real careful like, and when he got set in the saddle, he had a big grin on his face.

I figured those two Snake warriors were still below us, but there was way too much snow up over the passes to head up, so with Jimbo out in the lead, we headed downstream. Me and Runnin' Wolf was mighty grim when we passed those two dead Snake warriors. We didn't say a thing, but I was sure thinkin' how easy that could have been us lyin' there instead.

It had only been a bit over a year since me and Pa had left home and Pa was dead and I had been in three fights with Injuns, one while out huntin' on the plains and two here in the mountains. Men had been killed in all of them. This really was a wild and harsh land. I was comin' to understand what Pa was meanin' when he said "You fight to win, 'cause if you don't win, you don't survive."

Chapter VIII

The Fever

I FIGURED THE safest place for us to go and for Runnin' Wolf's leg to mend was the dugout, so we headed in that direction. We passed the creek comin' in from the east that I had done the trappin' on, and just a couple of miles below that, we climbed up out of the Bear River canyon, headin' east. I reckoned it would take us three or four days to get back to the dugout. I was tryin' to stay to hard rocky ground and high up in the timber as much as possible so's not to leave an easy trail to follow. I figured Runnin' Wolf's leg wouldn't let him stay in the saddle for a long, hard day either. But I figured he would never say a thing 'bout it hurtin' him like I knew it must. By midafternoon, I was lookin' for a safe place to camp, and we still needed meat. I headed down the hill and came out on the edge of a big meadow that had a small spring at the head of it and a beaver pond right out in the middle.

We stopped at the head of this meadow just inside the trees, and I got Runnin' Wolf down, hobbled the horses on the meadow grass, and brought in a little wood for a fire and nodded at Runnin' Wolf, and he nodded back. We had only been together for a couple of days but were learnin' fast what each other needed. I got back on Ol' Red and started along the edge of the trees, lookin' for some meat.

'Bout an hour later and a couple of miles below camp, I came across a well-used game trail. I turned around and headed back into the trees. Around a quarter mile away, I tied Red to a quakie then moved real easy like back down and waited sixty or seventy yards off the trail back in the trees. The sun was gettin' right low in the sky, and no game had come down to the meadow to graze. When it started to get dusk, I went back up to Red and started back to camp. I spooked a couple of deer but had no shot. All I could see was their white rumps bouncin' away through the trees. Then 'bout a half mile from camp, I saw a porcupine just climbin' down from a tree and got off Red, and with a stick, I smacked him a good, hard hit across its head. Skinnin' that critter wasn't fun, but I got it done. When I got to camp, Runnin' Wolf had a small fire goin'. I put the porcupine on a green quakie branch and set it up over the fire to roast. I still had coffee and flour, so I made up some pan biscuits and got some water to boilin' in the coffee pot. Jimbo came back with a snowshoe rabbit. I thought I should have taken him with me, and maybe he could have driven those deer I saw to me. I would have to try that next time I went out.

Next mornin' we headed out just after dawn and traveled much like we had the day before, tryin' to stay to rocky ground where we could and in the cover of trees. 'Bout midday we jumped a yearlin' doe that ran out just a few yards and stopped to see what we were, and I shot her. We now had some fresh meat. I figured on making today a short day of travel to let Runnin' Wolf rest his leg. Since we had seen no sign of the Snakes, it would give me and Jimbo a chance to check our back trail.

'Round noon we came out of the timber and had to cross a big, high bald ridge. There were several game trails up over this ridge, but we were gonna to be in the open on all of them. Runnin' Wolf didn't like it at all, and pointin' way up high to the timber, he said, "We should stay in the trees." It looked to be 'bout a hard half day's ride to where we could cross the ridge and stay in the trees, but he knew this country better than I did, so we started south in the trees.

It was a hard climb up through the timber, and we came to a couple of spots we had to backtrack to get around rock outcroppin's that we couldn't climb. By midafternoon the horses were gettin' mighty tired, and I saw Runnin' Wolf rubbin' his leg with a real grim look on his face. I knew we weren't goin' the make it across the ridge 'fore dark, so we started to look for a place to camp. We came up on a little shelf no more than ten feet across and maybe fifty feet long. There was no food or water for the stock, but it was level enough for us to sleep and the stock to stand comfortably, so we stopped.

After Runnin' Wolf was set, I unloaded the packs and unsaddled Red and the chestnut. Jimbo had taken off like he always did, scoutin' around and lookin' for somethin' to eat. I broke off a bunch of small branches and found part of an old squirrel's nest for tinder and left Runnin' Wolf to get a fire goin'. I cut us off some chunks of deer and put them on stakes to roast over the fire. My water pouch didn't have enough water left in it to do any more than wet the stock's mouths and give us just a swallow. I figured we would just move out at dawn, and when we found a stream on the other side of that ridge, we would have a good rest and drink there.

We had moved up in this timber quite a ways, and it was a right chilly night. Runnin' Wolf seemed fine under that bear robe, but I spent most of the night findin' and feedin' small branches into the fire. When it was barely light enough to see the trees, I was ready to head out. With Ol' Red and the horses havin' nothin' to eat or drink, they weren't very happy 'bout bein' loaded up for another day. Runnin' Wolf was tryin' to get movin', but it was real plain he was hurtin'. I got my arms around him to help him up and could tell he was gettin' feverish. We would have to rest for a few days before we got back to the dugout.

I let Red lead the way, and he picked as easy a trail as could be found. We came out of the trees just at the base of a straight-up rock face. It was 'bout a quarter mile across the ridge in the open, and we had to cross over an old rock side for part of that. By now we were up high enough and far enough away that bein' in the open for just the little while wasn't much of a worry. Runnin' Wolf was mighty weak, and I was worried 'bout the rock slide and knew it would be tough on him and the horses.

Red was followin' a game trail that led out under this cliff, and when we got to the slide, I was right pleased to see the trail went right on across it. It was narrow and windin' along, but these were all mountain horses. Ol' Red seemed right at home as he made his way across. One of the pack horses slipped and started to go down just as we were gettin' to the far side, but he managed to stay up. The chestnut Runnin' Wolf was ridin' was doin' fine and seemed to know his rider was hurt.

Just into the trees on the other side, the ridge dropped off into a sage flat, and I pulled up and stopped. Runnin' Wolf had beads of sweat runnin' down his face and was real pale. He needed water, and so did the stock, so with a nod, we rode on. The sun was gettin' close to center sky when we rode into a draw that had just a trickle of water runnin' down through the bottom. We followed it down 'bout a half mile and came to the edge of a meadow with a spring bubblin' up, and it turned that trickle of water into a right pretty little creek. There were quakies along the creek and a place to set up a camp, stayin' in the pines for shelter if the weather didn't hold.

I helped Runnin' Wolf off the chestnut, rolled out the bear skin on a bed of pine needles, and got him covered up. Ol' Red and the horses had stayed right there at the spring, drinkin' their fill. Jimbo had taken off as usual, scoutin' around. I filled the water pouch and got Runnin' Wolf to drink then went to work unloadin' the stock, hobbled them out on the meadow grass, built a fire up under a big ol' pine so the smoke would be broken up by the branches, and started cookin'. Jimbo came back with some pine hen feathers stuck to the side of his mouth, so I figured he'd had lunch. Roasted deer, pan biscuits, and coffee were lunch, but Runnin' Wolf hardly ate.

I'd seen the Cherokees back home make a tea usin' white bark, so I peeled some quakie bark and boiled it awhile. Runnin' Wolf didn't seem to care for the taste, but he drank it. After a while, he was sleepin' better, and the fever seemed to be down. Pa had told me once that aspen bark had medicines in it. It looked to be helpin' Runnin' Wolf rest, so I was glad I remembered that.

I put us together a lean-to and covered the top with pine boughs real thick and hung the deer way up in a tree a couple of hundred feet from camp. Then I went to gatherin' firewood, findin' the driest there was around. Much of it I broke off the dead lower branches of pines as they are almost always dry.

When the sun was 'bout midway 'tween center sky and the western horizon, I checked on Runnin' Wolf and told him I would be gone awhile, saddled Ol' Red, and called Jimbo, and we headed along our back trail, watchin' real close for any sign we were bein' followed. When we came out onto the bare ridge top by the rock slide, I stopped and just looked out over hundreds of miles of country. Lookin' for any movement or smoke or any sign of life. I saw what appeared to be an elk herd two or three miles northwest and below us, but they seemed content just grazin' in the open. I sat there in the saddle, just admirin' the view, when I noticed a haze between two hills way off to the northeast toward the Seeds-Kee-Dee. I figured this haze was out there maybe fifteen or twenty miles. I looked mighty hard for quite a while, but I just couldn't tell for sure if it was smoke or just a haze. There wasn't any haze in any of the other hollows or valleys that I could tell, so I figured it must be smoke.

I hightailed it back to camp to tell Runnin' Wolf, but when I got there, his fever was up again, and so I just kept it to myself. I boiled some more quakie bark and got him to drink the tea it made and built the fire up just a bit to help keep him warm. Then I just sat by the fire to ponder on our predicament. After rollin' it around in my mind for a while, I figured stayin' right where we were was the safest thing to do and the only thing with Runnin' Wolf in the condition he was in. We were up higher on the mountain than most huntin' parties were likely to come, and we had good water, shelter, and enough meat for a few days.

Runnin' Wolf had a bad time of it over the next three days. His fever would come, and I would try to get as much quakie bark tea in him as I could. When his fever seemed to break some, I tried to get him to drink some broth I made by boilin' some deer meat with plenty of fat in it, but he drank mighty little of that, and he didn't eat a thing.

On the mornin' of the fourth day, I woke up just before dawn to the howlin' of a wolf that wasn't far away. I just lay there real still, listening like I always did. That wolf was slowly movin' away from us with his mournful-soundin' howl. As dawn broke, the red-orange tint of the clouds was really something to see. I got the fire goin' and some coffee boilin' and watched the color fade from the sky as the sun came up. There were marmots below us in the rocks along the creek and a pair of camp robbers squawkin' in a tree not far away. I figured it was time to wake Runnin' Wolf and see how he was doin', when he sat up, smiled, and said. "Hungry." His color was back to normal, and I went right to work gettin' some deer strips roastin' over the fire.

As we sat there by the fire, eatin' roasted deer and biscuits and sippin' coffee, he told me his spirit helper, the wolf, had come to him in the night and had takin' his fever away. I figured he had been dreamin' and had seen Jimbo, as that dog had hardly left Runnin' Wolf's side for the last three days. But as I moved the stock from their picket line out to the meadow, I noticed another set of dog tracks just smaller than Jimbo's. I couldn't figure why Ol' Red and the horses or Jimbo hadn't made a fuss if there had been a wolf right in camp, and I said so to Runnin' Wolf. He just smiled and said, "They know he here to help."

I had been around the Cherokee enough to know they believed in a lot of things that didn't fit to our way of thinkin'. Most white people just figured it was all made up in their minds. But I could see the wolf tracks right in camp, and Runnin' Wolf's fever was gone and none of our animals had made a sound 'bout that wolf bein' here. None of this made any sense to me. I could tell I would be ponderin' on this thing for a long time to come.

Runnin' Wolf seemed to be gettin' better fast now the fever was gone. The next mornin', I stripped off the splint on his leg, and the swellin' had gone down a lot. The bruise was startin' to return to a more normal color. I wrapped his leg with some of the raw hide from that last deer, hair side against his skin, and replaced the splint and wrapped it as tight as I dared. I found a good strong stick with the fork on one end and made a makeshift crutch. He still couldn't put any weight on his leg. But now he could hobble around a bit.

I figured it was gettin' to be around the last of April by now, so I had 'bout a month before I would leave for Rendezvous. I told Runnin' Wolf 'bout the haze I had seen a couple of days ago and that we needed to get back to the dugout. I told him 'bout Rendezvous and asked if he would like to go with me. He figured the haze was what I figured, an Injun village. He reckoned it was Snakes, but he said the Arapahos and Cheyennes sometimes went to the mountains to hunt in the spring, that they were out of meat from the winter, and the buffalo hadn't returned from the south yet. So they went to the mountains to hunt deer and elk to get them by until the buffalo returned. He said we would have to be mighty careful movin' with huntin' parties 'bout. He said all these Injuns were his enemies, and if they found us, it would mean a fight. He said, "When you are ready to go to Rendezvous, I will know to go or not."

Next mornin' we broke camp and packed up the horses. Ol' Red seemed right ready to be goin' again. Runnin' Wolf was movin' much easier, but he still needed a lot of help. Once he was up on the chestnut, he seemed right at home. Jimbo took the lead, and we moved out, headed north by east. We were still high up, and we just followed the lay of the land, stayin' under the cover of trees as much as possible. I figured we were still two or three days from the dugout.

As the sun was gettin' low in the west, we were followin' a little creek that had become a rushin' torrent of water with the snow meltin' now mighty fast up in the high country. We moved away from the creek quite a ways so we could hear someone comin' without the rushin' water coverin' all other sounds, and we made us a simple little camp for the night. We set a small fire up under some trees to break up the smoke, and I made sure the firewood was dry. The grass was really greenin' up fast now, and there were a lot of wildflowers startin' to come up. I picketed the stock on a patch of grass close by, and we let the fire completely die out 'fore dark.

Next mornin' the sky was slate gray and lowerin'. The mountaintops were all covered, and it looked like we would be gettin' wet 'fore long. We loaded up, crossed the creek, and headed in a more easterly direction. We had traveled 'bout two hours, when we come upon a right pretty little valley with a creek runnin' down through it, and we started to follow it down. We had only been followin' it a little while, when it started to feel real familiar. I then realized this was the valley were Pa was buried. I told Runnin' Wolf the story of what had happened, and as we followed the valley down, it was only 'bout three miles when we came upon me and Pa's old camp. The lean-to frame was still up, but the boughs were all crumbled away. From there I went right to Pa's grave. Grass was startin' to grow right up over it, and I wanted to clean it up like me and Pa had done to Ma's 'fore we left Kentucky. But with Injun huntin' parties 'bout, I knew not to leave any sign we had been there.

Not wantin' to camp another night on the trail with a storm ready to break anytime, we pushed hard. Most all the way to the dugout, we could stay in the trees. The clouds kept gettin' lower as the afternoon dragged on, and by dusk, it was startin' to rain. That last hour gettin' to the dugout was cold, wet, and miserable. The only time I could see the trail was when the lightning would flash, and the thunder got so loud you could feel it shakin' the ground and the air. When we got there, I stripped the packs and saddles and turned the horses into the corral. I opened up the dugout, and it was so dark inside I couldn't see a thing, but it smelled mighty stale, bein' closed up for a few weeks. I had to feel my way to the fireplace and fumbled around for quite a while, gettin' a fire goin'. Once I had flames and we could see, I helped Runnin' Wolf in and got him settled by the fire. He was mighty weak. It had been a long, hard day of ridin', and I could tell his leg was really botherin' him. But he never said a word 'bout it.

Once I had the packs and saddles inside out of the rain, I put what deer meat we had left on the fire and made coffee. By the time the coffee was ready, the dugout was good and warm. Jimbo was curled up by the fire, and we ate roasted deer and drank hot bitter coffee. Then turned in and slept through the night.

Chapter IX

Making Meat

FOR THE NEXT COUPLE of days, Runnin' Wolf didn't move around much. I fixed him a spot by the outside fire, next to the logs of the dugout, so he didn't have to be in that dark dugout durin' the day. I figured it was 'bout the first of May, and the days were downright pleasant. My supplies were runnin' real low, the cornmeal and sugar were gone, and I figured we would be out of flour in another week or two. I had started usin' less of the bakin' powder 'cause it was 'bout gone. I still had some salt but not enough to cure much meat. There was still a little of the moose left in the smokehouse, but it had gone bad, so I threw it out for Jimbo. He wasn't very particular 'bout the condition of the meat he ate. We were back to havin' only jerky to eat, and we didn't have a lot of that left, so I knew I would have to go out and make meat.

Next mornin' I saddled Ol' Red and got Runnin' Wolf set. I left him the squirrel gun and had dug out Pa's old possibles bag that had his powder horn, patch knife, fire-makin' kit, two extra flints, and patch cloth, and I put eight .36-caliber balls in it. He had me get him the bow from the Snake warrior he had killed and the rest of the rawhide from the last deer. Once he had that, I got on Ol' Red, and we started out, with Jimbo takin' the lead as always. I thought 'bout leavin' Jimbo with Runnin' Wolf, but I really liked havin' him with me. So just like through the winter, the three of us headed out.

We went into several small parks that I had hunted with good success last fall but failed to see a thing. I was learnin' right fast the deer and elk didn't use the same areas in the spring as they did in the fall. I was headed in a west by north direction and came up over a small ridge and found a well-used game trail with both deer and elk tracks on it. I followed it for maybe another mile and came into a very protected little valley with maybe forty or fifty cow elk grazin' in it. I was still up in the trees, and the wind was in my face, so I got off Red and just let the reins drop to the ground. Red knew by now to stand where I left him when I let the reins just hang down. Jimbo was starin' real hard at the elk with every muscle ridged, and his tail was quiverin', but he never moved or made a sound.

It was gettin' to be late mornin' by now, and I figured those elk would be comin' back up in the trees to bed down for the afternoon in not too much longer, so I found us a spot 'bout forty yards off the trail in a little thicket of brush, and Jimbo and I just sat and waited. Maybe a half hour later, those elk started to move, but instead of followin' the trail up to where I was, they went the other way. It wasn't long 'fore they were all out of sight. There were a lot of mighty fat cows in that herd, and I figured it was 'cause they would be droppin' calves 'fore long. I figured I couldn't get around downwind of 'em before they smelled or heard me, so I just sat there and waited awhile. It was a right pleasant spring day. There were birds singin', some blue jays were squawkin' in the pines behind us, and a pair of hawks was circlin' in the sky overhead. There was just a slight breeze whisperin' through the pines, and the wildflowers were comin' up in the meadows where the sun had been hittin' each day.

I didn't know if I could make Jimbo circle around behind those elk and head them up this trail to me, but I figured it was worth a try. He knew what I meant when I would send him right or left and to stay with hand signals, and he knew the signal for him to go get Ol' Red, but I had never tried to teach him to circle animals before and herd them to me. I sat there, ponderin' on how to do this, and patted him on the head. He sat right up, watchin' me, and it was plain he wanted to go after them. Once the elk entered the trees on the other side of the clearin', I couldn't see where they had gone. I figured they wouldn't go far into the trees before they would bed down. But how I would get Jimbo to know how far to go to get to the other side of 'em before he jumped 'em was the question. I knew he would follow my hand signals, but he wouldn't be able to see me when he got to the other side and in the trees. He was payin' right close attention to me, and I made the signal for him to go left by pointin' left, then by pushin' my hand away from me, I was tellin' him to go farther away from me, then I made the sign to bring Red back to me. By now I figured he was goin' to be mighty confused, but I'd done it all a second time and a third. Then just pointin' left again, I whispered go.

He started off to the left slow and quiet, and when he was just 'bout out of sight, he looked back at me, and I signed to him to keep goin' farther by pushin' my hand away from my body again and again. He responded and was soon completely out of sight. I sat there and waited, not havin' any idea 'bout what was gonna happen. I moved a little closer and was sittin' by a big ol' pine maybe twenty yards above the trail we followed in here. I checked the prime in my pan and got in a good shootin' position. Right then I heard a loud crack of a branch and the thunder of hooves. Then there were elk runnin' out of the trees on the other side of clearin'. They were goin' in just 'bout every direction. They were runnin' through the meadow, runnin' through the trees, goin' right and left and straight ahead. I could now see Jimbo comin' out behind them. He had a cow and yearlin' calf right in front of him, and he was tryin' to herd them right to me. I was payin' right close attention to them, thinkin' that yearlin' was just what I was lookin' for, when I caught movement out of the corner of my eye. Not ten yards to my left, there were two cows followed by a yearlin' bull runnin' full speed up the trail. By the time I got the Hawken up to my shoulder, the first cow had passed and the second was right in front of me. I let her pass and fired just as the yearlin' had takin' her place. That yearlin' ran 'bout fifty more yards and fell. I stood up and could see Jimbo still tryin' to herd those other two elk, but they were gettin' farther away. We both found out herdin' elk wasn't like herdin' Ol' Red.

While I was dressin' him out, Jimbo came back, and I rubbed his ears and told him he was a good boy. Then I cut off a good chunk of the liver for him. When I got finished, I put the rest of the liver and heart in the saddlebags, and we headed back to camp to get the horses to carry this elk out.

When I entered camp, Runnin' Wolf was workin' there by the fire pit. He had that bow stripped down to the wood. He had the hair scraped off the hide and had been to the stream and soaked the raw hide and had it cut into strips. He was learnin' to get around pretty good with that crutch. As I rode up, he smiled, and I got down and told him the story of how Jimbo had scared the elk and how the three had run right past me. We had a good laugh at Jimbo as I told Runnin' Wolf of him tryin' to herd those elk. I set the liver and heart on a tall stump I was usin' as a table, put the pack saddles on the horses, and headed back to get the elk.

It took 'bout an hour to get back to the elk, and we were movin' right along. I figured it to be six or seven miles. There was a pair of coyotes that was eatin' on the gut pile when we rode up, but they scattered mighty quick like. It didn't take long to get the hide off this yearlin' and then strip the meat. This time of year, the elk had started to shed his long winter hair, so I figured the hide would make good leather but not much of a robe, so I cut it in half and lined the packs with it to carry the meat so the blood wouldn't soak into the canvas of the panniers. Once I got all the useable meat packed and Jimbo had ate his fill of the scraps, we headed back to the dugout.

Just as we topped the first rise, a black bear stood up in the trail, maybe seventy-five yards in front of us. Jimbo had been distracted from findin' that bear first as he was draggin' the bone of a whole elk haunch with him and was bringin' up the rear. That bear had smelled the dead elk and was headed right down the trail to his carcass. Since we didn't need more meat right now, I took Red and led the horses off the trail a couple of hundred yards, and Jimbo, although he was followin' along with us, was growlin' and makin' sure that bear knew there would be a fight if he came any closer. We just circled way out around him while he stood in the trail, watchin' us. But when we got past him, he dropped down and continued on his way down to what we had left of the elk carcass.

We were back in camp in a little over an hour, and I figured it was midafternoon. Runnin' Wolf had that Snake's bow all rewrapped with rawhide strips and had braided the rawhide just above and below the handle. He had it settin' by a small fire, dryin', and he grinned and said "Now can be used by Ute." He then grinned and said, "Snake's bow not good for Ute."

I hung the elk meat in the smokehouse and walked up the stream, gatherin' dead limbs from the currents and chokecherries to use for smokin' that meat. Last fall, me and Pa had used some cottonwood to smoke meat, but we found the flavor was much better usin' the wood from the berry bushes. I built a small fire in the fire pit in the bottom of the smokehouse and closed it up, goin' back every couple of hours to add a few more of the branches. The jerky strips would be done in a day or two, but the roasts might take a week.

After Runnin' Wolf had finished his bow, he said it would take a few days to dry and harden. Then he took his crutch and started up the trail along the stream. He was gone long enough I was wonderin' if I should go see if he needed some help, when I heard his laugh and here he came almost runnin' down the trail right into camp. He found a match to his crutch stick, and with one under each arm and holdin' his broken leg up, he was comin' down that trail faster than I could walk and was laughin', havin' fun doin' it. He almost fell when he came to a stop by the fire, and we both had a good laugh. It felt good to laugh again, and Jimbo came up to see what was goin' on. He was waggin' his tail and tiltin' his big ol' head to the side, tryin' to figure us out. Then we started laughin' at him. It felt so good just to laugh. We laughed at everything till my sides were hurtin', and I had to make myself stop. It felt mighty good to have a friend again, a friend to talk to and laugh with. I still missed Pa a lot, but that low-down, miserable feelin' that would come over me was comin' less and less. I knew it wasn't 'cause I missed him less, just that I had so much to take up my thoughts these days.

Over the next couple of weeks, Runnin' Wolf's leg was gettin' stronger and healin' fast. Every few days I would take the splint off and check his leg. The color was almost back to normal, and as he used the crutch sticks, he was puttin' more weight on his leg each day. Around the third week of May, he was back to usin' just one crutch and would ride the chestnut to take Ol' Red and the horses out to the meadow to graze each day. He spent time every day makin' arrows from the good, straight willow limbs from along the stream and then practiced with that bow. He was mighty good and unbelievably fast with the bow and arrows. I had him practice every day as well with the squirrel gun, and he was gettin' much better with it, but he still preferred the bow.

I was spendin' my days gettin' ready to leave for Rendezvous. I had dug up me and Pa's cash, and Runnin' Wolf seemed amazed at the number of plews I had. I double-checked all the packs and made repairs where needed, braided new rawhide lead ropes, cleaned and checked all the horses' hooves, and filed them down where needed. I came to believe we needed one more pack horse for all the plews and big pile of furs we had. Two pack horses just couldn't carry it all.

Runnin' Wolf said, "Make travois like moving a village until we find more horses. I will go to Rendezvous with my friend."

Next day I cut enough narrow lodge pole pines to lash together two travois, and by what I figured was 'bout the first of June, we left the dugout and headed west by north to hit the Bear River and follow it up all the way to Willow Valley. Runnin' Wolf said he had never been there, but from what he had heard, it should take us 'bout six to eight days to get there.

Chapter X

Warm Springs

AS WE TRAVELED northwest and dropped out of the foothills of the still-snowcapped Bear River Mountains, we traveled over hill after hill covered with sage and across countless miles of tablelands of nothin' but sage. The antelope were everywhere, and on the second day out, Runnin' Wolf showed me how to lure them into range by hidin' in the sage and settin' up a little flag on a stick just above the sage, and those little prairie goats just came right in, tryin' to figure out what that flag was. I didn't like antelope as much as deer and elk, but the fresh meat still tasted mighty good.

The size of this western country was beyond discribin'. You could see for a hundred miles or more, and it was all the same. There was mountain range after mountain range with miles and miles and mores miles of empty land in between. The sky was so big it almost hurt the eyes to stare at it, and the mountains so high the clouds even have a hard time gettin' over them. The wildflowers were now really comin' out. There were Injun paintbrush, yellow daises, bluebells, and many more. I had no idea what they were. And they were growin' right out around the sage. Along the creek bottoms, the grass was a foot high already, and we saw game every day.

Pullin' those two travois made for slow goin', as we would have to find a way around most rough spots. I figured it would take us a couple of extra days to get to Willow Valley. But we hit the Bear on the third day and just followed it along, goin' north, stayin' up on the benchland on the east side of the river. We found a nice, wide trail goin' down to the river a couple of hours 'fore dark and made a camp in a grove of cottonwoods not far from the river. The river was runnin' mighty high and was makin' quite a roar with all the snow meltin' mighty fast up in the high country. I didn't like not bein' able to hear good over the roar of the water, but there was no shelter, and we figured the fire and smoke could be seen for a long ways off if we were just out in the sage, and the only trees were right along the river.

Runnin' Wolf was walkin' now without the crutches but still favorin' that leg a lot. I figured it would take several more weeks before he was all healed up. But it had only been five or six weeks since I had set that leg, and with him bein' young and strong, it was healin' mighty fast. He would take off the splint at night and rub the leg and sleep with it off, but he would wrap it good and put the splint back on each mornin' before he would walk on it.

By the time we had the stock watered and hobbled to graze on the grass along the river, Jimbo came into camp with the largest rabbit I had ever seen. It was double the size of the big black-eared jackrabbits that we jumped so often out in the sage. He just dropped it and went out again. It wasn't long 'fore he brought in another one. Before dark, he had brought in three of these big rabbits. They reminded me of the snowshoe hares, and I figured they must be a hare of some kind. Runnin' Wolf just called them big *doovapooch.*[1] He said their fur made warm clothes for the winter. I skinned, cleaned, and put two of them

---

[1] Ute name for rabbit.

on a spit over the fire and gave the third one back to Jimbo, along with a whole bunch of ear rubbin' and a little roughhousin' that he seemed to like so much. We had very little coffee left, maybe enough for another day, and no flour or sugar. I sure hoped we didn't have any trouble gettin' on into Rendezvous and they would have plenty of supplies.

When those rabbits were done, we sipped on hot, bitter coffee and ate roasted rabbit that tasted mighty good, but I sure had been missin' my biscuits. As we sat around the small fire that we had made sheltered in this thick grove of cottonwoods, Runnin' Wolf started to tell me 'bout his people and village. He told me 'bout his sister Shinin' Star, whom he had to provide for, and how she had lost her man on a hunt for *cooch*,[2] what the white man calls buffalo, last fall, just a few months after they were together. He said she was the prettiest girl in the whole village, and her man had been his friend. He talked of how his father had been killed in a raid on the Arapaho a couple of summers ago, and his mother, after much mournin', had taken another man from the White River band and had moved away, and he talked of how he and his sister had stayed. He said he wanted to take me, whom he owed his life to, to his village and how I would be an honored guest. He told me that when we met, he had been on his way back to his village from the Yambow,[3] a valley to the west. He had gone there to visit friends and relatives in another village and to see a girl, but she was not there as she had gone with her family to visit relatives in Timpanogos[4] valley. He had stayed there just a few days, visitin' some relatives, and had decided to go back to his village along the northern route, when he came upon that Snake huntin' party on the Bear River.

He continued telling me more of the trappers from General Ashley's brigade that he spent those many moons with

[2] Ute name for buffalo.
[3] Ute name for Kamas Valley, Utah.
[4] Ute name for Utah Valley, Utah.

and how they had taught him their tongue, how they had paid him by givin' him his knife and a cookin' pot that he gave to his sister and lots of beads and copper rings that they called *foofarraw* and said, "If I gave them to the girls, they would all like me." He said he gave most of them to Shinin' Star but had kept some of them for Pale Moon, the girl he had gone to see, but when the Snakes had killed his horse, he had lost everything includin' the rest of the foofarraw.

I went out and brought in Ol' Red and the horses and put them on a picket line right close to camp. With Jimbo and Red bein' right with us, I figured we were safe without standin' guard all night.

Next mornin' after eatin' leftover rabbit and just drinkin' water, I figured we had 'bout enough coffee for one more pot and I would save that for supper. We loaded the travois and started north again. 'Bout midday I was lookin' around for a place to rest the stock for a bit and came upon a spring that smelled a little of brimstone and had just a bit of steam comin' off the surface. There was good grass goin' out a ways from the water, and I figured the stock could rest and graze an hour or so. When I got down to taste the water, it was almost hot to the touch. Now I hadn't had a real bath since last summer, and then it was in a mighty cold mountain stream, and when I turned around to tell Runnin' Wolf I was fixin' to take a bath, he was already strippin' out of his buckskins.

We spent the next couple of hours soakin' and scubbin' in that warm water. It took a bit to get used to the heat, but after a few minutes, it was right down relaxin'. I tried to get Jimbo to get in, but he wanted no part of that hot water. My hair hadn't been trimmed for many months, and it took a lot of scrubbin' to get it feelin' clean again.

My skin was so white it started to burn from the sun, so I figured it was time to move on. Just then, Jimbo growled and took off. Me and Runnin' Wolf both jumped out of the water, naked as jaybirds, and I picked up my Hawken, and he, his bow. Just then I heard three shots go off, and someone yelled in accented English, "OK to come in!" I wasn't goin' to put down my Hawken to get dressed, and Runnin' Wolf just slipped behind the chestnut with arrow ready and stood still. I answered, "Come in if'n you're friendly."

As they came on in, I could see there were more than just the three of them, and I wasn't at all ready to put down the Hawken. Then I could see the others with them were three Injun squaws, and those squaws were each leadin' three pack horses. I was standin' there naked with the Hawken, and one of the men just started laughin', then the others joined in, and it was catchin', 'cause I started to laugh, and I glanced over at Runnin' Wolf, but he was lookin' at me like I was crazy. What he didn't know was by them shootin' off their guns, they was tellin' me they was unarmed and friendly. I set the Hawken down in easy reach and put on my buckskins as they rode on in. I couldn't see Jimbo, and Runnin' Wolf was lookin' real worried and not ready to put down his bow.

I told him they were trappers and said I thought it would be all right. But he just signed *Snakes* back to me. Them trappers came on in and climbed down and, talkin' in Snake, must have told the Squaws to unload the horses, and the trappers came over and introduced themselves. The one in the lead was Jean Luc Lamont, the next was Jacques Basile, and the third was Lucien Mineau. They said they were free trappers and had been with Fontenelle up on the Popo Agie, that their squaws were Shoshone, and that they were headed to Rendezvous.

Runnin' Wolf had figured they were friendly by now and had slipped into his buckskins as well. I told them my name was Zach Connors, and then Runnin' Wolf came around that chestnut, and I told them his name and that we were headed to Rendezvous as well. Jean Luc spoke real good English even though it was hard to understand through his accent. Lucien could speak a little, but it was he who was talkin' in Snake to the squaws, but it didn't appear Jacques spoke anything but

French, and he was younger than the others, I figured 'bout my age or maybe a bit younger.

I hadn't seen Jimbo since just before those Frenchies had rode in, and I figured he was just out in the brush. And that made me a little worried 'cause he seemed to have a better feelin' for people than I did. So it made me wonder just what kind of men these were.

Those squaws had their horses unloaded mighty quick and then said something in what sounded like mixed Snake and French and walked right up to the edge of that hot spring and pulled their dresses up over their heads and, naked as could be right there in front of all of us, got down into that hot water. It looked like they were enjoyin' themselves. My eyes must 'bout popped out of my head, 'cause those Frenchies started to laugh at me again, and Jean Luc asked what the matter was that I was standin' just like that a few minutes ago. I must have turned red as a beet, 'cause they laughed all the more. Then they stripped down and got into the water themselves.

I had only seen one naked girl before in my life, and that was 'bout three years ago back home just 'fore Ma passed on. There was gonna be a dance and social at the church over in Pottersville on Saturday night. I had been on a hunt with my Cherokee friends and had stayed at their village Friday night. I was really lookin' forward to seein' Emma Potter and maybe dancin' with her Saturday night. Emma was my age and was real pretty. She had long auburn hair and green eyes and, at seventeen, was shapely enough she turned all the men's eyes in her direction wherever she went. I had been sweet on her for years, and I knew she liked me too.

As I headed home, I crossed buckhorn ridge and was followin' the trail down Potters Draw, kind of daydreamin' 'bout the dance, when I heard some splashin' in the creek up ahead. I slowed right down and snuck on down the trail real quiet. When I could see some movement out in the creek, I just real careful like moved through the brush so I could see. Standin' out in the creek in water just up to her waist was

Emma. She was completely naked and washin' her hair. Now I knew I should look away, but I just couldn't. She had her head back with soap in her hands, workin' her hair over; her eyes were closed. There were beads of water glistenin' off her skin, and the sight just 'bout took my breath away. I was feelin' mighty guilty, but I just couldn't look away. Ma had always told me the good Lord was always lookin' over my shoulder, so never do anythin' he wouldn't want me doin', but I just couldn't look away. Then I wondered if he really was lookin' over my shoulder, if he was enjoyin' the view as much as I was.

I was hidden real well in a thicket and knew I couldn't be seen if I didn't move and just sat there and watched her finish her bathin'. Then she walked right up out of the water and picked up a towel and dried off. I'd never been so uncomfortable, sittin' there in the thicket, not darin' to move a muscle. I had feelin's I never felt before, and my manhood was growin', and I wanted to get out of there but couldn't. I was breathin' so hard I was 'fraid she was gonna hear me, and I had started sweatin', but I just sat there and watched her get dressed and leave.

The trail down Potters Draw led right down past the Potter Homestead and then on into town, and our place was way out on the other side of town. But instead of followin' the trail past the Potter's place, I climbed back up on the ridge and stayed in the forest all the way back home.

At the dance that night, Emma was there wearin' a newly made dress and lookin' just as pretty as a picture. When she saw me, she came right up and said she wanted to dance. I must have turned mighty red, and I couldn't look her in the eyes, and she wanted to know what the matter was, if I was feelin' all right, and I just couldn't say a thing. All I could see was her standin' in the creek, naked. I started breathin' real heavy and gettin' lightheaded and had to sit down for a few minutes. She brought me a cup of punch and sat with me until I could breathe and talk again.

When me and Pa left home, the thought of leavin' Emma behind was 'bout the hardest part for me, but the adventure of seein' the country we had heard tell of and bein' with Pa after Ma had passed on were a stronger pull for me.

I wanted to talk to them Frenchies 'bout the best way into Willow Valley, but I was havin' a mighty hard time keepin' my eyes off all those naked breasts splashin' around in that water, and when I saw Runnin' Wolf lookin' too, I decided we better move on before these Frenchies took offense, and I said the same to Runnin' Wolf. He smiled and nodded in agreement.

By the time we had the travois tied to the horses and loaded, Jean Luc had gotten out of the water and, wearin' just a breach cloth, came over, admiring my bundles of plews and other furs we was tyin' on to the travois, and asked where I'd gotten them. He said he hadn't seen any one man get that many in a season before. I just smiled and told him "In the mountains." Then he asked if I wanted to do some tradin'. He turned around and said something in French, and the youngest and prettiest squaw came out of the water, naked as ever, and walked right up to us. He shoved her toward me and said he would sell her to me for twenty of my plews. Her eyes were down, starin' at the ground, and she looked mighty afraid and sad. He slapped her hard on the rump and said something else in French, and she looked up and forced a smile on her face. I shook my head no and said I'd like to trade for a couple of horses. He grabbed her by the hair and pulled her away from me and brought up his hand to hit her, and I unloaded with my right fist just has hard as I could and caught him right on the nose. I felt it break, and he went down hard.

I had never really considered my size before, but I was taller and heavier than most men I ever met. I was even an inch or so taller than Pa had been, and he was known back home as a mighty big and powerful man. I had grown strong with workin' all the time, and I had put every ounce of strength I had into that punch. Jean Luc didn't move when he hit the ground. This naked squaw jumped back with a look of fear. Lucien and Jacques started for their guns, and Runnin' Wolf stepped up with his bow drawn, pointin' it at them, and at the same time, Jimbo stood up out of the brush, showin' his teeth and growlin', and those two Frenchies just froze right where they were standin'. The two squaws still in the water were holdin' on to each other and starin' at Jimbo, and the one by me took a step behind me, away from Jimbo. He was a mighty fearsome sight.

I motioned with my hand for Lucien and Jacques to sit down in the water. They did, and so did the squaws. I got down and checked on Jean Luc. His face was a bloody mess, but he was still breathin'. I had only hit him the one time, but his nose was broke and his upper lip smashed and his left eye was already turnin' color. I shook him some, and he started to come to.

I told Jimbo to stay and had Runnin' Wolf tell them squaws to get dressed. It was mighty distractin' bein' around naked women. Seems the Ute and Snake tongues are kind of alike, and Runnin' Wolf could speak a little Snake, and between that and the hand signs, he seemed to be makin' them understand. The ones in the water climbed out away from Jimbo, but the one behind me didn't move. The look in her eyes told me she was afraid, and then I realized Jimbo was sittin' right by their dresses. I called Jimbo over to me and told him to sit, and she grabbed hold of my arm and was standin' right up against me. I could feel myself turnin' red again just like when I saw Emma in the creek back home, and it seemed to be gettin' mighty warm, but I just walked her over to where their dresses were.

Jean Luc was groggy and just crawled over to the water and was washin' off his face. I motioned for the other men just to stay in the water, and I went over and gathered their weapons and put them in a pile a little ways out in the brush. Runnin' Wolf was talkin' to the squaws, findin' out what their situation was. He could speak a little Snake as Snake and Ute are kind of alike, and what they couldn't understand of each other, they would use sign language.

I motioned for the two in the water to get out and get dressed. I had been in such a hurry to leave I hadn't put my grizzly claw necklace or possibles bag on yet and did so now. Jimbo was sittin' on his haunches right by me, and when that real pretty younger squaw looked at me again, she pointed at me and said something in Snake. The others just looked at me and stared.

Jean Luc was sittin' there at the water's edge, starin' at me as well. After a minute, he said, "So you're the one they call Grizzly Killer, and that is the Great Medicine Dog." He slowly got to his feet and looked at me and said, "You got no call to hit me like that," and I simply told him I would abide no man strikin' a woman. He said that she wasn't no woman, just a squaw, and I told him there was no difference.

I motioned him over to the others and told them now we would talk. I asked them, if they had been trappin' with Fontenelle, where all their plews were as their packs were carryin' some but not many for three trappers. Jean Luc told me they lost most of them and half their traps crossin' the Seeds-Kee-Dee. He said they'd looked for a few days downriver, but it was runnin' so high with the snow meltin' in the high country they never found one. I asked them why he wanted to sell the woman, and he told me they needed the plews to resupply for the comin' year or they would have to sign on for just wages with one of the brigades. He said they were just squaws anyhow and he could get another later. I asked him how he knew of me. He told me that I was a great warrior to the Shoshone, and they were singin' songs around their campfires of the Medicine Dog. That I killed the great bears all alone and killed enemies farther away than an arrow can fly. He said the Shoshone believed me to be both their friend and their enemy, that I had killed many warriors and had given of the great bear to others, and that I had great medicine.

I asked them how they came by the squaws and why they had the right to sell them. He told me they stayed in their Shoshone village through the winter, and the squaws were given to them. Then Runnin' Wolf told me these Snake squaws had been given to the trappers as a sign of peace, but after they left the village, these men treated them like slaves and beat them if they didn't do just what they said.

I asked Jean Luc how many plews he figured it would take to get outfitted for another year, and he said maybe sixty if they was sellin' for the same as last year. I figured, lookin' over their packs, they had maybe thirty or forty, and I told him I would give him forty plews for all three squaws, the squaw's horses, and two pack horses. He laughed and said that was robbery. I told him I had the plews and he needed supplies and that was my offer. Those three Frenchies talked and cussed and wasn't happy, but they agreed. I held my hand out to shake, and Jean Luc just looked at me and told me he would get even for his broken nose and bein' robbed. I simply told him he didn't have to take my offer, that he wasn't bein' forced, and he could find me at Rendezvous if he wanted to get even.

I counted out forty prime plews while Runnin' Wolf told the Snake squaws they now belonged to us. I had Jimbo sit by their weapons while we loaded the horses with all our truck off the travois. I had Runnin' Wolf lead out, with the Snake women followin', and I rode Red over to Jimbo and told him to stay again by the weapons. My meanin' was clear to those Frenchies that they couldn't get their weapons till Jimbo was gone. When I was 'bout a quarter mile out from the hot spring, I whistled real loud, and a minute later, Jimbo was right by our side. I trotted Ol' Red up to Runnin' Wolf, and he looked at me and said, "They come after us." I just smiled and said, "I know."

Chapter XI

Sweet Lake

WE TRAVELED AS FAST as we could the rest of the day and on into the twilight. We passed a spot that the river widened out in a place it looked like we could cross. But I motioned for Runnin' Wolf to just keep on goin'. I sent Jimbo along our back trail to see if there was trouble close and went up to tell Runnin' Wolf to keep goin' 'bout another mile and then drop down to the river and follow it back to this crossin' and we would make camp on the other side. He just nodded and went on. He was leadin' a pack horse, and each of the three Snake women were too. I dropped way back behind the others until they were out of sight, seein' how clear of a trail we were leavin' and how easy it would be to follow in the dark. The moon would be settin' in 'bout an hour, and it would be a dark night. I didn't think they could follow our tracks after that.

I caught up to the rest 'bout the time Runnin' Wolf was turnin' down to the river. We followed the river back down to where it widened out, and although crossin' in the dark wasn't pleasant, we had no trouble. We made a dark camp, just eatin' a little jerky and drinkin' water. Jimbo came into camp then, and the women jumped when Jimbo came out of the dark and up to me. It was real plain Jimbo made them all real jumpy. He came up, and with his low growl, he was tellin' me we were bein' followed. Runnin' Wolf grabbed his bow, and I asked him to stay with the women, and Jimbo and I would go. He looked disappointed but, I had got us in this fix, so it was my place to fix it.

I saddled Red again and followed Jimbo out into the night. We went less than a mile when Jimbo stopped and got down on his belly. I turned Red off the trail and went back down by the river and let the reins hang as I always did then hurried back up to the trail. I had Jimbo stay in the brush on one side of the trail, and I got on the other. 'Bout ten minutes later, here came the three of them, and I heard Jean Luc whisper something in French, and one of the others cussed. When they were right between us, I yelled "Get 'em!" and fired my pistol into the air. At the same time, Jimbo jumped in, growlin' and goin' after the horses. Those horses started buckin'. Lucien was thrown off first, and his horse and the pack horses took off back down the trail. Then Jacques's horse went down with him on it, and Jimbo jumped up onto Jean Luc and bit his leg, and he lost his balance and went down. Their horses were scattered all over the place, and since I didn't know if any of them still had their guns, I stayed out in the brush, out of sight. When things had quieted down and I had moved down a ways from the trail, I yelled back up at them, "Next time you come sneakin' up my back trail in the dark, you won't walk away!"

Next mornin' we were on the trail 'fore light, and Runnin' Wolf told me these squaws knew a shorter way to Willow Valley over the mountains that would save us several days of travel over followin' the Bear River. We were now on the west side of the Bear and followin' it along, headin' 'bout straight north. We jumped several deer just after it got light, and Runnin' Wolf motioned for us to stop, and he went on ahead. I was just startin' to wonder where he had gone, when he came ridin' back to us with a deer across the back of his saddle. We tied it onto one of the pack horses and headed north again.

We found a grove of cottonwoods on a bend in the river and stopped to eat and rest the horses. Jimbo was now in the habit of headin' down our back trail whenever we stopped, and he was just watchin' me for the signal, and when I pointed, he took off. Those Snake women went right to work, skinnin' and butcherin' that deer, and they had a fire goin' and meat cookin' by the time Runnin' Wolf and me had the horses watered and hobbled on grass along the river bottom. We sat down, and as I looked at these three women now with their dresses on, there weren't much difference in their ages. The one was a little younger and looked a lot like one just older. I figured maybe they were sisters, and both of them were mighty pretty. The other I figured was 'bout the same age as the older sister, if they were sisters, and was nice lookin' too, although she didn't have the natural beauty of the other two. Me and Runnin' Wolf sat down by the fire, and I asked Runnin' Wolf to have them come over 'cause I wanted to know their names.

They came over to the fire with worried looks, and as I stood up, the two older ones stepped back, but the younger one just looked right up into my face and smiled. Her older sister said something to her and tried to pull her back, but she pulled away and kept lookin' right at me. Runnin' Wolf laughed a little and was smilin' at the three of them. I asked what was funny, and he said, "The others are afraid of you, but Sun Flower Woman is not afraid."

I said Zach and pointed to myself and repeated Zach several times. Then Sun Flower Woman said Zach. It took a few tries, but she got it out pretty good. Then her sister looked up and said something and made the sign for *grizzly* and *kill* and pointed at me. Runnin' Wolf chucked again and told me I was mighty big medicine to them and my name was Grizzly Killer, not Zach. I asked in sign if they were sisters, and with Runnin' Wolf's help, they understood and said yes. Then I asked the sister's name, and she said something, and Runnin'

Wolf told me Raven Wing, and pointin' to the other, I asked her name. She didn't look up, and I could tell she was mighty worried. Sun Flower Woman said her name was Kimama and made a sign for *butterfly*. I asked Runnin' Wolf to tell them they were safe and we would not hurt them, that they were free to do what they wanted and they could stay with us till we could get them to their village. Runnin' Wolf looked at me and said he wouldn't be safe in the land of the Snakes. Raven Wing then spoke in part English and part French, but she made me and Runnin' Wolf understand that Grizzly Killer owned them now and they would do what he told them and that Runnin' Wolf had helped them, that he was a great warrior, and he would be safe with Grizzly Killer and the Shoshone women in the land of the Shoshone. I asked her where she learned to speak our tongue, and without lookin' at me, she said, "White man's in village." I was wonderin', if the Snakes were friendly to trappers, why they had attacked me.

Jimbo came up to the fire, and all three women just froze. But Butterfly was tremblin' all over. I walked over to her, and she didn't dare move. I told Jimbo to sit, and he did, waggin' his tail, and his big ol' tongue was hangin' out the side of his mouth. I patted him on the head and told Butterfly he would not hurt her, that he would protect her. Then she looked up at me, and with tears in her eyes, she said, pointin' at Jimbo, "Big Medicine Dog kill brother."

I looked at Runnin' Wolf, and he said something in Ute I didn't understand and walked away down toward the river.

It took me a few minutes to put it all together, then I tried to make her understand that the warrior Jimbo had killed was tryin' to kill Runnin' Wolf and Jimbo was just protectin' Runnin' Wolf and me. If that warrior was her brother, I was sorry, but when we were attacked, we were warriors too, and we would always fight. I told her that she was with us now and Jimbo would protect her and Sun Flower and Raven Wing, just like he had protected Runnin' Wolf, and that me and Runnin' Wolf and Jimbo would only kill those who were tryin' to kill us. She seemed to relax a little, but I could tell she was still mighty scared. Then Sun Flower and Raven Wing came over and talked to her in their own tongue. I figured they were tryin' to comfort her.

I walked down by the river where Runnin' Wolf was standin' and asked if he was all right. He said, "Her brother had killed his horse and tried to kill him, and he didn't know if he should trust her or any of them." He said, "The Snake and Ute are enemies, and the women can be more vicious than the braves."

I told him I believed these Snake women were just afraid and away from their own people, that if we showed them we would protect them, they would be our friends, and that it was Jimbo that scared them. If we were kind to them and provided for them like good men, they would be good women too. He nodded, but I could tell that trust on both sides would have to be earned.

We traveled another ten miles or so before we stopped for the night. Those three women made camp mighty fast, had firewood gathered and deer meat roastin' while me and Runnin' Wolf took care of the stock. Now we had eight horses and Ol' Red, and waterin' and hobblin' them for the night took a bit longer. Runnin' Wolf's leg was gettin' stronger every day, and he was walkin' with almost no limp, and he wasn't wearin' the splint anymore. I had Jimbo go back down our back trail, and he was gone quite a spell, but when he came back, he was carryin' part of a half-rotten deer leg. So I figured all was clear. The women each had a buffalo robe to sleep under, so when it was time for sleep, me and Runnin' Wolf brought in Ol' Red and the chestnut and tied them right close. With them and Jimbo, I figured we wouldn't need to stand guard.

A couple of hours before light, Jimbo licked my face, and I was instantly awake and listenin', but I couldn't hear a thing. Jimbo made his very low growl, and I rolled over and got up and instantly saw Butterfly's robe was gone. I checked on the horses, and her horse was gone as well. Jimbo was waitin' for me to tell him to go after her, but I just motioned for him to stay.

I threw a few small sticks on the coals and blew some life into them and got what few coffee beans we had left and made our last pot of coffee. Everyone was awake by now, and Sun Flower and Raven Wing were talkin', and Runnin' Wolf said, "They are afraid we would be mad 'cause we paid for all three of them, and they were worried 'bout Kimama."

I brought them over to the fire and, with Runnin' Wolf's help, told them I did not buy them to own them but to get them away from Jean Luc and the others, that Butterfly could have left anytime she wanted to, and so could they, that me and Runnin' Wolf would help them and protect them if they stayed with us, but if they wanted to leave, they could, just like Butterfly did. Sun Flower, who seemed the boldest of them, asked why we helped them, that we paid for them, and we didn't make them come to our robes at night, and now we told them they could go anytime. She asked, if we didn't want them, why we bought them.

I looked at Runnin' Wolf, tryin' to find an answer for them, and he just had a puzzled look on his face as well. Then I told them that Runnin' Wolf had a sister just like them, and he would want someone to help and protect her if she needed help just like we were helpin' them, that it made our hearts good to help those that needed help.

Runnin' Wolf still had a puzzled look on his face, but it was somehow different, and Sun Flower just looked at me and smiled and said, "I stay with Grizzly Killer, and it makes my heart good too." Raven Wing was watchin' Runnin' Wolf, and I could tell she was seein' him different now. He was not just a Ute and an enemy but a lovin' brother that cared for his sister.

The women were puttin' some meat over the fire, and it was plain Runnin' Wolf was ponderin' on what had been said. Finally, he said to me, "They are just like Shining Star, and helpin' them makes my heart good too."

We were loaded and movin' north again just after dawn, and 'bout midmornin', Raven Wing pointed to a break in the hills to the west and told Runnin' Wolf that was the trail to Sweet Lake and then we go over the mountain to Willow Valley. We turned on to a fairly plain but not well-used trail and left the Bear River, headin' west. As we came out of the pass in the hills, the biggest water I'd ever seen filled the whole big valley, spreadin' off to the north. It was so big you couldn't see the north shore, and it looked to be at least a half day's ride to the west side of the lake. I was just starin' at it, and I asked Runnin' Wolf if'n he had seen this lake before, and he just shook his head no. He said, "I've had heard stories about it, but I have not been here."

Jimbo had been scoutin' up ahead as usual, and he came back to see why we had stopped. The women seemed to be gettin' excited 'bout something, and Raven Wing told Runnin' Wolf, "We stop by lake to rest horses for climb over mountain."

We followed the trail down, and it was plain it was leadin' around the south end of the lake. Just after midday, we came to a big sandy beach. There were trees back a ways from the water and grass for the horses and no sign of anyone bein' around. We stopped and unloaded the horses and hobbled them on the grass. I figured it to be the first part of June, and it was a right pretty and warm day. The weather had been clear ever since we left the dugout. And I figured by lookin' at just the sage-covered hills, it didn't rain here in the summer like it did back home. We built us a fire maybe twenty-five feet back from the water, in the sand, then Sun Flower and Raven Wing just pulled their dresses up over their heads and ran out into the water, completely naked again.

Bein' naked didn't seem to bother them a bit. It was just as natural to them as any other part of their lives. I was just standin' there, starin'. Bein' around naked women wasn't natural to me at all. Then Sun Flower came runnin' up out of the water, splashin' and laughin' right to me. She grabbed my arms and pulled me out into the lake. I must have had a real strange look on my face, 'cause Runnin' Wolf started to laugh at me, then he stripped down and went in the lake too. I was standin' in water up to my middle in soakin'-wet buckskins with this beautiful girl completely naked, laughin' and splashin' water right in front of me. I was gettin' mighty uncomfortable, and my manhood was stickin' straight out, pushin' against the buckskin. Then Sun Flower jumped up on me and threw her arms around my neck and kissed me. I held on to her as tight as I could. She drew her head back and smiled and looked at me with those dark shinin' eyes like they were teasin' me. She had her legs wrapped around my middle, and she pushed her upper body away from me and started to undo the laces on my shirt. I let her do it, just watchin' those dark eyes of hers. When she had the laces undone, she unwrapped her legs from around me, and I pulled the shirt off, and she started to undo my pants.

In just a minute, I was as naked as she was, and she took my hand and placed it on her breast and kissed me again and again. I had never been with a girl before, and I had no idea what to do, but she just took my hand and led me out of the water and we lay down in the grass. She taught me how to make love over and over all afternoon. There was no wrong in it. It was just another part of the natural world. I still was not at all comfortable at bein' naked in front of a woman, but Sun Flower was so natural 'bout it, it all seemed right.

By late afternoon, I had not seen Runnin' Wolf or Raven Wing since we went into the water earlier, not that I had been lookin', and I knew it was gettin' to be time to be fixin' a meal 'fore dark. But I was havin' a right hard time wantin' to move. Lyin' in the grass with my arms around Sun Flower, holdin' her tight up against me, was the finest feelin' I could ever remember havin'.

Then I noticed movement across the way and could see Raven Wing and Runnin' Wolf walkin' hand in hand toward the fire pit. A couple of hours before, Sun Flower had spread my buckskins out over some brush in the sun to dry, and now we got up and got dressed. My buckskins were still a little damp, but they would dry with me in them by the fire soon enough.

Jimbo was chewin' on the remains of a rabbit he'd caught, and I figured we needed to spend the night and get an early start tomorrow, but I wanted to have a look around before dark. I saddled Ol' Red and whistled for Jimbo, and we went out scoutin'. I rode east along the lakeshore for a couple of miles and then made a big half circle around camp, endin' a couple of miles from camp on the west side at the lake shore. I saw no tracks but our own, and Jimbo hadn't smelled anything wrong, so I just headed back in. There was deer roastin' on the fire, and I noticed the bedrolls were spread out. Mine on one side of camp and Runnin' Wolf's on the other, and right next to each was a buffalo robe. I looked at Runnin' Wolf, and he just smiled at me.

After we ate, me and Runnin' Wolf went out and gathered the stock, watered them, and brought them right in close and set up a picket line for them. While we were doin' our chores, Runnin' Wolf said, "Snake women are good, not like Snake warriors," and he had a big ol' grin on his face. I figured life on the trail was gonna be mighty different from here on out.

Next mornin', after gettin' almost no sleep all night and eating a little leftover meat, we were loaded up and were on the trail by dawn. 'Bout midmornin' we were roundin' the southwest side of Sweet Lake[5] and started north along the western shore. By midafternoon we came to where a canyon came down the mountain from the west, and Raven Wing pointed and said, "Willow Valley." We turned and went

---

[5] Sweet Lake is what the Shoshone and early trappers called present-day Bear Lake. It spans the Utah and Idaho border. It is approximately twenty miles long and eight miles wide.

another five miles or so and found a campin' spot alongside a grassy meadow full of flowers with a fast-movin' creek runnin' right down through it.

We set up a camp mighty quick, and Runnin' Wolf said he would go make meat and left me in camp to care of the stock. Once I had the stock hobbled in the meadow, the women had a small fire goin', and we were waitin' for Runnin' Wolf to come back. I had the women come over and sit down by the fire, and with what Injun talk I had learned and with sign language, I got them to understand I wanted them to speak English. And so I started the long process of teachin' these two Shoshone women the English tongue. The only way I knew how was by pointin' at something and sayin' what it was in English. It was the same way I had been teachin' Runnin' Wolf, but Runnin' Wolf already knew a fair amount 'fore I started with him.

But these two sisters seemed to make a game and a competition out of it. They were pointin' at everything and waitin' for me to say the word, and they would try to repeat it. I would point to my nose and say *nose* and then my ear and say *ear*. Then Sun flower lifted her dress off and pointed to her breast and waited for me to say the name, but I just turned bright red, and Sun Flower and Raven Wing both just laughed at me. They seemed to take particular delight in makin' me turn red. I didn't know it at that time but would find out later that Raven Wing already spoke mighty good English and Sun Flower knew some as well. They were still laughin', and Sun Flower was slidin' back into her dress, when Runnin' Wolf came ridin' into camp. He had a small buck on the back of his horse with its antlers just startin' to grow for the year. Then I could see he was hurt; his right arm was bloody. I jumped up, but Raven Wing beat me to him. She was helpin' him down, and I got the deer off the back of the chestnut and noticed a good-sized gash down the haunch of the deer. When I got over to the fire, Raven Wing and Sun Flower had his buckskin shirt off, and I could see a couple of nasty scratches a few inches long runnin' from his shoulder, almost to his elbow. But those women were cleanin' it up, and by the time I had his horse taken care of and went over to find out what had happened, his arm was wrapped up tight, and he had a big ol' smile on his face.

When I asked what had happened, he said he needed the Grizzly Killer with him. He told me after he shot the deer with his bow, he gutted it and got it tied onto the chestnut. He had gone just a few feet when a grizzly stood up in the trail and swiped a paw at him. He said, "The chestnut reared up, and that saved me. Just the tip and the bear's claws caught my shoulder, and I fired the squirrel gun at the bear. I don't know if I hit him or not, but then the chestnut was running and the grizzly wasn't following." The more I pondered on this, the more worried I was gettin'. If Runnin' Wolf's shot had hit the grizzly, we had a wounded bear in the area, and if it didn't hit him, we had a grizzly on the prowl in the area. Both were mighty fearsome to deal with.

I pulled the balls from the Hawken and Harper Ferry rifles and put in an extra charge of powder and then did the same for the squirrel gun. It was a lot lighter load, but we might need all we could get out of all the guns if that bear showed up. I brought the stock right close and said we would all have to watch tonight. They all agreed, and the women started to bring in more firewood and built two more fires in a triangle around us.

Long toward mornin', Jimbo started to growl, and Ol' Red let loose with a loud bray, and the horses were all mighty uneasy, but we never saw a thing.

Just as the sky was turnin' gray along the eastern horizon and some of the stars were startin' to disappear, we ate some of the deer Runnin' Wolf had brought in and loaded up. We headed up the trail just when it was light enough to see into the trees pretty good. I didn't want to be surprised by a wounded grizzly feelin' real cantankerous comin' out of the shadows. Jimbo was out in the lead, and I was next with two pack horses, then Sun Flower and Raven Wing, with Runnin' Wolf bringin' up the rear with the other two pack horses. If that bear came at us, I didn't want the women slowed down with the pack horses to pull along. I kept whistlin' Jimbo in a bit so's I could see him most of the time. I didn't want him as far out in front of us as he usually was.

As we climbed up toward the pass, it was mighty steep, and we stopped to rest the horses often. By midmornin' we came out on a flat bench, and it appeared we only had another mile or two to reach the top. But with the horses lathered and winded and us not gettin' any sleep last night and very little the night before, we stopped and pulled the packs to let the horses rest. I figured we could all use a couple of hours sleep.

The view from here was like none I'd ever seen before. Lookin' east, you could see forever. The bright blue of the sky with its fluffy white clouds just seemed to blend into the horizon. To the southeast, you could see the snowcapped peaks of the Bear River Mountains, and lookin' down at the clear blue water of Sweet Lake as it filled this huge valley that it was set in, you could see every shade of blue you could think of. You could see mountain ranges to the northeast that I had no idea what they were, and in the distance, you could see there was no tellin' how far away they were. This was a mighty big land and as beautiful as anything you could imagine.

We lay down in the warm June sun with the horses ground-picketed right close by, and with Jimbo on guard, I was asleep almost at once. When I opened my eyes and lay there listenin' as always, I could see the sun was past center sky, so I knew we'd been asleep more than two hours. I could hear a whisper of wind shakin' the quakie leaves that were just gettin' to full size from their buds, and I heard the cry of a hawk and then caught his movement as he soared high overhead. I sat up and looked at Sun Flower lyin' there by me and the beauty of her face. I wondered what Ma and Pa would think of me with this Injun girl. Then I thought of Emma Potter and wondered if she was married now and if I would ever see her again. I didn't think so, 'cause I doubted I'd ever leave these mountains now; they were my home. As I stood up, the others came awake, and we all took our time gettin' movin'. The sleep helped, but it wasn't at all enough.

As we loaded up, I noticed Jimbo was starin' at the trees off to the south. They were maybe two hundred yards away. He wasn't growlin', but something over there had his attention. Just as I was ready to saddle up, Jimbo stood up, and all the hair down the middle of his back stood up, and he started with his deep-down low growl, and I knew there was something over there. I didn't cotton to the idea of bein' followed whether it was by man or beast, so I told the others to stay there while I checked it out. I checked the prime in the Hawken, Pa's old Harper Ferry, and the horse pistol and started over to the trees. Jimbo was out in front, but he wasn't gettin' very far ahead.

When we were 'bout fifty yards from the trees, Jimbo started to growl and then took off toward them. I caught a glimpse of movement, and an ol' silver-tipped grizzly came out from behind the branches of a pine and started right at Jimbo. He was limpin' on his front leg, and Jimbo was able to stay out of range of those claws. Red was way too nervous to hold still, so I jumped off to get a good shot. I aimed right for his front shoulder and fired. When that ball hit him, it threw him off-balance, but he didn't go down. And then he started after me. He wasn't movin' very fast now, but I didn't have time to reload, and Red had taken off with the other rifle, goin' back to the others. I started to reload as fast as I could make my hands move, and then Jimbo attacked him from the rear. That bear turned to take on Jimbo, and that gave me time to finish loadin'. That ol' grizzly was turned, fendin' off Jimbo, and I had a clean shot at his other shoulder from only 'bout fifteen yards, and my shot was true. The bear roared his hatred of me to the world, but with two broken shoulders, he couldn't get up. As I started to reload again, I heard the thunder of hooves and saw Runnin' Wolf bearin' down on me at a full run. That chestnut could really run. He jumped off and fired the squirrel gun, and I was ready and fired again. That grizzly tried to roar again, but no sound came out, and just as I was reloaded and ready to fire another shot, his head collapsed, with his sightless eyes starin' right at me. Runnin' Wolf turned and looked at me, and with a big smile on his face, he simply said, "Grizzly Killer."

We spent the rest of the day right there, skinnin' that bear and then scrapin' the hide. I slept sound that night, and the next mornin', we were loaded and back on the trail just after light.

Chapter XII

Willow Valley

AFTER WE CRESTED the pass, we followed a creek down, goin' through meadows so full of wildflowers you could hardly see the green of the grass for the colors of the flowers. We went through stands of timber and scattered stands of quakies. There were sage flats, and even the dry sage-covered hills had flowers bloomin'. We traveled what I figured was 'bout twenty miles and made camp where another stream came in from the north. We hobbled the horses and Jimbo set out on his routine scout.

The game was plentiful; we'd seen deer and elk throughout the day. There were wolves howlin' to the north just as it was gettin' dark, and several moose came down into some beaver ponds that were just above us on the stream comin' in from the north. Although his antlers were just half grown this time of year, one bull looked to be bigger than Ol' Red, and Red was bigger than any of our horses.

We continued with the English lessons each night around the fire and every time we got the chance in our travels each day. I was startin' to pick up more and more Ute and even a few of the Snake words. But the women were learnin' English much faster than I was learnin' Injun. When we got under the robes for the night, I had a mighty hard time goin' to sleep with a naked girl snuggled right up against me.

We entered Willow Valley 'bout midday the followin' day, and none of us knew where to go. The valley was mighty big. I could see maybe thirty or forty miles to the north and another ten or so to the south, and it was at least ten miles across to the west to another high, rugged mountain. We climbed up to a high point of land just north of where the river had cut its course through the foothills and just looked 'bout. Runnin' Wolf noticed a smoky haze way off to the south, so we headed that way.

We hadn't traveled but a mile or two, when we saw a half dozen riders comin' toward us. As they got closer, the hair on Jimbo's back started to stand up, and Runnin' Wolf came up from the rear to my side and said, "Snakes." Then Sun Flower kicked her horse and took off toward them. When she got to them, there was hand wavin', and it was clear she knew them, and then Raven Wing took off to go meet them. Runnin' Wolf had a mighty serious look on his face, and I checked the prime in my pans. In just a few minutes, they all headed our way. Jimbo slipped off into the brush and disappeared.

When they were 'bout forty yards out, a very tough-lookin' brave ridin' beside Sun Flower held his hand up in the sign of peace, and I did the same, and then Runnin' Wolf held his hand up in peace, and these six braves along with Sun Flower and Raven Wing came on up to us. It was clear Sun Flower and Raven Wing were excited, and she started to talk way too fast for me or even Runnin' Wolf to understand. Raven Wing must have noticed the confused look on our faces and said something, and Sun Flower slowed down and started to use sign. I then started to get the gist of what she was tryin' to say.

It seemed this fierce-lookin' brave to her side was their brother and their village was here, camped on the Little Bear River just an hour's ride south of where the Little Bear runs into this river we were followin'. If it had a name, I missed it. Her brother's name was Spotted Elk, and he was leadin' this huntin' party to bring meat to their camp. He was lookin' real serious at Runnin' Wolf, and Raven Wing started talkin' and then rode over to Runnin' Wolf and signed he was her man. I'm not sure whether Runnin' Wolf was more concerned 'bout bein' a Ute in the middle of all these Snakes or 'bout bein' called Raven Wing's man. He was mighty uncomfortable; it was plain to see. Raven Wing talked to her brother, and although I didn't understand any of what was said, it was plain the look on Spotted Elk's face and the others with him changed, and then he signed to Runnin' Wolf that the protector of his sisters was welcome in their village. Then he looked at me and signed and, along with some English, said, "We have met before in battle." I must have had a confused look, and he continued. "I steal horses. Mule kill my friend. You Grizzly Killer, great warrior."

There didn't seem to be any hatred toward me for killin' their friends, only respect of a warrior in battle. He told us the village elders would want to meet Grizzly Killer and this Ute that was the protector of Shoshone women, that seein' Sun Flower and Raven Wing would make the hearts good of everyone in the village. Then he asked me, if I was Grizzly Killer, where was the big Medicine Dog?

I whistled, and Jimbo came out of the brush behind them and trotted up alongside me. They all had a surprised look, and Sun Flower said something to them in Snake, and they all looked a little nervous. Then she said something else and got down from her horse and walked over to Jimbo and rubbed his ears. Spotted Elk smiled at her and then motioned for them to go. I ask Runnin' Wolf if he knew what she said to him, and Raven Wing answered in sign and English that Sun Flower told them they didn't need to worry, that she would not let the Medicine Dog eat them. I was still laughin' at that as we headed toward the Little Bear River and the Shoshone camp.

I was right pleased I could understand their sign talk, 'cause I could only pick out a word or two every so often of the Snake tongue. I was havin' a mighty hard time with Ute talk, and I could tell it was goin' to take a while to learn Snake. I was findin' out that Raven Wing spoke more English than I had figured she did, but she wasn't real sure of herself with English, so she didn't use it much. I figured with Sun Flower and Raven Wing's village bein' here at Rendezvous, that they would stay with them when we left. So I might not learn much Snake anyway. I was ponderin' over why everyone called them Snakes but they called themselves Shoshone. But that seemed to be more than I could talk 'bout with knowin' so little of their tongue.

As we approached their camp, I whistled Jimbo back to me 'cause there were dogs barkin' and comin' out to us. As the people of the village noticed us, they moved back away, pointin' at Jimbo, then Sun Flower and Raven Wing rode on ahead. Then two very serious-lookin' young warriors stepped out in front of us, and we all stopped. Sun Flower and Raven wing talked to them for just a minute, and one of them took off, announcing our arrival throughout the village.

People started to gather, watchin' us. Sun Flower motioned for me and Runnin' Wolf to follow. The lodges were all set with their openin's to the east, and there were paintings on the outside of most of them. There were scenes of huntin' and battles, some of the sun and moon, others of animals. There were stands set up with totems hangin' off them in front of most of the lodges and a small fire ring just outside as well. Most of the children were completely naked, some hidin' behind their mothers, peekin' around them, watchin' us. Others were more bold right out in front. I had the thought that Sun Flower would have been one of them right out front 'cause there was nothin' bashful 'bout her at all.

We passed fifteen or twenty lodges and came to a larger one with a big space around it, and Sun Flower stopped us and motioned for us to get down. This was clearly the chief's lodge, and then I noticed Runnin' Wolf. I never saw anyone look to be in such misery. He was mighty uncomfortable bein' in the middle of a Snake village and with the warriors that had tried to kill him just a couple of months ago probably right here as well. As I got off Ol' Red, I told Jimbo to stay, and I rubbed his ears a bit.

Sun Flower and Raven Wing just stood off to the side of the lodge openin', and in just a minute, a man stepped out. He was wearin' a full headdress of feathers that trailed clear down to his knees. He appeared to be in his forties and was wide in the shoulders and looked to be a very powerful man. He was much shorter than me, but he had a look that told me I didn't want to make him mad. Two beautifully dressed women stepped out behind him and stood one on each side of the lodge openin'. Their dresses were almost white and decorated with colored quills and what looked to be colored glass beads. He spoke to Raven Wing, and she nodded. Then he turned to Sun Flower and spoke. Both women looked surprised, and Sun Flower turned and left. He spoke again, and Raven Wing said he wished for us to sit.

When we were all seated around the fire, he spoke again, this time in heavy accented English. He said his name was Charging Bull, and he was chief of this village of the Shoshone people. Then he started talkin' in Shoshone, and Raven Wing Spoke in English, tellin' us what he was sayin'. She spoke much more English than I would have believed. Just then, Sun Flower returned, and with her was Butterfly. He motioned for Sun Flower and Butterfly to sit down. He told us of Butterfly meetin' them on the trail, and they had taken a shorter way to Willow Valley through the canyon of the Little Bear River. He said that Butterfly had told him of the French trappers' treatment of the women and of bein' bought from the Frenchmen by Grizzly Killer. Butterfly had not looked up; she was just starin' at the ground. He said that Butterfly had shamed them by runnin' away, and I could take her back now, and she would not run away again.

Lookin' at Raven Wing, I asked her if I could speak, and she nodded. I spoke slowly so Raven Wing would not miss anything I wanted to say. I told him that Butterfly had the right to leave anytime she wanted, that I bought them not for myself but to get them away from the Frenchmen whom I did not think had good hearts, that Sun Flower and Raven Wing could leave us if they wished. I told him that these brave Shoshone women were worth much more than furs, and my heart was happy to see Butterfly back with her people. Butterfly looked at me with a look of surprise. Sun Flower had a worried look on her face. I told him we were honored to be welcomed into his village, but we had to meet General Ashley at the Rendezvous and asked if we could return later.

He said it would make his heart good if we returned, and he hoped to get to know Grizzly Killer and this Ute warrior better. Raven Wing then spoke again, tellin' her chief that "this Ute's name is Running Wolf." Runnin' Wolf had not said a word since we entered the village. As we got up and went to the horses, Jimbo was right by my side, and Chargin' Bull asked and Raven Wing repeated where the big Medicine Dog came from. I turned and told him, "From your camp. This is the pup your warriors left behind when they stole my horses."

He looked surprised then shook his head and smiled. As we got in the saddle, Sun Flower came over and reached up to my hand. She looked at me with questioning eyes and asked, "You come back?"

I looked into those dark beautiful eyes, smiled, and said, "Yes, I come back."

As we rode out of the village, a Shoshone boy came ridin' up to us and signed he would lead us to the camp of Ashley. Runnin' Wolf asked his name, and he said it was Little Horse. We hadn't rode far when we saw another Injun village on the other side of the Little Bear. The Shoshone boy with us pointed and said "Nez Pierce." Their horses were right pretty with most of them havin' spotted rumps.

It didn't take long, and we were seein' white men and their camps. I hadn't seen a white man since last rendezvous. We waved and yelled greetin's, and not much farther, I saw the tents set up that Ashley done his tradin' from. As we rode through the camps, Jimbo seemed to be gettin' a lot of attention, and men were wavin', pointin', and yellin' at others to come and see this huge dog.

When we got up in front of the tradin' tents, some of Ashley's men came out and helped us unload all the plews and furs from the horses. The horses were all mighty tired as they hadn't had these heavy packs off all day, and it was gettin' to be late afternoon now. When I asked, they said the general was out with a group, scoutin' the valley to the south of here, and they didn't expect him back till sometime tomorrow. As they were gettin' the furs weighed, several men that I knew from last year came up. William Sublette and Jedediah Smith were among them, but neither of them knew me. Mr. Sublette came up and asked who it was that got all these plews, and I smiled and said Zach Connors. He just stared at me for a minute, and Jed Smith walked up and said, "Boy, you've changed."

I hadn't thought 'bout it, but I guess my looks had changed. My hair ain't been cut in over a year and was way down past my shoulders, plus now I had a beard. Mr. Smith asked where Captain Jack was, and I held out my grizzly claw necklace and told them that it was what was left of the grizzly that put Pa under, that he was buried along a creek in the Bear River Mountains. They looked at me and said they were awful sorry that this was a mighty rough country. Then one of the others said it was a lot easier to go under out here than to survive.

Just then, Jimbo came around the corner of the supply tent and right up to me. Another one saw him and asked me if I was the one that the Snakes were callin' Grizzly Killer and if that was the big Medicine Dog. I patted Jimbo on the head and nodded. Mr. Sublette then said, "Boy, you've got you a mighty big name with the Injuns." He told me that Grizzly Killer was bein' talked 'bout all over the mountains now, that word was spreadin' that I had mighty powerful medicine, and that I could talk to that dog and he could understand me.

'Bout then, the supply clerks were weighin' the furs and told me I had 248 pounds, and that would give me $1,240 in credit. That sounded like a fortune to me. Back home, you could buy a pair of good mules for forty dollars and a year before we left a neighbor sold his whole farm with barns, cabin, stock, and fifty acres planted all for $1,250. For the first time in my life, I felt rich. I knew I wouldn't have near this much if it wasn't for Pa, and I really wished he were here to see this much money. I knew he'd never had that much before. I picked out some beads and brass loops, a good-sized cookin' pot, a few yards of bright-red trade cloth, and several twists of tobacco. When they had tallied up what I had, I told them we would be back tomorrow or the next day to get the rest of our supplies after General Ashley got back. The clerks offered me whisky at five dollars a bottle and seemed surprised when I turned it down. Pa had never been a drinker and had always told me it robbed a man of his senses. I had tasted it a couple of times at socials back home and never had a taste for the stuff.

We said our good-byes and headed back to the Shoshone village. Runnin' Wolf was still bein' mighty quiet, and I asked him if he wanted to go back there. He said no, but he wanted to be with Raven Wing, and he believed Chargin' Bull was a man of his word. But he wasn't sure 'bout all the other warriors in their village.

It was only 'bout three miles back to their village, and we were followin' along the Little Bear. We passed the Nez Pierce village again and watched a huntin' party cross the river into their village with several pack horses loaded with game.

When we approached the Shoshone village, there was a new lodge put up on this south end, and as we rode past, Sun Flower stepped out, smiled, and ran over to us. Then Raven Wing stepped out and motioned for us to come over. She said that the village had given them this lodge, and we would stay here. Little Horse said that he would take the horses out to the horse herd and they would be safe. We kept Ol' Red and the chestnut with us and led them over to the side of the lodge and picketed them on a good-sized patch of grass that went on down to the river bank. We pulled the packs over by the lodge, and I pulled out the trade cloth, beads, and brass rings and loops, and we gave them to the women. Their eyes lit up, and the smiles they had were really something to see. I brought out the cookin' pot, and they got even more excited. They pulled us both inside the lodge, and there was a small fire pit right in the center and a large openin' at the top for the smoke to go out. They had their buffalo robes laid out one on each side of the fire pit against the outside walls, and I thought of my dirty and smelly bedroll and knew it wouldn't do. I told them all I had to go back to Ashley's camp, and I would be back in just a little while. Sun Flower got that worried look on her face again, and I told Jimbo to stay with them, and she smiled at that. I figured she was still afraid I wasn't comin' back.

Ol' Red wasn't very happy 'bout bein' saddled again, and he made it plain he figured he had done enough for today. But we came to an understandin', and he finally stood still. I put him in a lope and was back at the tradin' tents in no time at all. I picked up six good Hudson Bay–type blankets and headed back. The sun was just an hour or so from settin' when I got back. Sun Flower and Jimbo were standin' out in front, waitin' for me. I knew I had only known Sun Flower for a mighty short time, but it was almighty comfortin' to have her waitin' for me when I got back. I handed her three of the blankets and stepped inside and set the other three on Raven Wing's robe. I looked at Sun Flower and asked where they were, and she pointed down toward the river. I took care of Red and went back to the lodge. She was makin' up a bed with the new blankets. She had cut a strip off the red cloth and was usin' it as a sash. She had it tied around her waist, and she was wearin' some of the brass rings around her arms. I walked over and picked her up in my arms and just held her, and I realized that I really had feelin's for this girl.

Just as the sun went down, Runnin' Wolf and Raven Wing came back, and Raven Wing said we were to go back to the chief's lodge and eat with him and dance. When we arrived at the chief's lodge, he was sittin' in front of the outside fire on a buffalo robe, and there was a grizzly robe spread out on one side, and he indicated for me and Runnin' Wolf to sit there. Across the fire from me was an elk robe, and across Chargin' Buffalo was another buffalo robe. The chief said something, and Raven Wing went over to his side and knelt down while Sun Flower stood behind me. In just a few minutes, there was a crowd of Shoshones circled around us, formin' a ring. Then Spotted Elk and three others came up to the fire, and they took their places, with Spotted Elk across from me and the others sittin' around between Spotted Elk and Runnin' Wolf. Raven Wing had a smile and look of pride on her face as her brother took his place by the fire, and I wished Sun Flower was by my side, but she was standin' behind me where I couldn't see her. When all was seated, Chargin' Bull said we would eat.

His wives came and gave each of us around the fire a wooden bowl of what I could only describe as stew. They started with the chief then Spotted Elk and then me then the others, and Runnin' Wolf was last. I couldn't identify all that was in it, but it tasted pretty good. I didn't know for sure, but I figured that was the order of importance they placed on each of us around the fire. There was no talk at all while we ate, and when all was finished, Chargin' Bull said, "Now we smoke." The older of his wives went into his lodge and brought out a small rolled-up hide that was almost pure white like her dress. It had beads and quillwork, and she unrolled it in such a way as everyone around the fire could see a drawin' of a chargin' buffalo. When it was unrolled, there was a pipe very ornately decorated with buffalo hair and an eagle feather, and it was painted in the same colors as the paintin's on his lodge. I pulled out the pouch I had the tobacco twists in and offered the tobacco to Chargin' Bull. He reached out and accepted it and spoke. Raven Wing said, “Chargin’ Bull thanks Grizzly Killer.”

He slowly filled the pipe, and his younger wife picked up a stick from the fire and held it while he puffed the pipe to life. He blew out a big puff of smoke and started to chant softly as he moved the pipe through the smoke first up and down then left and right. Then he passed the pipe to Spotted Elk. He went through the same motions, but then he spoke. Raven Wing spoke softly when he was finished and said, “Spotted Elk says he is honored to smoke the pipe with such great warriors. Even though Grizzly Killer and Runnin’ Wolf have been our enemies in the past, they have proved themselves honored friends and are welcome in the land of the Shoshone.”

He then passed the pipe to the next brave, and he went through the same motions. When he spoke, he was lookin’ right at me, and he spoke slowly enough for Raven Wing to keep up. He said his name was Badger. As I looked at him, he looked like I’d seen him before, but with the fancy dress and feathers he was wearin’, I couldn’t be sure. He said he was one that helped me skin the grizzly on the mountains to the south and the robe that I gave him that day was the one that me and Runnin’ Wolf were sittin’ on now, that I was not only a good warrior but a good hunter and that I had big medicine to kill the great bear all alone. And he passed the pipe to the next.

As the pipe went to the next two, it was like they were tryin’ to outdo each other with the praise, and then the pipe was passed to Runnin’ Wolf. He spoke mostly in English as he moved the pipe up and down. He said he thanked the one above, creator of all things, for his life and the lives of his new friends, the Shoshone, that he hoped there could be peace between the Shoshone and the Ute, that he would return to his people and tell of the honor the great chief Chargin’ Bull and his warriors had placed on him, that in his time bein’ a friend of Grizzly Killer, he had learned it was better to help people when they needed help than to be their enemy. And he passed the pipe to me.

I followed along the same as the rest had, and when I spoke, I simply said it made my heart good to be friends with the Shoshone people, that their warriors I had met in battle were brave men and did the Shoshone proud, that they went to the one above bein' proud of how they fought, that my mule and my dog, who had also fought the brave warriors, were my friends just like Runnin' Wolf and now the Shoshone people., that they fought with me 'cause they were my friends. I did not own them like I did not own slaves, and they stayed with me of their own will, and we took care of each other. I protected them, and they protected me. And I handed the pipe back to Chargin' Bull.

The chief said, "There has been much good spoke here tonight, and my heart is good that other people have honored our dead warriors and had protected our women. Now we dance to celebrate our new friends."

Chapter XIII

Trouble at Rendezvous

THEY DANCED to the beat of drums till near mornin', and I was dead tired when we finally got back to our lodge. Runnin' Wolf and Raven Wing were nowhere to be seen. When I crawled under those new blankets, I fell asleep almost at once. I could feel Sun Flower lie down next to me, but the next thing I remembered were the sounds of a village wakin' up and the light comin' through the smoke hole at the top of the lodge. My arm was around Sun Flower's naked body, and as I looked down at her, those dark eyes were smilin' up at me.

Runnin' Wolf and Raven Wing were still asleep on the other side of the lodge, and I had never even heard them come in. I was as quiet as I could be gettin' up, and Sun Flower pulled her dress on, and we moved the door cover to step out. Jimbo was curled up right in front of the door and had to move before we could even step out.

I walked down toward the river to check on Ol' Red and the chestnut with Jimbo leadin' the way. They were still on good grass, and I led them down to the water. While they drank their fill, I washed my face and drank of the clear, cold water.

When I got back to the lodge, Sun Flower and Raven Wing had a fire goin' and were puttin' some deer on to boil in the new pot, and I wished I would have thought to get some coffee along with that pot. I asked 'bout Runnin' Wolf, and they said he went out to check on the other horses.

Runnin' Wolf got back, and we ate the boiled deer along with some pemmican that someone had brought over. I had never tasted anythin' like it. Runnin' Wolf really liked it. He said it was like the pemmican that the Ute women make. It appeared to be pounded meat, berries, nuts, and fat all pounded together and stuffed in a gut casing. We sliced it off and ate it like a sausage. It tasted different but good since we had been eatin' just meat for many days now.

I told the women we would go to the tradin' tents again today and get supplies for the next year and that I needed to know if they wanted to go with us when we left Rendezvous or if they were gonna stay with their people. Sun Flower looked almost hurt that I would ask, and Raven Wing smiled at Runnin' Wolf and said, "We will go where your trail takes you. If it is to follow the wind, we will follow the wind with you." Then Sun Flower looked at me and asked, "Do you want me to follow the wind with you?" I smiled at her and nodded. She jumped, almost knockin' me over as she threw her arms around me.

Since we needed the pack horses and packs to get our supplies, me and Runnin' Wolf saddled Ol' Red and the chestnut then went out and brought the other horses in. We got the empty packs on them and asked Sun Flower and Raven Wing if they wanted to go with us. They looked at each other, and Raven Wing said they wanted to see friends and family today. We nodded we understood and headed for the tradin' tents with two empty pack horses. Along the way, I started figurin' just what we would need for supplies. I figured if we got triple what we had last year, we would be in pretty good shape. I still didn't know what would happen when we got back to Runnin' Wolf's people. Would he stay with them or come trappin' with me? We had talked a bit 'bout that, and I figured he didn't know for sure himself. But I had the feelin' he liked the adventure of seein' new country. So I figured I'd have a partner whether he knew it or not.

We had plenty of traps that were all still in good shape. I still had a keg of powder at the dugout, cached, but we would want more. We needed lead and flints, awls, and needles. We needed knives for the women and, if there was one to be had, a better rifle for Runnin' Wolf. I had won my Hawken in a shootin' contest at last year's rendezvous that we had to give five dollars for a chance at it, and Ashley had made over 150 bucks on that twenty-five-dollar rifle. I was hopin' he might do that again this year.

As we neared the tradin' tents, Runnin' Wolf waved at a group of trappers that was sittin' around a fire pit, talkin', and then headed right for them. He jumped down, and as I rode up, there were backslappin' and greetin's goin' on all around that fire pit. When Jimbo came up beside me, one of the men jumped back and started to pull out a knife. I told Jimbo to sit, and Runnin' Wolf started laughin' at the worried look on his friend's face. It took just a minute, but that trapper started to chuckle himself and then said that was the biggest, meanest-lookin' dog he ever saw. That trapper then carefully stepped around Jimbo, held out his hand to me, and said, "I'm Ely Tucker, and you must be the one they're callin' Grizzly Killer."

I shook his hand and told him, "I'm Zach Connors, and my friend here is Jimbo," and Jimbo lifted his paw toward Ely, and everyone had a good, hard laugh. We sat around that fire, and I learned this was the group of trappers that had been in Runnin' Wolf's village last year, and these were the men he had guided and had learned English from. One of the men named Grub Taylor, whom they just called Grub 'cause they said he was always hungry, asked Runnin' Wolf how his sister was doin', and then he looked at me and said she was just 'bout the prettiest woman he ever saw anywhere, red or white. They asked Runnin' Wolf where he was stayin', and when he said with the Snakes, they all looked surprised. Ely said that he thought the Snakes and Utes were enemies. Runnin' Wolf then told them that I had a knack of makin' friends out of enemies, and he told them the story of us findin' Sun Flower, Raven Wing, and Butterfly and of buyin' them from those three Frenchies. Ely said he knew Jean Luc and he was a mean one, and he'd seen him and the other two he didn't know ride in just this mornin'. Then Grub laughed and told Runnin' Wolf he was just makin' friends with the Snakes so's he could get their women, that the Snakes had mighty fine women. Runnin' Wolf just smiled and said, "They do have mighty fine women."

These were men that you could ride any trail with and know you could count on them. Like most of the men me and Pa had come west with, they were tough and rough, but if you needed help, you could count on every last one of them, and I could see why Runnin' Wolf was glad to see them again. I would count them as friends from this day on.

It was early afternoon when we heard a commotion over by the tradin' tents, and it was clear that General Ashley and his men had just come back to camp. I figured I'd give him a little time to get settled after he got back, and then we said our farewells to Ely, Grub, and the others and went on over to Ashley's tents.

As we walked up, the general was lookin' in his ledger book, and when he looked up, it took him just a minute, and then he smiled and said, "Zach Connors, you've done well." He asked 'bout Pa, and it was painful all over again as I told him the story of the grizzly and of buryin' Pa. He told me that Captain Jack would be mighty proud of the man he had raised, that it took a powerful will to spend a winter in these Rocky Mountains all alone. I told him the story of the Snake women and the Frenchman Jean Luc and his two companions and that I had paid them for the women and horses with forty plews. That they accepted it but wasn't happy 'bout it, and they might make trouble. He told me they couldn't make trouble, or they would be thrown out of camp and they would need supplies too. We picked out our supplies, and I got a few more things for the women. He had a few large coffee pots, so I picked one of them and got a lot more coffee and sugar than I figured we'd need, but I didn't want to run short again on that. I really had been missin' hot coffee.

I asked him 'bout a rifle, and he said he couldn't get a Hawken this year, that the Hawken brothers had every one in their shop spoken for. But one of his mule packers had a mighty fine Pennsylvania rifle made by Johnson that he figured would shoot as true as a Hawken, and he sent a man to fetch this packer. He said the packer's name was Liam McKinney, and he might be willin' to part with it if the price was right.

In just a little while, Liam came up, and I introduced myself and Runnin' Wolf and told him we were needin' a good straight-shootin' rifle. He was smilin' as he handed me the gun and told me it was as true as any he had ever seen. He said it was .54, and if he was to sell it, he would need at least seventy-five dollars for it. I asked if I could shoot it, and he just smiled again and said sure. I picked up a rock 'bout the size of my fist and walked out there around fifty big steps and set it on top of another rock. When I came back, there were six or eight others standin' there, watchin'. One of them said, "That's a mighty small target at that range." I checked the prime and pulled the hammer back and put the sights on the little rock. When I shot, the little rock just exploded into tiny pieces.

I turned around and asked the general how much I still had on his books, and when he told me $608, I started thinkin' I was bein' robbed. These prices we were payin' were ten times higher than they were back home. But back home was a mighty long ways away. Then Runnin' Wolf stepped up and pulled his medicine pouch from his belt and opened it up. He told me that when he found these rocks last year, Ely had told him it was valuable and asked if it was enough the buy the rifle, and he pulled out two gold nuggets. The small one was the size of the end of my thumb, and the other was twice that size. I had never seen pure gold before, and I had no idea what they were worth.

Liam's eyes were as big as could be, starin' at those nuggets, and General Ashley said that small one would buy the gun. Runnin' Wolf handed the smaller nugget to Liam, and with a big smile on his face, he nodded and said deal. Runnin' Wolf then turned to General Ashley and asked him if he would give me credit for the worth of this big nugget, and he said, "Running Wolf wants to help pay for supplies."

The general took the nugget and felt its weight. He set it on the fur scale, but it was too light to weigh. He threw it up in the air a few times and caught it and said he figured 'bout a half pound. He then handed it to me and asked if I agreed. It felt like it weighed 'bout half as much as a plews, and I told him as much. And he looked at Runnin' Wolf and said he would put $150 in my books for the nugget and asked if that was what he wanted. Runnin' Wolf nodded and said, "Next year I will have beaver of my own to trade," and I knew then I would have a partner through next winter.

We had all four horses loaded down heavy. We had put most of the supplies in barrels and had to change the packs a lot to carry barrels, and it was gettin' to be late afternoon as we headed back to the Shoshone village, just leadin' Ol' Red, the chestnut, and two pack horses.

While we were at the tradin' tents, several groups of Injuns came by lookin' and doin' some tradin' with furs they had. Some of it was tanned and some dried green like our plews were. There were a few Injun women tradin' with trappers for a turn under the robes. And others just watchin' the white men with hairy faces that they had not seen before. We were only 'bout a mile from the tradin' area, when I noticed the hair rise all the way down Jimbo's back, and then he took off on a dead run. I handed Runnin' Wolf the lead rope of Red and the pack horse I was leadin' and took off, followin' Jimbo.

Jimbo headed toward the river and through a bunch of cottonwoods and then thick willows. The willows were too thick for me to get through; then I heard Jimbo attack and a man yell and then scream. I had to find an openin' and then fight my way through the willows with my Hawken in one hand and my tomahawk in the other. I broke through the willows into a grassy area that was hidden between the willows and the creek. I could see two naked women lyin' in the grass, one partly in the river and one naked man tryin' to stop his leg from bleedin', and Jimbo had another naked man down on the grass. I couldn't see his face, for Jimbo was holdin' him by the throat, but I could see he had several bad bite marks all over his body. The woman lyin' partly in the water was cryin', and I knelt down and checked the other and saw she was breathin' but not awake, and I rolled her over and saw it was Butterfly. She had been beaten up something awful. Then I saw the man holdin' his leg was Lucien, and I called off Jimbo, and when he stepped back, it was Jean Luc. Jean Luc was just barely conscious, and I told Jimbo to go get Sun Flower, and he took off. I told Lucien, if he moved, I would kill him, and I cut a good strip off one of their leggin's and tied Jean Luc's hands behind his back. I picked up Butterfly and was just settin' her down by the water when Runnin' Wolf came into this little clearin'. I quickly told Runnin' Wolf that I figured Jean Luc and Lucien had attacked and raped Butterfly and her friend and Jimbo had heard what was happenin' and had stopped it. Then I asked him to go back and get General Ashley just as fast as he could.

Butterfly was comin' awake, and I was tryin' to clean up her face a little. One side of her face was badly swollen. Her eye was black and blue and swollen shut, her lips were smashed, and her nose was still bleedin' some. She had deep teeth marks over one of her nipples, and she was holdin' her ribs on her left side. The other girl had quit cryin' now, and she had got up and pulled her dress back on and came over to help Butterfly. She had a black eye, and bruises were comin' out on her arms and the side of her face, but she hadn't taken near the beatin' Butterfly had. Once I had most of the blood wiped off Butterfly's face, she just leaned into me and was softly cryin'. The other girl brought her dress over, but butterfly didn't move away from me at all. She was just sittin' with her knees up to her chest, one arm holdin' her ribs and the other around her knees, and leanin' into me and not movin'. I put one arm around her, tryin' to comfort her, and looked at Lucien sittin' there, holdin' his leg. He had a real scared look.

That was a mighty big mean-lookin' gash that Jimbo had ripped in his leg, and I figured he wouldn't be movin' without help. Jean Luc was awake now, and he was starin' at me with hatred on his face. He had a lot of deep-lookin' tooth marks poking in him. His butt had a big open tear on one side, and one arm was ripped up real bad, and he had tooth marks on his neck. I was kinda surprised Jimbo hadn't just ripped his throat out and killed him on the spot. It would have been easy enough for him to do. It looked to me like Jean Luc must have been on top of Butterfly when Jimbo came in here, and Jimbo had just bit him real hard on the butt and pulled him off, did the same thing to Lucien, and then went back and made sure Jean Luc wasn't goin' anywhere.

In just a few minutes, Runnin' Wolf came back with General Ashley and a group of men. Ely Tucker was among them, and when he looked at Butterfly, he turned and yelled, "Someone go get a rope. We's havin' us a hangin'." He then took the dress that was lyin' by her and gently laid it over her shoulders to cover her up. I didn't move, and neither did she. She just sat there, leanin' against me. A couple of the men went over and picked up Jean Luc, and were not bein' gentle 'bout it either. Then General Ashley asked me what had happened.

After I told what I knew for sure and then what I thought, Jean Luc yelled, "That wasn't what happened at all!" He said my dog attacked him and Lucien for no reason, that they had made a deal with the women to buy them some foofarraw, and that my dog was a killer and needed to be killed, or no one was safe.

I told them all I had sent Jimbo to go get my Shoshone woman to help Butterfly, and they would find out what happened for sure in just a little while. Jean Luc was complainin' him and Lucien was hurtin' and needed some doctorin'. Ely just walked over to him and, without sayin' a word, hit him in the face just as hard as he could. Jean Luc's legged buckled, and he hit the ground out cold. It took 'bout another half hour 'fore Sun Flower and Raven Wing showed up, with the Shoshone village bein' 'bout two miles away. Jimbo was leadin' the way, and he came right over and sat down right by me. When Sun Flower came through the willows, she had a mighty surprised look when she saw all these men here and me sittin' with Butterfly naked, leanin' against me. I motioned for her and Raven Wing to come over. The other Shoshone woman was still standin' there nearby, and when she saw Sun Flower, she ran over to her and started talkin' real fast. I couldn't pick up any of it. While Sun Flower was talkin' to this other girl, Raven Wing went over to Butterfly and started talkin' with her. After a few minutes, Raven Wing asked me to help her get up, and while Raven Wing and I were helpin' Butterfly stand, Sunflower came over and pulled her dress on her. She had to lift her arms up, and that hurt her, but she did it. Then Runnin' Wolf came to take my place, and I asked him to take Sun Flower and Butterfly back to their village while Raven Wing and I stayed to tell everyone what was said. I asked him to bring Chargin' Bull or Spotted Elk back with him.

Raven Wing told them all that Butterfly and Spotted Fawn had come to this secluded place to wash their hair and bath. They thought that no one had seen them come in here. But they got here and in the water when Jean Luc, Lucien, and Jacques came through the willows, and when Jean Luc saw Butterfly, he got real mad. He said she belonged to them, and she told him that he sold her to Grizzly Killer, and then he got even madder and started beatin' her. Then Spotted Fawn came over to help her, and he hit her too. Then Lucien came and grabbed Spotted Fawn's arms and pulled her back, and then Jean Luc started to beat Butterfly again. Then she fell down, and he kicked her, and her ribs were broken. Then they raped them both. She said that Jacques had left when Jean Luc started to hit her, and they didn't see him again.

Grub had left the group right at first when they first heard what I thought had happened, and now he was back and was tyin' a noose in a rope. Jean Luc saw that and was gettin' real worried and said they couldn't hang them, that those women were nothin' but squaws. I spoke loud enough for everyone to hear when I said, "He is right. They are squaws, and we don't have the right to hang them." They all looked at me like I was touched in the head.

The general just looked at me and asked what I had in mind. I said, "These are Shoshone women, and this is a Shoshone matter. We should give these men to the Shoshone for justice, and I expect the Shoshone chief Chargin' Bull here in just a short time."

The color drained from Jean Luc, and for the first time, I saw Lucien had tears in his eyes. This was a hard group of men, men that could and would do whatever they felt justice would require, and everyone of them nodded. General Ashley said, "We will wait until Charging Bull arrives." He told Ely to get them back to camp and tie them securely to a couple of trees, and we'd see what Charging Bull had to say 'bout them.

Ely, Grub, and a few others tied them standin' up. They were facin' the trees with their hands tied on the other side of the trees. They were still naked, and there was still blood seepin' from the worst of the bites Jimbo had given them. There were a lot of trappers coming by to see what had happened. The feelin' in camp was the Snakes were friendly to the trappers, that we were mostly welcome in their lands, and we couldn't let a few rotten men turn them against us. One man said there were already too many Injuns wantin' to put us under, that we should just hang 'em and give their bodies to the Snakes.

I asked if anybody had seen their friend Jacques or knew where they were camped, but no one knew.

It wasn't long before someone yelled the Snakes were comin' in. Chargin' Bull, Spotted Elk, Badger, and maybe a dozen others came ridin' in. Runnin' Wolf was out in front, and he came right over to me. They were dressed in full headdresses and all their finery, showin' the importance they placed on this meetin'. Chargin' Bull rode up to where I was standin' and stopped. Raven Wing was still with me, and he spoke to her, and she nodded. After lookin' at the men tied to the trees, he looked at me and spoke. Raven Wing was speakin' softly, standin' right next to me, and I asked her to speak loudly enough for everyone to hear. She said the chief said his heart was good to see that Grizzly Killer, Running Wolf, the Ute Warrior, and the Great Medicine Dog were still protectors of Shoshone women, that by making prisoners of the bad white men, we all showed we were true friends of the Shoshone people. He said that Spotted Fawn had said only one of the men did the beating of the women but that both had raped them. He wanted the one that did the beating and said we could do what we would with the other.

General Ashley stepped up and told the chief it was his honor to have the Shoshone chief at his camp and he would have a feast and gifts for the chief and his people tomorrow. The chief nodded and turned and said something to Badger, and Badger rode over and put a rawhide braided rope around Jean Luc's neck and tightened it up. He took his knife and cut Jean Luc's hands free from around the tree, and Jean Luc looked with hatred at all of us but never said a word. Badger retied his hands, mounted his horse, and led Jean Luc back to the rest. I asked the chief what would happen to Jean Luc, and after he spoke, Raven Wing said that it was not for Charging Bull to decide, that the squaws would decide the punishment. It was a silent and solemn camp as Chargin' Bull and his warriors rode out, with Jean Luc limpin', tryin' to keep up with that lead rope around his neck.

Chapter XIV

Indian Justice

THE SUN WAS just settin' when me, Runnin' Wolf, and Raven Wing led Ol' Red and the horses back to our lodge at the Shoshone village. We had the packs unloaded and was just takin' care of the stock when Sun Flower came in from the village. She told us Butterfly was in her family's lodge and Blue Fox, the medicine man, was with her. He said she would heal, but the bones in her chest would take time to be whole again. I asked her 'bout Jean Luc, and she just looked at Raven Wing. Raven Wing said it was a matter for the Shoshone women, and we were not to be concerned with him anymore. She said that me and Runnin' Wolf were to stay at the lodge tonight and Sun Flower and herself would be back later.

After they left, I asked Runnin' Wolf what was gonna happen, and he told me the women would likely torture him to death. That they would make him live in much pain for as long as they could before he died. 'Cause his brutality was against women, they would either cut or burn his manhood off to make him a woman in the next life. They would take his eyes so he could not find his way in the next life. Runnin' Wolf said it was the worst possible death for a man, 'cause he would be a man no more. A man should die in battle or old age 'cause he survived all the battles in life. I told Runnin' Wolf a man like Jean Luc was not a real man in this life or the next. And I believed his next life would be far worse for him than this one.

I roasted some coffee beans and ground them up, and me and Runnin' Wolf had hot coffee with a little sugar, ate some jerky, and turned in. I heard Jimbo whinin' a while later and, just after that, a man screamin' way off in the distance. I just lay there, starin' at the few stars I could see through the smoke hole and shuddered at the thought of what was happenin'.

I figured it was 'bout three hours later when Sun Flower and Raven Wing came in the lodge. Sun Flower slid under the blankets and wrapped her arms 'round me and just held on tight. She didn't move at all the rest of the night. Nothin' more was ever said 'bout Jean Luc Lamont or 'bout that night.

The next mornin' Sun Flower and Raven Wing was quiet and a little distant. I asked 'bout their mother and father. They said they were not here, that they were visitin' family in another village and did not make the trip to Rendezvous. Spotted Elk came by and said he was leadin' a huntin' party again tomorrow and asked me and Runnin' Wolf to go with them. I told him we would be honored, that we needed meat too. He nodded and then spoke to his sisters in Shoshone for a bit, nodded at us, and left.

Me and Runnin' Wolf saddled Ol' Red and the three saddle horses, and I told the women we were goin' over to Ashley's camp, and I would like them to join us over there in 'bout an hour. They both had puzzled looks but said they would be there. I wanted to see that Lucien had been dealt with before they got there.

As me and Runnin' Wolf rode into the tradin' area, we both noticed Lucien was not still tied to the tree. There was a large group of men standin' in front of the tents, and we stepped out of the saddles and joined them. They said they was fixin' to have a Trappers' court and had been waitin' for us.

Since I was the one that found them, they wanted my input to decide their fate. Lucien was tied to a stump, and Jacques was standin' by him. Lucien had his buckskins on and looked mighty rough. I could tell by the way he was sittin' to one side his leg was really hurtin' him. Jacques was just lookin' scared and had dark circles under his eyes from not sleepin'.

Most of the men there I did not know, but some I'd seen last year over on Burnt Fort at the Rendezvous. There was Jim Beckwourth, Bill and Milt Sublette, Ely, Grub, and their friends. I could see Jed Smith was talkin' to General Ashley. Then Ely brought over a man 'bout my age and, with a big ol' smile on his face, said to meet Jim Bridger, that he was as young and foolish as me. We shook hands, and he just kept starin' at Jimbo. He finally looked up and just said he was surprised there was anything left of those two guys after a dog that big got after 'em.

General Ashley stepped up and said we was gonna hold court to figure out what to do with Lucien Mineau. I heard someone say "Hang 'em and be done with it."

Another said, "He didn't kill nobody, so he don't deserve to hang."

Then the first one said, "Maybe not yet, but with what he did, he could have got a bunch of us killed," and there was a lot of agreement with that.

I stepped forward and said we should hear what he had to say 'bout it.

Ashley turned to Lucien and asked if he wanted to speak for himself. He said he didn't beat those women and Jean Luc told him if he didn't go along, that Jean Luc would make him pay. That he and Jacques were afraid of Jean Luc 'cause he had such a bad temper. Jacques was just starin' at the ground, lookin' mighty scared. I didn't think he was understanding what was bein' said. Lucien said that Jean Luc had told them they would get rich comin' out here to trap, but they were doin' all the work, and Jean Luc told them he would just leave them to the Injuns if they didn't do what he said.

I heard a murmur go through the men, and someone said, "Would you look at that."

When I turned, I saw Sun Flower and Raven Wing ridin' into camp. They were both wearin' new soft leather dresses trimmed with colored quills and beads. They each had a sash of the red cloth around their waists and headbands of the cloth. They had cut ribbons off it and tied them in their horses' manes. They were truly beautiful women, and the men just looked at them in awe. Me and Runnin' Wolf stepped toward them, and as they stepped down the horses, the group of men parted to let them pass. They saw Lucien and Jacques there, and Sun Flower looked at me with questioning eyes. I spoke softly just so they could hear and told her and Raven Wing we were decidin' what to do with them.

I asked them if they could talk to Jacques, and Sun Flower nodded and asked me what I wanted to know. I said I wanted to know why he left the others and if Lucien was afraid of Jean Luc. She looked at me and said, "Yes, we were all afraid of Jean Luc." She then walked over, and in some French and some Shoshone, she talked to him for a few minutes. She turned and said he didn't want to hurt anyone, and he was afraid Jean Luc would kill Butterfly, so he ran away, but that Lucien was closer to Jean Luc and couldn't get past him in those willows.

I told everyone that Sun Flower and Raven Wing were the other two women I had bought from the three of them, so these women knew these two Frenchmen. Then I asked Raven Wing if she believed Lucien should die for what he did to Spotted Fawn. She looked at Sun Flower, and both of them shook their heads no. General Ashley then asked Lucien and asked Sun Flower to ask Jacques what they would do if we let them go. They both said go back home. The general said, "Let's take a vote. Who says let them go?"

The majority of hands went up. The general turned to the two of them and told them to leave this country at once or face the same fate as Jean Luc. Sun Flower stepped up right close to me, and someone walked over and cut the ties off Lucien. Raven Wing then told the two of them that many of the Shoshone warriors weren't happy that Charging Bull didn't take Lucien too, and she did not think they would make it out of Shoshone lands if they did not go at once.

The last I ever saw of those two was them walkin' away from the tradin' tents, headin' to where they had their horses. Lucien was limpin' real badly, and I knew he was in for a mighty rough time.

Everyone started to break up and go back to their camps. But Ely and Grub came right over, and with a big ol' grin, Grub said he couldn't believe that we had found the purtiest girls in the whole Snake nation. I introduced these two rough Ol' mountain men to Sun Flower and Raven Wing. Grub made a big bow and kissed Sun Flower's hand, and we all had a big laugh. Runnin' Wolf put his arm around Raven Wing, and Grub smiled and told her that Runnin' Wolf's sister, Shining Star, was just as purty as she was, and he didn't know how Runnin' Wolf could be so lucky to have such purty women in his life.

General Ashley's men were settin' up makeshift tables from small logs lashed together, and they already had whole haunches of deer and elk roastin' over fires. They were makin' cornbread and had several pots of coffee goin' and were settin' out gifts for the Snakes and for the Nez Pierce, but they were settin' out mostly goods to trade with the Injuns for furs.

Me and Runnin' Wolf took Sun Flower and Raven Wing through the tables, lookin' at all the trade goods Ashley had brought here all the way from St. Louis. They had never seen so much before. We picked out a few more things that caught their eye. The brightly colored trade cloth was what they really liked. We picked up some blue and yellow too. I picked out another ax and made a deal for a couple more of the pack saddles they wouldn't be needin' on the way back. I found one of the spade shovels they had been usin' and made a trade for that as well.

I had a few blacksmithin' tools along with Pa's harness repair kit and other stuff in the cache back at the dugout, but I wasn't much of a hand at smithin' work. I had watched Pa work iron before, but I had only tried a few times. So I figured it wouldn't do much good to get more of that stuff. But I did pick up a few iron hoops from broken barrels to have.

We had moved off to the side by a fire when the Nez Pierce rode in. It was quite a sight with them in all their finery, and I had never seen such pretty horses. They called them Appaloosas, and a couple of the Britishers that had come down from their land said they had been breedin' them special for the spots on the rumps for as long as any of 'em could remember. They were puttin' on a ridin' show with some of their finest horses, and it was the best ridin' I'd ever seen.

They had lots of furs to trade, and it looked like General Ashley was doin' real well. It wasn't long after that the Shoshones came ridin' in. Sun Flower and Raven Wing went over to meet their brother and some friends.

There was a lot of drinkin' goin' on, and with a lot of mighty lonesome trappers and the Injun women, I was afraid there was goin' to be more trouble. But the women seemed right friendly, and there were couples headin' to the bushes real often, and no one seemed unhappy. Many trappers, it 'peared to me, were tradin' their entire last year's work for a few bottles of whisky and turns in the bushes with a willin' Injun girl. Ashley made gifts to the Injuns and traded for all their furs. The food was plentiful, and everyone seemed to be havin' a good time.

Runnin' Wolf was with Ely and Grub, and I found Sun Flower still with Spotted Elk and asked 'bout Butterfly. Sun Flower said she was still mighty sore and was scared to come back here. I told Sun Flower I wanted to talk to her and asked if she would go with me.

It took but a few minutes for Red and Sun Flower's roan to get us back to the village, and Sun Flower led me to the lodge where Butterfly was. We entered, and Butterfly seemed surprised, and she asked Sun Flower why we weren't with the others. Sun Flower told her I wished to speak to her. I didn't know if Sun Flower could tell Butterfly exactly what I was sayin', but the meanin' seemed to get across to her. I told her she was a strong Shoshone woman and that she should not let a few bad men make it so she didn't enjoy herself, that Lucien and Jacques were gone and would not be back, and the other trappers were good men that wanted the best for her. I asked her, if me and Sun Flower helped her, she would come with us to see all the things at the Rendezvous. I also said Jimbo would be there to protect her and he wouldn't leave her side.

I don't know what all was said between those two friends, but Butterfly smiled up at me and nodded. Her face was still swollen and bruised, and her ribs were mighty sore, but in just a few minutes, Sun Flower had helped her into a fringed dress and had put some of the yellow cloth in her hair. I got her horse ready and put my hands together to help boost her up on the horse. We just let the horses walk back to the tradin' area.

As we walked the horses toward the crowd, it got quiet, and everyone was watchin' us. Spotted Elk came right over, and the two of us helped Butterfly down. A man I did not know came toward us, wantin' to give Butterfly a necklace he had made from beads, and Jimbo stepped in front of him and growled. He stopped with a surprised look on his face and said very sincerely that he was sorry for what happened and he wanted her to have this. I told Jimbo to sit, and he did, but he stayed between this stranger and Butterfly. Butterfly reached out and accepted the bead necklace and smiled at him, and everyone cheered.

We stayed with Butterfly and looked at all the trade goods, and Spotted Elk gave her some of the foofarraw. Nothin' was said, but I got the feelin' Spotted Elk liked Butterfly a lot. I thought back to when we first rode into the Snake village and the naked kids some hidin' behind their mothers and others not, and I thought again Sun Flower would have been right out front, not bashful at all, but Butterfly would have been one of the ones hidin' behind her mother.

This part of the Rendezvous reminded me of the town socials and dances back home in Pottersville, 'cept there was more drinkin' and gamblin' goin' on here. That made me think of Emma again, and I wondered where she was and what had become of her. I must have been kind of daydreamin', 'cause when I looked at Sun Flower, she was watchin' me with kind of a puzzled look on her face. Those dark eyes of hers lookin' up at me could make me forget everything in the past and just want to hold on to her forever.

As evenin' approached, I was tired, and I figured from Sun Flower's look she was too. Neither of us hardly slept the night before. We found Runnin' Wolf and Raven Wing, and I let them know we were goin' back to the teepee, and they said they would be along shortly. I saw where Spotted Elk and Butterfly were, and we walked over to them. Sun Flower asked her brother if he needed any help gettin' Butterfly back to the village, and he said no then said we would leave on the hunt tomorrow before light. I nodded, and he spoke to Sun Flower in Snake for just a minute.

We were just walkin' along, leadin' Ol' Red and the roan, enjoyin' the evenin'. It was a mighty pretty evenin' at that. As the sun set, there were a few fluffy clouds that turned bright red orange, and as long as we stayed a ways out from the river, the mosquitoes weren't much of a bother either. I asked Sun Flower what her brother had said to her. She just smiled and shook her head then said she did not know how to say in English. I could tell she knew more English than she made on, but she wasn't sure 'bout it. I was still amazed at how much English Raven Wing really knew. And bein' with Runnin' Wolf was helpin' them both out with English 'cause they spoke English all the time to each other. It was a lot easier for them to understand that than Runnin' Wolf speakin' Ute and Raven Wing speakin' Snake. But it seemed to me that Raven Wing must really have a gift for speakin' different tongues 'cause she was pickin' up Ute mighty fast as well.

The evenin' star was out and shinin' bright when we reached the teepee, and I could hear a few night birds callin' from the trees along the river. We went inside and climbed under the robes. She slid her naked body up against me, and we made love and fell asleep in each other's arms. I woke for just a few minutes when Runnin' Wolf and Raven Wing came in but didn't stir again till I heard Jimbo whinin' just outside the openin'. I got up and looked out and could see a couple of fires gettin' started and figured it was time to get ready for the hunt.

Chapter XV

The Hunt

I WENT OUT and got our pack horses in the dark, and when I returned, Runnin' Wolf had Red and the chestnut saddled. We threw the empty packs on the horses and were ready when Spotted Elk rode over. He just nodded his approval and motioned for us to leave. Sun Flower and Raven Wing had a fire goin', but there wasn't time for coffee, so they just handed us a bag of jerky, and we rode out, each of us leadin' two pack horses. There was Spotted Elk, a brave that was called Red Hawk, Badger, and the young man that had takin' me and Runnin' Wolf over to the tradin' tents that first day, Little Horse. Little Horse was leadin' three pack horses as well.

We made our way toward the mountains to the east. By the time the sky started to get gray along the eastern horizon, we were followin' a trail alongside a fast-runnin' good-sized creek up a narrow rocky canyon. We were headin' due east, and I figured we had traveled maybe eight or ten miles by the time it was light enough to see. Then without warnin', the canyon opened up into a large, broad basin that went off to the south, farther than I could see. The sun wasn't up yet, and there were coyotes yippin' at each other on both sides of this basin. We continued to follow the creek and jumped a cow and calf moose that took off, stayin' 'bout two hundred yards away from us. Spotted Elk stopped and pointed across the basin. Maybe a mile away, we could see a herd of a couple of dozen elk.

We sat there, studyin' the lay of the land, and I figured we all were figurin' out a plan. There was a mornin' breeze blowin' right in our faces out of the east. The elk were grazin' in a big grassy meadow where the creek made a big bend off to the north. There was kind of a bottleneck between a rocky point on the hill and the creek. It looked to me like if we could get set along the creek at the bottleneck and have Jimbo and a couple of others spook the elk from above, those elk would just naturally run through the bottleneck within just a few yards of those of us by the creek. I suggested to Spotted Elk my plan, and he nodded. I told him that me and Runnin' Wolf with our guns needed to be by the creek and two of them with their bows. I thought that Little Horse could take Jimbo with him and one of the other braves and circle way out around the meadow and come into it from above, and hopefully the elk would run out through the bottom. Spotted Elk said it would take more than two men and the dog to keep the elk from scatterin' in every direction. Badger and he talked 'bout it for a few minutes, and Spotted Elk signed he would go with Grizzly Killer and Runnin' Wolf, and Badger would lead the others around and come in on the elk from above.

We tied all the pack horses along with Ol' Red, Spotted Elk's pinto, and the chestnut right where we were. I showed Little Horse very quickly how to give Jimbo hand signals for where he wanted him to go. Then Badger led out, leadin' Little Horse and Red Hawk, and I told Jimbo to go with Little Horse. Spotted Elk led the way across the creek, makin' real sure we were stayin' out of sight of the elk. I was carryin' the Hawken and Pa's old rifle, and Runnin' Wolf had his new long rifle. But he was also carryin' his bow and quiver over his back.

We worked our way along, stayin' on the outside edge of the brush, walkin' real quiet on the far side of the creek away from the elk, when all of a sudden, right in front of us, a big buck deer with four points on each side of his antlers bounded up from the creek and headed off to the north. They were callin' these deer mule deer 'cause of their big ears. They were bigger and had much bigger antlers that grew in a different shape than the white-tailed deer from back home. They also seemed to like open country more. The whitetails always stayed in the thickets and tight cover, but these big mule deer would run right out across open country but most often too far away to shoot.

It took us 'bout a half hour to get across from the rocky point. We couldn't see the elk, but we could see those rocks. Spotted Elk checked the breeze again by droppin' a couple of leaves and watchin' 'em fall. Even though it wasn't as strong as before, it was still comin' from the elk toward us. We very slowly moved across the creek again, and Spotted Elk, signalin' us to stay, worked his way to the edge of the willows and brush. In just a minute, he came back. Without makin' a sound, he drew a little map in the dirt, showin' the creek where we were and where the elk were. He showed a possible route the elk might take and run across the creek a little above us and indicated for me with the two guns to go there and block that route, and he and Runnin' Wolf would stay here. I nodded and, watchin' where I placed every step, headed for that spot.

In less than five minutes, I was there and could then see just what Spotted Elk was worried 'bout. There was a very well-used trail where the elk was comin' down to the water, and it looked like a natural route for them to follow. I was only 'bout a hundred yards from the closest elk, and very slowly I got set where I figured I'd have good shots no matter if they came toward me or straight down through the bottleneck where Runnin' Wolf and Spotted Elk were waitin'.

I didn't know how long it would take for the others to get in position above the elk, so movin' as little as possible, I got as comfortable as I could and checked the powder in the pans again. I watched several of the little ground squirrels that looked a lot like prairie dogs playin' along the edge of the meadow. I heard a couple of the trappers at Rendezvous call 'em pot guts. They did kind of have pot bellies when they stood up. The elk were grazin', movin' around a little, and in what I figured was maybe twenty minutes, I could see seven of them from where I sat. Then all at once, all their heads came up, and they were all lookin' up the hill, away from me.

All of a sudden, they were all runnin' right at me. I took a bead on the chest of the first one, and when she was maybe thirty yards out, I fired the Hawken, and she collapsed. When she hit the ground, the others behind her turned off the trail and headed right down toward the bottleneck. It took me but a couple of seconds to have Pa's old rifle up, and a bull with good antlers grown out 'bout two feet long already for this time of year was runnin' by, and I followed him along and fired. He jumped but didn't fall. I then heard Runnin' Wolf's rifle fire, and Badger came chargin' past me with his horse, runnin' full out. His reins were just lyin' across the horse's mane. He had his bow in hand and fully drawn and was guidin' his horse with his knees. I ran out where I could see, and in just a few seconds, he was right up alongside a runnin' cow and let fly with his arrow. It was only a few seconds, and he had another arrow in her, and as the third arrow buried deep into her side, she stumbled and fell. Jimbo was then comin' right to me, and I gave him a hard ear rub and patted his head, and he took off again down toward Runnin' Wolf.

I could see the bull I shot with Pa's rifle had only run 'bout a hundred yards and was down. As I looked down into the bottleneck, I could see two more down. Five elk on the ground, and I started to wonder if we had enough pack horses. We had a mighty lot of meat to carry back, and in the heat of summer, it would start spoilin' mighty fast. I reloaded just as fast as I could and started to dress out the first one of mine. Red Hawk and Little horse were just now gettin' to us, and Badger sent them for the pack horses.

When I finished the first one and started for the second, I could see the pack horses were just headed this way and would be here in no time. Badger had his elk gutted, and Spotted Elk was walkin' over to help Runnin' Wolf finish his. Just as I was pullin' the guts from this bull and had cut out the liver, Badger walked up, reached down, and cut a thin strip off the liver and ate it raw and then sliced another off and handed it to me. I just shook my head, and he laughed at me. I started skinnin' this one, and Badger stayed right there, helpin'. By the time we had the hide off him, Little Horse and Red Hawk were back with Ol' Red and all the horses. We all knew time was a real factor with meat this time of the year, and there was no wasted time in gettin' all their hides off.

We cut and packed all this meat just as fast as we could and had the weight spread out on all the horses in no time. We used the hides to cover the meat for shade and to help keep the flies off. I figured we were between ten and fifteen miles from the village, and with heavy loads and a narrow rocky canyon, I reckoned we'd be maybe three or four hours gettin' back. It was 'bout midmornin' when we left that open basin and started down the narrow canyon.

By the time we reached the mouth of the canyon and entered Willow Valley, there was a cloud of flies around each of the pack horses, and I was mighty happy to see the tops of the teepees, or lodges as the Injuns called them. When we rode into camp, there were dryin' racks set up, with fires ready to start under them, and more than a dozen women met us and started to unload the meat. They spread the hides out on the ground and laid the meat on them and just ignored the flies. 'Bout half of them went to cuttin' the meat into strips, and the others were hangin' the strips onto the dryin' racks and gettin' the fires started.

It was hard to believe how fast they had those racks filled and the fires goin'. The smoke was keepin' the flies off. They had gathered chokecherry branches for the fires, which burned with kind of a sweet smell. Runnin' Wolf cut off a big ol' chunk of meat from one haunch, and he headed for our teepee with it while I helped Little Horse care for the horses. Spotted Elk was takin' the livers and hearts we brought back and was givin' them to several families. He had me take one liver over and give to the older wife of Chargin' Bull.

When I got back to our teepee, Sun Flower and Raven Wing had staked out that still-green grizzly hide. Sun Flower was on her knees, workin' a mixture of brain matter and water into it. Raven Wing was settin' up a spit over the fire with that chunk of elk so we could turn it as it roasted. Runnin' Wolf was just comin' back from takin' his chestnut to the river for water, and I headed down to do the same with Red.

It had been a real good hunt this mornin', but with a village like this, huntin' and bringin' in food was a constant thing. There were two other huntin' parties that went out today, but neither of them had returned yet.

It was fixin' to be a right warm day 'bout the middle of June. There were fluffy white clouds and a mighty blue sky. There was the green of the trees along the rivers and wildflowers with every color you could imagine. The air was so clear it made you think you could see forever. I knew I'd never get tired of the beauty of this land. I could just stare off into the distance all afternoon and never look at the same thing twice. It didn't rain near as much here in these western mountains as it did back home. It had been quite a spell since we had any.

There was quite a commotion comin' from the other side of the village, and lookin' that way, I could see another Injun village was comin' into Rendezvous. Sun Flower stood up and walked over by me and said they were Bannocks, another tribe of the Shoshones that lived west of the mountains. Those Bannocks, after wavin' and shoutin' greetin's to the Shoshone village, went over to the east a couple of miles and camped along the creek we had followed this mornin' on our hunt.

Not long after that, the other huntin' parties came in, and they had both deer and elk, and the second huntin' party even had a black bear. Everyone pitched in and, in no time, had more dryin' racks lashed together and smoky fires goin' to cure all this meat. The game was plentiful, but it wouldn't last with this many people all in the south end of Willow Valley and everyone huntin' for their food.

As the elk roast was gettin' done over the fire, I made up a pan full of biscuits and got a pot of coffee goin'. Raven Wing had been down by the river and had pulled some wild onions and a few camas roots. She said they were for later. We sliced off pieces of the roast, ate biscuits, and drank coffee. This was the first time Sun Flower or Raven Wing had tasted sugar, and when I put it in their coffee and saw the smiles, I figured I best get another sack or two of sugar 'cause this would never last. After we ate, we just lay back in the afternoon sun and napped.

A couple of hours later, Spotted Elk, along with Butterfly, came to our teepee, and Spotted Elk had three of the elk hides from this mornin' and gave to us. He said these were the ones me and Runnin' Wolf had shot. He looked at the grizzly skin that the women had been tannin' with the hair on most of the day with a look of surprise then, lookin' right at me, said, "You are the Grizzly Killer." He helped Butterfly sat down. Her ribs were still really hurtin' her when she got up and down. She looked and me and started to speak in Shoshone. Raven Wing started to tell us what she was sayin'. She told us when we first got herself, Sun Flower, and Raven Wing from Jean Luc and the others, she was afraid I would kill them, that she knew the Great Medicine Dog had killed her brother, and that I had killed some of his friends that were with him, and she really believed I had bought them to use them and then kill them, so she ran away. She said she told that to Sun Flower, and Sun Flower told her she was wrong, but she was scared and went away alone. She said now she knew she was wrong, that all white men did not have bad hearts, and that she was sorry for thinking that way.

She asked if she could give something to the Medicine Dog. I called Jimbo over, and she reached out to him, and he stepped right up to her and licked her face. She rubbed his ears and whispered to him for a minute then opened up a leather pouch and pulled out a turquoise stone that was on a piece of rawhide. The rawhide went through a hole that had been ground through the turquoise. She very carefully wrapped the rawhide around Jimbo's collar and centered the stone between the grizzly claws. She said that was the most cherished of her possessions, and she wanted the one that saved her life to have it. Jimbo loved the attention and lay down right in front of her with his huge ol' head sittin' in her lap.

After Spotted Elk and Butterfly left, I wanted to go back over to the tradin' area and talk more to the other trappers 'bout the land, to learn as much as I could 'bout which way others were goin' for the fall trappin' season. It wasn't that I wanted to tag along, but just the opposite, I wanted to stay far away from where most of the trappin' was bein' done. Last season me and Pa hadn't seen another trapper after we left Rendezvous and had had a great trappin' season, so I figured the fewer trappers in an area, the better trappin' we would have.

Sun Flower and Raven Wing stayed while me and Runnin' Wolf saddled up and headed for the tradin' area. We were just takin' our time, walkin' along the river. It was early enough in the day; the mosquitoes weren't bad yet. Twice we passed groups of naked Injun kids and women playin' and bathin' in the river, and as we got closer, there was even a group of trappers out in the water, their skin so white it 'bout hurt your eyes. One ol' trapper that I didn't know walked up to the river and said, "Jack, you need to sit down in some of that mud over on yonder bank. That ass of yours is so white it's 'bout to blind the rest of us." Everyone was gettin' a good laugh from that bein' said, and as the one doin' the talkin' stripped down to get in the river, everyone laughed even harder. This trapper had whiter skin than Jack.

There was a small group of men standin' and looked to be just jawin' away, when I saw one of them was Ely. When he saw me and Runnin' Wolf, he motioned for us to come over. We stepped off our mounts and walked on over, and Ely, with a big smile on his face, said we was just in time for the fun.

Ely told a story of an old trapper they called Stinky Johnson and that he smelled so bad no one wanted him around. Ely said, "Last night after an ample amount of whisky had been drunk, Grub and a couple of the boys was gonna take Stinky over to the river ta give him a bath. It had became clear that Stinky wasn't as drunk as the rest of them, and it turned out to be quite a fight." He said, "Grub has a black eye, and Frank and Marcus both have fat lips this mornin', and well, Stinky, he still stinks." He told us, "I don't think Stinky has bathed since he come to the mountains more than five year ago."

And Henry Finn added, "Or put on a different set of buckskins." After the fight was over, Grub had yelled at Stinky that the only company he was fit to keep was with a skunk.

Well, several of the boys heard that, and some of them went out and caught a couple of skunks last night, and now they were just gettin' ready to throw them in the tent with Stinky, and maybe that would make him take a bath. There must have been two dozen men in on this, 'cause they was forming a circle 'round Stinky's tent. Ely said he was still sleepin' off last night's drunk.

Then I saw Grub and Marcus walkin' real quiet, each carryin' a little willow cage with a skunk in it. When they got right up by the tent flaps, each of them reached in their cage and grabbed the skunk by the tail and threw them right through the tent flaps. Then they grabbed the tent flaps and held them closed as four or five other men ran up with sticks and started to beat on the canvas tent. It was only a few seconds, and we all started to back up as the sickenin' smell of them skunks started to come out of the tent. Stinky was tryin' to cuss through all his coughin' as he fought his way out. When he got clear, there was a roar of laughin' and men scatterin' in every direction, tryin' to get farther away from that smell. Stinky was cursin' to the heavens as he was strippin' out of them old greasy buckskins. He picked up his knife, and yellin' at the top of his lungs, he told us all we was the most low-down dirty bastards that ever walked the earth and he was gonna slow-peal the hide off every one of us sons of bitches. He went on and on, tellin' us he had never seen such a bunch of goddamned bastards before, that we was all so low-down we would all fornicate with animals, and he would get even if took till his last breath.

He was headed to the river, and just before he got there, he stopped and started to wretch his guts up. I figured the smell, along with the hangover, was just too much for even his iron belly. He was sittin' in the water on a little sandbar, usin' the sand to scrub the smell off, and another group went over to his tent and pulled out all his buckskins and bedroll and, with sticks, picked it all up, including the tent, and took it to the closest fire and burned every last bit of it. They all said if he didn't have enough on the books to get a new bedroll, clothes, and a little tent, that they would take up a collection.

I had never met Stinky before, and I wasn't right sure just how serious his threats were. But Ely said he'd calm down after a while, and even if it took a while longer, he would see it was for his own good. He had been out in the river for quite some time, and another trapper walked over to the river's edge and tossed him a piece of what looked like a cactus and told Stinky to use the pulp on his hair and it would help. He was a mighty red- and tender-skinned man when he finally climbed out of the river. Grub picked up a tanned elk hide and walked over to him, and he wrapped it around himself, and he simply said thanks. He was shiverin' from the cold water as he walked over and stood by the fire to dry off and get warm.

Me and Runnin' Wolf was standin' with this group of trappers, and I asked if anyone had seen where them skunks ran off to, and everyone just shook their heads. One of them said, “They’s probably down to the river too, tryin’ to wash Stinky’s smell off them,” and everyone roared with laughter.

We talked ’bout where they had all spent last winter, and it seemed most of the Rocky Mountain Fur men stayed right here in Willow Valley, and they planned on doin’ that again this winter. I told them I had a place in the Bear River Mountains, and I figured there were still plenty of beaver to be had in that direction. But we were goin’ down into Ute territory first, and I didn’t know what I’d find down there. Grub and Ely both said I had me a right fine guide for that country in Runnin’ Wolf and there were beaver to be had. Ely told me that the Spanish claimed that land as their own. They had given a license to trap that country to a man by the name of Provost, said he was a Frenchy but worked with the Spanish out of Taos. But he said when they went with Ashley into that area, they stayed and trapped ’bout six months and never had any trouble.

There was still a lot of drinkin’ and gamblin’ goin’ on. There were trappers and Injuns bettin’ on all sorts of contests. There was knife and tomahawk throwin’, foot races, and wrestlin’ matches. There was a horse race gettin’ started. It appeared to me the Injuns loved to gamble as much as the trappers did.

The tradin’ area had been busy ever since we had got here, with the Bannocks tradin’ all the hides they had brought in, and then someone said there was a village of Flat Heads camped ’bout twenty miles north of us, and they would be comin’ in to trade tomorrow. It ’peared to me General William Ashley was makin’ a fortune.

I made my way over and found General Ashley and talked to him for a while ’bout what he had found scoutin’ to the south of here a few days ago. He described a round valley not far, maybe ten or fifteen miles south, with three rivers that met in the middle of it. They formed one river, and it cut through a mighty steep, narrow rocky canyon goin’ down through the mountains to the west. He said that all three forks of this river looked like mighty good trappin’ grounds with plentiful game, and with it bein' so close to Willow Valley, he figured one of his brigades would trap those forks for the fall hunt.

I told him I was goin' to be headed for Ute country in just a few days and thought I might go through that area on the way. He suggested we go on through this valley, and maybe ten miles farther to the south, we would come upon a bigger river that would lead us right up into the western end of the Bear River Mountains. He told me his men were callin' the river Weber River after their leader, John Henry Weber, who was leadin' one of his brigades for Rocky Mountain Fur.

I started wonderin' 'bout all the supplies we'd picked up, and with the teepee and our other camp stuff, I thought we might need a couple more pack animals. I asked General Ashley if he figured he was goin' to need all the mules for his return trip or if he might sell a pair of them to me. We made a deal for the mules, a couple more sacks of sugar, and a couple more empty barrels, and I still had over $600 on the books.

Me and Runnin' Wolf had just put the packs on our new mules, had the extra sugar in the barrels, and were ready to head back to our camp when somebody yelled from the other end of camp, "We got Injun trouble! They's is two dead white men up on the big bend of the Bear!"

Chapter XVI

Dead Men Don't Tell

WE TIED OFF the mules, Red, and the chestnut and went with all the others to where these trappers had just come in. Ely said he knew one of them. His name was Lucas Fuller, but he didn't know the others. The one doin' the talkin' said his name was Clay Sanders, and the two youngsters with them were Noah Hart and Samuel Perkins. Said they had been up in the Absaroka country and spent the winter with the Crows, that they had run into a party of Blackfeet in Jackson's Hole and had to turn back and go way out east and come down across the Popo Agie and then west to the Bear. That was why they were so late gettin' here. 'Cause they sure didn't want them Blackfeet cuttin' their trail.

He said 'bout midafternoon yesterday, they were followin' the main trail along the Bear, and just where it started to turn south again, they came across a mighty gruesome thing. He said it was just by chance they saw them, 'cause they was off the trail apiece. He told us they were just ridin' along, and he caught a scent of smoke and burned meat, so he rode over through the trees to see, that they found a little clearin', and in it, two men had been staked out on the ground, stripped naked, and a fire built right 'tween their legs.

He said red-hot coals had been put in their eyes and on the bottoms of their feet. He said he figured it took them a considerable amount of time to die. He said one of them had been castrated, and then it was all put in his mouth, and he had been scalped as well. While the other one wasn't cut up at all, he said they cut them from the stakes and gave them a proper burial, but we'd not know what happened, 'cause dead men don't tell.

Someone said it had to be those Frenchmen, and everyone just nodded. Then someone else explained to Clay and the rest of them what had happened here at Rendezvous and what the Shoshones had done 'bout it and what we had done and that the Shoshones had warned them if they caught them, this would happen.

Clay said, "I thought the Snakes was friendly to us trappers," and someone else said, "They are, until we're not friendly to them." He pointed at me and said, "Grizzly Killer there and his Ute partner are livin' right in their village with a couple of their squaws right now with no trouble at all."

Clay looked over at me and said, "So you're the one they's callin' Grizzly Killer." He said, "The Crows is even talkin' 'bout your medicine up in Absaroka and out on the plains with the Sioux and Cheyenne." He said, "Listenin' to the stories they're tellin', I figured you must be bigger than a grizzly and your dog the size of a buffalo." He walked over and looked up at me, then he said, "Well, you are mighty big man, but with all them stories they're tellin' 'round the fires at night, I sure thought you'd be bigger. Now where's this buffalo-size dog of yours?"

I whistled, and the group parted as Jimbo came to me.

Clay jumped back and then laughed. He looked at Jimbo and shook his head then said, "Well, he ain't as big as a buffalo, but he is the biggest damn dog I ever saw."

I patted Jimbo on the head and said, "Jimbo, meet Clay," and Jimbo lifted his paw to shake, and everyone around had a good laugh.

Someone asked Clay if them Blackfeet was a raidin' party, a village, or what? Lucas spoke up for the first time and told us they weren't there long enough to find out. Once they figured they was Blackfeet, they was hightailin' it out of there mighty fast. He went on to tell us they was with the Crows last winter when them Blackfeet devils attacked a Crow village that was on the Yellowstone or, as the Injuns called it, the Elk River, maybe twenty miles from our village. When most of their warriors were on a hunt, they butchered everyone in the village—man, woman, and child—then burned it to the ground. Every lodge was lost. "When that huntin' party came back and saw what was left, they sent a runner over to our village, and we got up a war party mighty fast. Clay and me went with them, but these two youngsters was out huntin' with some young men from the village at that time." He went on that they had followed them devils for near a week when a big norther blew in and they lost all sign of their trail. He said they were lucky to make it back at all with three feet of new snow and wind blowin' so hard you could hardly see your horse's ears. "After we saw what those Blackfeet do to people, we didn't want to be anywhere they might find us."

Death was just accepted by all of us in these Shinin' Mountains. No more was said 'bout the fate of Lucien and Jacques. I didn't know for sure, but I, just like the rest, figured that was who these four latecomers had buried. That the Shoshone had done it, I had no doubt, but I didn't think any less of them for it either. I had been raised on the edge of the frontier, where mostly the law was what good men believed was right and wrong, where men had the will to enforce what they believed was right. Those of us that chose to live this far from the civilized world just accepted this as part of life. I had no desire to change their ways and no desire to leave these mountains either. So I, like most all the trappers and explorers that just had to cross the next horizon, accepted the Injuns and their justice like we accepted our own. Their ways were harsh and cruel, just like this land they lived in, where every day was a struggle to survive.

It was near dark when we got back to the lodge. Sun Flower and Raven Wing had those three elk hides staked out, fleshed, and the hair scraped off two of them. That grizzly hide looked like it had been worked hard as well. The cookin' pot was settin' on coals by the edge of the fire, and what they had in it was smellin' mighty good. Me and Runnin' Wolf unloaded and then picketed the mules with Red and the chestnut. I figured they would try to go back to the other mules they had been with for so long. So we made sure the picket line would hold and there was good grass for them so they didn't try to move.

When the chores were done, we sat down by the fire, and Sun Flower handed me and Runnin' Wolf a carved wooden bowl, then Raven Wing filled them with a stew. It was made with the leftover elk roast and the wild onions and camas root and the root of a flower I'd heard called sego lily. Then they just stood back, waitin' for us to eat. I motioned for Sun Flower to sit by me, and she seemed hesitant, but she did so. I asked her why she and Raven Wing weren't eatin' with us, and she looked at me and said, "Men eat first then women."

I looked at Runnin' Wolf, and he was just grinnin' at me. I asked Sun Flower if this was my fire. She looked puzzled but nodded. Then I asked her if this was my camp, and she nodded. Then I said to her and Raven Wing, "If this is my camp and this is my fire, then this is my food, and we will do things my way."

They both had very puzzled looks, and Sun Flower said, "You are not pleased with the food."

I said, "The food is good, the eatin' is not. I want all of us to eat together. I want my woman to eat by my side when I eat. I want her to be by my side always. My woman is not my slave. She is my partner, and I will not eat until she does."

Sun Flower looked at her sister and then at me and said, "We have only two bowls."

I grinned at her and said, "We will share this bowl then." I reached in the bowl and pulled a very tender piece of meat out and put it to her mouth. Those beautiful dark eyes of hers were starin' right into mine as she opened her mouth, and I slowly pushed the piece of elk between her lips.

The next day we just stayed around camp most of the day. The women worked on finishin' the hides. I walked out and found some suitable cottonwood pieces and went to work carvin' a couple more bowls and some spoons. Eatin' stew with your fingers is a messy process. Ma always had a bunch of wooden spoons, and when one would break, Pa would make a replacement. He liked usin' hickory, but that doesn't grow out here, so cottonwood will have to do.

Runnin' Wolf went out and checked on all the horses and brought in the women's horses. Sun Flower's roan and Raven Wing's dun where both nice mounts, not what I would call great horses, but they did what was asked of them. I wondered what it would take to trade the Nez Pierce out of a couple of their Appaloosas. But then I figured what we had would do just fine.

As we sat 'round the fire, drinkin' coffee and eatin' some of the fresh smoked elk for lunch, Runnin' Wolf asked Sun Flower and Raven Wing if they could use weapons. Raven Wing said, "With warriors like us to protect them, why would they need to?"

Sun Flower didn't say a thing but took her knife and threw it. It stuck in the piece of firewood 'bout ten feet away, and then with a sly smile on her face, Raven Wing threw hers, and it stuck in the same piece of wood, only a couple of inches from Sun Flower's. I must have had a surprised look on my face, 'cause Sun Flower smiled at me and said, "We grew up tryin' to compete with Spotted Elk." Then she looked at Raven Wing and said, "Raven Wing is good with a bow."

Runnin' Wolf got up and got his bow and handed it to Raven Wing and said, "Show me."

Without sayin' a thing, she took the bow and stuck an arrow in a cottonwood sapling 'bout thirty yards out. I asked Sun Flower if she could do that, and she nodded. She said she wasn't as good with one as Raven Wing, but she could shoot. I was both surprised and pleased.

We sat back down, and I asked Runnin' Wolf what this was all 'bout. And he said we was gonna be travelin' without a village to protect the women, that if we were out huntin' or trappin' and the women were alone, he wanted to know they could defend themselves. I was mighty glad he was figurin' ahead like that. It showed I was still a greenhorn, that I hadn't thought that far ahead. So I set my mind to teachin' Sun Flower to shoot the squirrel gun and said, "We needed to make a bow for Raven Wing."

Runnin' Wolf just smiled and said, "It will be done."

I spent the rest of the afternoon smoothin' out the spoons and bowls I had roughed out in the mornin'. By dinnertime, I had us each an eatin' spoon and two big ones for the pot. We now had four bowls. We had six tin cups, two tin plates, a small and large coffee pot, the large cookin' pot, and two fry pans. We now had two axes and two spades, we had our ridin' mounts, and now with the two mules, we had six pack animals and enough food staples to last us a year, and we now had a buffalo hide lodge. We had our weapons with plenty of powder, lead, and patch cloth, and our traps. We had some blacksmith tools and harness repair kit back at the dugout. I figured we were outfitted as well as anybody in the mountains and a lot better than most. And I wished Pa could see everything we had accomplished.

Next mornin' we were goin' out to start teachin' the women to shoot, when a group of eighteen trappers came by with all their pack animals fully loaded. They said they had nothin' left to trade and was headed up to the Wind River country for the fall season. Their leader was a man by the name of Henry Clayson, and he told me to watch my hair, that with what stories were bein' told all over the mountains 'bout me, that there would be a lot of young warriors wantin' to be the one that took the scalp of Grizzly Killer. He told me many Injuns out there figured the greater the warrior they kill, the greater their own medicine. He said most would fear me 'cause of the stories. But many would want to take my medicine for their own.

We shook hands, and I wished them good huntin', and we watched as they headed north to the Bear River trail that would lead them 'round the big bend where they would leave the Bear and head east toward the headwaters of the Seeds-Kee-Dee. From what many of the trapper had told us, that was mighty pretty country up there. I figured maybe we'd have to go up that way next year, since that was the home country of Sun Flower and Raven Wing.

We headed out toward the creek we'd followed up when we went huntin' a couple of days ago. The trappers were callin' it Blacksmith's Fork, and we found a right nice spot that had a cut bank of sand. We set up some pieces of bark for targets in front of that sand so we could dig the balls out easy enough and remold them. I figured we had plenty of lead but no need to waste it anyhow. You just never know when something might happen, and you lose it crossin' a river or use more that you figured in a battle or just whatever might come up. Whenever Pa had practiced shootin', he had always dug up the used balls, and we'd remold them even when we were back home.

I had used this squirrel gun since I was 'bout ten years old, and I was well used to the weight of the long barrels of all the rifles. But Sun Flower, bein' just a small woman and never heftin' a rifle before, was strugglin' to hold that barrel still, so I tied together a couple of good sticks to make a rest for her to set the barrel in. The first time she shot, she jumped, and I could tell she was embarrassed. I figured she was as competitive and determined a girl as I'd ever met. She learned to reload, and she shot till she was hittin' a piece of bark with every shot. Then she started to practice without the forked sticks to rest the barrel on, and in another half dozen shots, she was hittin' them bark pieces again. She had a big smile on her face when she handed the rifle back to me. I wouldn't take it back, and I told her it was hers now.

While Sun Flower and I had been there, shootin', Runnin' Wolf and Raven Wing had ridden on up the creek. While I was digging the lead balls out of the sand, they came back, and Runnin' Wolf was carryin' three oak branches 'bout six feet long and maybe a little over an inch thick. He said he could make good bows with these. We loaded up and headed back. On our way back, we came across where an old beaver pond had been, and it was clear full of willows. Runnin' Wolf stopped and said he was goin' to cut a bunch of arrow shafts.

We went on back to camp and spent the rest of the day and the next just workin' on things that needed doin'. Sun Flower and Raven Wing were finishin' up those hides and had that grizzly robe downright soft. It was gonna make a mighty warm bed come winter. I made up a possibles bag for Sun Flower with a new patch knife, flint, a small roll of patch cloth, two dozen .36-caliber balls, most of which I remolded from the ones she had shot, the round ball mold, and meltin' spoon. I even put a couple of sewin' needles in it and some sinew wound around a small stick.

Runnin' Wolf worked on the bows and arrows. He had peeled all the bark off the willow arrow shafts and made a little rack he set by the fire to dry them, bein' real careful to keep them turned so's they'd dry even and stay straight. He had found some small pieces of flint and was chippin' out arrowheads. We would visit with others of the village, and many trappers came by to visit. It was a right pleasant thing to pass the time that way.

The next mornin', I saddled Ol' Red and the roan, and Sun Flower and I took a long ride up the canyon of the Little Bear River. I just wanted to do some scoutin' and see some more of the country. We jumped several groups of deer. Sun Flower wanted to shoot one by herself, and so the next group we saw, we stopped, and with me stayin' with Red and the roan, she started her stalk. She disappeared in the brush by the river, and I just waited. 'Bout twenty minutes or so later, I heard her shot and heard deer runnin' away through the brush.

I climbed up on Ol' Red, and leadin' her roan, I walked on up alongside the river. I came out in the clearin' and just started to laugh. Sun Flower was guttin' a small buck. She was bloody up to her elbows, and the only thing she was wearin' was a big smile. She was completely naked. As I rode up, I could see her dress was laid out on a bush, and she said she didn't want to get it bloody. That was a picture I'd remember forever, her standin' there, smilin' at me, bloody and naked and so proud of her kill. We finished up with the deer and went to the river. I really can't remember enjoyin' myself more than watchin' her wash the blood off herself in the cold mountain stream then sittin' on a rock in the sun to dry before puttin' her dress back on. I tied that deer behind the saddle on Ol' Red, and we headed back. I was right proud of Sun Flower and as happy as I could remember bein'.

It was late afternoon when we got back, and most of the lodges were down. Runnin' Wolf said a runner had come to the village and told of a big Blackfoot raidin' party attackin' Shoshone and Crow villages and the Shoshone needed help. I found Chargin' Bull and asked if they needed our help. With Sun Flower with me, she said Chargin' Bull said his heart was glad that Grizzly Killer offered his help, but where they were goin' was many days' travel and farther away from the land where we were goin', that the Blackfeet were longtime enemies of the Shoshone, and it was matter to be settled by Shoshone. He said most of his warriors had already left, and he was followin' with the village. He said we would meet again and to take care of our Shoshone women. I just nodded and shook his hand. He spoke for a moment more, and Sun Flower nodded, smiled, and then spoke another moment to her chief.

They were now mostly gone, and Chargin' Bull mounted up and left ridin' to the head of the column. I asked Sun Flower what the chief had said, and she told me he said to take good care of Grizzly Killer and Runnin' Wolf, that we were good men. She said she asked Chargin' Bull to tell her father and mother of her and her sister and how happy they were.

Just as we got that deer on a rack and a good smoky fire goin' under it, several riders came by and said there was big trouble at Rendezvous, and several men were hurt bad.

Chapter XVII

Too Many Ways To Die

NOT KNOWIN' what had happened, I wouldn't leave the women, so we all saddled up and headed to the tradin' area. There were several men laid out on the ground and a few more sittin' on stumps with bloody bandages on their heads, arms, and legs. Two that was on the ground were bein' totally left be, and it was plain they were dead. We tied off our mounts, and I asked Ely and Grub what we could do to help. He just said, "Maybe start digging some graves. Two are already dead, and there are two more ain't gonna last much longer." As I asked what had happened, Sun Flower and Raven Wing just went right over and started to help doctorin' them. General Ashley had a bolt of trade cloth out, and two of his clerks were cuttin' it in strips for bandages.

Raven Wing came over and said they needed my help, so I left Grub and Ely and followed Raven Wing. She told one of the men that I could fix a broke leg, that I had fixed Runnin' Wolf's broke leg, and it was fine. This man was in a lot of pain and was drinkin' some whisky to help. I yelled at Runnin' Wolf, askin' him to go find some bark and splints like we'd used on his leg, and he and Grub took off together. I still didn't know what had happened, but these injuries weren't from weapons or a fight.

I'd seen these men in camp but didn't know them. This one here with a broken leg I'd heard was called Smokey. His leg was twisted in a mighty bad way, his head was bloody with a big knot on one side, and two fingers on his left hand were smashed. Then I heard someone say behind me they was comin' back from a hunt and got caught in a rock slide. Someone else said there were too many ways to die in these Rocky Mountains.

Runnin' Wolf and Grub came up and laid out what they'd found, and Grub asked if that would do, and I just nodded. Raven Wing had come back over and was tryin' to bandage his fingers. I told him I ain't no doctor and I'd only done this a time or two and never on a break this bad. This trapper just looked at me through bloodshot and pain-filled eyes and said, "Just do your best. There ain't nobody here any better."

I had Grub and Runnin' Wolf hold his shoulders and asked Ely to hold his head and Raven Wing to hold his hand. Sun Flower came over by me as I carefully picked up his foot and pulled hard and turned it straight. He screamed, and Jimbo howled, and he passed out. I held his foot in place while Runnin' Wolf wrapped his leg with a piece of elk hide and then the bark and splint sticks, and Grub tied it up with wide strips of the trade cloth. His breathin' was fast and shallow, and I wondered if he would make it. Someone else said, "Looks like Bonner just went under."

Next mornin' there were three graves by the banks of the Little Bear River and seven injured men. Smokey was alive and awake but in a lot of pain. I figured it would be a long time 'fore these men were up and trappin' again. But with the Rocky Mountain Fur Co. brigades gonna winter right here, I figured there would be men to care for 'em. We got some aspen bark tea started to see if that would help them some. We had been up all night, and when everything quieted down, we headed back to our camp.

As we approached our lone teepee, I could see where the Injun village had been was a mess. There were discarded items thrown here and there, bone piles that the dogs had scattered, and all the grass was worn down. It didn't look like a place I wanted to stay any longer. But we ate some of the deer Sun Flower had shot yesterday that was still on the rack and got the smokin' fire started again and went inside and slept for a few hours.

When I woke, Runnin' Wolf was already up by the fire, workin' on arrows. He said he needed some good rawhide to finish the bows. We talked 'bout leavin' Willow Valley and headin' to the Ute country and findin' his village and his sister. He figured his sister and others would be worried 'bout him. He had told them he would be back before summer. The women were up and fixin' a meal. Raven Wing said they needed more elk hides and said we should go where we could hunt on the way. This time of the year, most of the elk were up in the high meadows. So we decided we would leave the next day and take the trail up Blacksmith's Fork to the basin where we found the elk before and turn south from there instead of goin' through the valley to the south and on to the Weber River.

Late in the afternoon, we went back over to the tradin' area and said our farewells. Smokey looked a little better, but he was gonna be down for quite a spell. He thanked me for doin' what I'd done for his leg, and I told him not to rush the healin'. A couple of the injured men were up and 'bout, but the others hadn't moved much at all since they were brought in. We visited with Grub and Ely for a while and said our good-byes. Grub, with a twinkle in his eye, told us to take right good care of those purty girls of ours, or he'd be 'round to steal 'em from us.

I found General Ashley, and he was havin' a parley with Jed Smith, Bill and Milt Sublette, Jim Beckwourth, Tom

Fitzpatrick, and Davy Jackson. Jim Bridger, Robert Newell, and Joe Meek were standin' by a fire nearby. We said farewell and good huntin' to all of them, and they bid us the same. Jimbo was gettin' a lot of attention, and he was even lettin' some of the men he knew rub his ears a bit. When the farewells were over, we headed back to our teepee. I made up a pan of cornbread, and we ate more of the smoked deer, cornbread, and strong sweetened coffee.

Next mornin' we were up at dawn, and after biscuits and coffee, we started right in packin' the horses. I was amazed how fast the women had the teepee down and was usin' two of the lodge poles for a travois to carry it. The Buffalo hides were mighty old and worn, but there were enough all stitched together, and it was still heavy. When we had everything loaded, I was mighty glad I'd made the deal for the two extra mules, 'cause all the animals were fully loaded. The mules were good solid packers and had been on the trail for months, so they didn't mind goin' at all. Jimbo took off scoutin' ahead as usual, and me and Runnin' Wolf would trade off the lead. The women were in the middle, each leadin' two pack horses. The last pack horse had the travois, and either me or Runnin' Wolf would bring up the rear with the mules. This was how we would travel each day.

The trail goin' up Blacksmith's Fork was right narrow and rocky. We had to lift the travois a couple of times over rocks, and by the time we reached the basin at the top of the canyon, the animals all needed a rest. We found a grassy spot by the creek and let them rest and graze for a couple of hours. While the rest was restin', there I rode Red off a couple of miles to the south to get a better idea of the land. This basin was a valley a couple of miles wide with just grass and brush in the middle and timbered mountains to both the east and west. I figured the Bear River was only twenty or thirty miles to the east over the mountain and the Weber River maybe thirty or forty miles to the south. Goin' over the mountains to the east looked rough for how we were loaded, so I planned on followin' the valley we was in to the south and find an easier crossin'.

We hadn't talked 'bout the route Runnin' Wolf wanted to take into Ute country, but as heavy as we were loaded, I figured we needed to head to the dugout and cache most of our supplies. Runnin' Wolf agreed and said from the dugout we would follow the Bear River up over the pass and follow what the trappers were callin' the Duchesne River down to where Rock Creek runs into it, and he figured, by now his village would be camped somewhere along Rock Creek for the summer.

We only traveled another five miles or so and made camp along a small stream that was lined with willows and was runnin' down from the west. We didn't set up a shelter at all, with the weather still bein' dry and warm. I figured we were in friendly country right now, so I didn't worry much 'bout a fire. But still, just out of caution, we built the fire in a little clearin' in the willow so it wouldn't be easy to spot.

With the high mountain to the west, the sun set real early, but it stayed light a mighty long time afterward, and we enjoyed the long summer evenin'. There were deer comin' down to the creek for water. Some were right near camp and didn't seem bothered by us bein' here at all. Just as the evenin' star showed up, a wolf started its mournful howl across the valley and was answered by one just to the south. The darker it became, the stars appeared, and I was still in awe lookin' at the night sky. I'd been in the Rocky Mountains for over a year now, and the number of stars lookin' like you can reach out and touch them was a sight I never got tired of. The smoke from the fire had been keepin' the mosquitoes at bay, but as we let it burn down, they got so bad we had to crawl under the bedrolls for protection. The next mornin', we were all scratchin' the bites, even Jimbo.

The horses and mules had been on good grass all night and seemed well rested and ready to go. We loaded them all and continued south. We saw several moose that mornin', but we were fully loaded and couldn't carry that much meat, so we just watched them as they ran from the creek and headed into the timber, away from us. The abundance of game in this country was really something to behold. I asked how anyone could ever go hungry in a land with so much game. Runnin' Wolf said, when feedin' a village and the deer and elk are pursued all the time, they leave and go places they are hard to find. He went on sayin', "It takes many animals to feed a village, and the hunters must travel farther and farther from the village to find the game. That is why the villages must move often, or the people will go hungry." He said it was easy to find game to feed just a few like us, but hard to find enough for a village, and people do go hungry in the winter.

We made good time goin' through this wide valley, and by late mornin', we came to a large canyon runnin' east and west, endin' this wide valley we had been in. We turned east, headin' up the canyon through grass covered hills and large stands of quakin' aspen. The climb up was steady and at times so steep we would have to switch back and forth, movin' sideways along the hills, and that became hard on the horse with the travois. We would stop and rest often after crossin' these steep areas. We jumped deer right regular as we traveled through the stands of quakies and watched as they bounded away. We nooned in a small clearin' that had a spring comin' out of the ground and formed a creek less than a foot wide.

As we neared what I figured was the top of the ridge we were climbin', the quakies started to give way to pines. We would have to skirt around most of the stands of pines 'cause the trees were so close together and had so much deadfall the horses couldn't get through, so our progress had slowed a lot.

It was gettin' to be late afternoon when we came upon a little clearin' with a pond out in the middle, and as we approached, Jimbo started to growl, and all his hair stood up down the center of his back. Then he just took off toward a pine thicket on the other side of the clearin'. He had just started off, when a small black bear took off out of this thicket and ran for all he was worth out into the forest, with Jimbo 'bout a hundred yards behind. I whistled real load for Jimbo, since we weren't in need of a bear right now and decided we would camp here in the trees not too far from the clearin' and water.

We started unloadin' the packs and gettin' hobbles on the stock so they could wander this little meadow all night, 'cept Ol' Red. I don't put hobbles on him 'cause I trust him not to wander off. We were still sleepin' in the open as the weather was still warm and dry. The women were gatherin' firewood and gettin' camp set up when Jimbo come back. He looked at me real disappointed like. He knew he had done his job on that bear, but he didn't understand why I hadn't done mine and followed him after it. I noticed Jimbo's nose was swellin' up and called him over. He had a big ol' bee sting right on his nose, and it was gettin' bigger. I wondered why a bee would sting him and where he got stung. I walked over by where I'd first seen the bear, and there were bees swarmin' all 'round that thicket, and it didn't take long for me and Jimbo to get away.

I figured that young bear was after honey, just like they did back home. Me and Pa had robbed beehives for honey before, and some fresh honey on some cornbread sounded mighty fine. So I went back to the others and told them my plan. Sun Flower said she was no bear, and the bees were too angry. Raven Wing just smiled and shook her head. Runnin' Wolf looked mighty skeptical, but he said he would help. I made up a couple of torches usin' grass and pine pitch, one for each of us. Then we wrapped a blanket around us and headed for the bees. We lit the torches when we were 'bout thirty yards out, and when they was smokin' real good, we moved in. It was workin' real well, and the bees were stayin' away from the smoke and heat of the torches. We got up to where I could see the hive and where that bear had ripped it open, when a little bit of a breeze came up and blew the smoke away from the hive and bees. The bees were on us like flies on a fresh kill. I was gettin' stung all over my face, and when I dropped the torch and ran, Runnin' Wolf was just jumpin' in the pond. I followed right behind him, only to find out the pond wasn't deep enough for us to get all the way under. I was swattin' at bees, just sittin' in and splashin' water all over me till all the bees finally left. And then we could hear the laughter. Sun Flower and Raven Wing were standin' by the campfire, laughin' and pointin' at us, and they would laugh some more. Jimbo was sittin' on his haunches between them, and I really believe he was laughin' too.

We both stood by the campfire and stripped out of our wet buckskins and hung them by the fire to dry. Raven Wing went to the pond and got a big handful of mud and some moss and mixed it together, and they started coverin' all the bee strings with the mud. When Sun Flower was done, my whole face was covered with mud, and she laughed all the harder. She told me I might be the great Grizzly Killer, but I was no bear to get honey. At this point, I figured she was right.

After the bees had settled down, Sun Flower walked around to the other side of the pond and picked up the blankets me and Runnin' Wolf had dropped runnin' for the pond. We wrapped up in those blankets and sat by the fire, drank coffee, and ate smoked deer. Just before dark, we walked to the pond and washed off all the mud and went to bed. There was a pack of coyotes yippin' at the moon just down the hill a ways and some owls hootin' back and forth to each other in the forest. Sun Flower backed her body up against me, and as I wrapped my arms around her, holdin' her tight, I thought how natural this felt. It was hard for me to believe we had only known each other such a short time, 'cause this felt like we had known each other forever. I remember Pa sayin' many times as I was growin' up that him and Ma was meant to be together, and as I went to sleep, I figured that me and Sun Flower were meant to be together too.

Next mornin', I woke to Raven Wing's laughter. I sat up to see what was goin' on and saw Runnin' Wolf. One side of his face was swollen up something terrible. He had three or four stings on the right side of his nose and a couple more right under his right eye. His eye was swollen shut, and his nose was all distorted. I had to chuckle a little, but I don't think Runnin' Wolf figured it was funny. I had bumps all over my face as well, but my stings didn't swell up as bad as Runnin' Wolf's. Sun Flower was gettin' coffee goin' and some biscuits started while Raven Wing went for a walk out through the forest. When she came back, she was carryin' a handful of plants. She took a coffee cup and started to break up the plants in it. Then she added just a little bit of water and heated it on the fire. She took a stick and mixed it up as it heated into a paste then set it aside to cool. By the time the coffee and biscuits were ready, Sun Flower handed me a coffee cup that had a big chunk of honeycomb in it. The honey was drippin' out of that honeycomb and the cup was almost clear full of thick, sticky honey. Sun Flower just smiled at me and said, "Bees not angry at night."

Runnin' Wolf drank a little coffee and tasted the honey, but he didn't feel like eatin'. That honey on the warm biscuits was mighty fine. After we ate, the plant mixture Raven Wing had mixed up was cooled, and she smeared it on Runnin' Wolf's face. It looked worse than the mud did, but she said it would make the swellin' go down.

We got loaded up and started off to the east and again. We were still havin' to go around the thick stands of pines, but within an hour, we had started to descend the ridge. As we started off the east side, there was mile after mile of sage coverin' the hills. There were stands of quakies, but they were stunted in their growth and thick like the oak brush that grows here in the west. As we would approach these patches of quakies, deer would run out and head across the open sage toward other stands of those quakies that might be a mile or two away. There was a line of cottonwoods, makin' a green line, twistin' its way down off the mountain that was obviously a creek, and we headed for that. I figured we could follow it all the way to the Bear River.

By midday we were by the creek and stopped under some cottonwoods to rest the stock and eat. I was amazed at how the swellin' was down on Runnin' Wolf's face. He looked almost normal. My stings were now 'bout like mosquito bites, but they itched worse. I figured we wouldn't be tryin' for honey again anytime soon, at least not in the daylight.

We could now see the channel of the Bear River, and I figured we would make it easy 'fore nightfall. This side of the mountain was mighty dry. This creek we were followin' was the only water I could see. It hadn't rained at all in over month now, and I thought no one would ever be able to farm this land 'cause the crops would just dry up and blow away. We jumped a few rabbits and two different flocks of prairie chickens as we descended these barren hills. Jimbo had a run-in with a big ol' diamond-back rattlesnake, but his reflexes were fast enough that he killed the snake and brought it back to us. Runnin' Wolf said it would make a good dinner and skinned it. I kept the rattles to add to Jimbo's collar.

While we were noonin' here, Runnin' Wolf took his bow and walked out through the sage and disappeared. 'Bout an hour later, he came back with three big prairie chickens. He said he needed feathers for the arrows he was makin' and the birds and snake would make a good dinner. We moved on toward the Bear. We were down in the foothills far enough now, and there was nothin' but sage and a few little prickly pear cactus, 'cept along the creek.

By midafternoon there were clouds buildin' up over the mountains to the west, and a gusty wind had started to blow. As the afternoon passed, the clouds kept gettin' thicker and darker, and by the time we reached the Bear River, we all knew we were in for a storm. We unloaded the horses and mules and hobbled 'em just as fast as we could, and the women went to work settin' up the teepee. The wind was gustin' so hard by then it took all four of us to set it up. I had never set one up before and didn't know what I was doin', so 'bout all I could do was hold things down to keep them from blowin' away.

It took some doin', but once we got the coverin' over the poles, I was amazed how stable it was in the wind. We barely got the bedrolls inside when the rain hit. There was lightnin' and thunder that shook the ground. Me and Runnin' Wolf went out and gathered just a couple of armloads of firewood and were soaked to the skin when we came back in. Then the hail came, and Jimbo pushed his way inside with the rest of us. The hail was hittin' the teepee and ground so hard it made a mighty loud roar. The lightnin' was flashin' so bright it would light up the inside of the teepee, and the temperature fell till it was downright cold. Once we got a fire goin' inside, it warmed right up, and the women put the chickens and that snake to roastin' over it.

We heard a big crash, and I looked out to see what had happened, and not fifty yards away, a big cottonwood had split down the middle and was burnin' even in this hard rain. I couldn't see Ol' Red or the horses and hoped they were all OK. The storm seemed to be gettin' worse, and water started to run in under the hide coverin' 'cause we didn't have time to shovel dirt up over the flap that touched the ground. So me and Runnin' Wolf went out and covered it with mud the best we could. I couldn't have been any wetter if'n I'd jumped in the river. I was gettin' mighty concerned 'cause we still couldn't see any of the stock.

We stripped out of the wet buckskins and just wrapped a blanket 'round us and ate, hung the buckskins over the fire to dry, and listened to the storm rage outside. I don't think any of us slept. We just lay there and listened to the poundin' rain. I wondered what had become of the mules and horses and just what we'd find in the mornin'.

Chapter XVIII

The Badger

THE NEXT MORNIN' we got up to low-hangin' clouds, and everything outside the teepee was wet. I was mighty glad we had the flour, cornmeal, sugar, and bakin' powder in barrels, or it all would have been ruined. I sent Jimbo out to find Ol' Red, and we tried to build a fire outside. Everything was so wet we had to use coals from the little fire inside the teepee to finally get it started and then set all the packs 'round it to start to dry things out. Every so often it would start to sprinkle a little, but the hard rain seemed to have stopped. The river was runnin' mighty high and looked like rollin' mud. This was the first time I'd seen a river muddy since we'd left the lower parts of the Platt last year. It was runnin' way too high to try to cross this mornin'.

Sun Flower and Raven Wing were gettin' the coffee goin', when I saw Ol' Red trottin' through the brush from upriver with Jimbo right alongside. That ol' mule came right up to me like he was comin' back to the barn. He sure was a pretty sight. I threw the saddle on him and followed his tracks back along the river, hopin' the other mules and horses would be together.

I went for a couple of miles and saw the other two mules just standin' in the brush, and as I approached them, I could see the horses were scattered along the river for another couple of hundred yards. I was surprised they all had traveled that far with the hobbles on.

I took the hobbles off each one as I got to them, and they all followed along pretty good. One of the pack horses was favorin' one leg a bit, and I figured that was from her tryin' to run with the hobbles on. Jimbo was a right convincin' herder when he needed to be. We set up a good strong picket line when I got 'em back to camp on the best grass we could find, but it wasn't much. We would have to find 'em better graze soon.

We kept rearrangin' the packs and such 'round the fire, tryin' to dry it all out, and 'bout midmornin', the sun came out for a little while. But by midday, the clouds were lowerin' again and gettin' darker. When we heard the first thunder off to the west, we started loadin' everything in the teepee. I took the spade and shoveled dirt up over the ground flap good. We hurried and brought in enough firewood for the rest of the day and night, just in case it came down on us again like it did the day before.

Runnin' Wolf was over checkin' on the stock one more time, and he took the horse favorin' his leg and was walkin' him some, when up in the sage, maybe a hundred yards, Jimbo got into a mighty fierce fight. I could see Jimbo up over the sage, but I couldn't see what he was a fightin'. From the sounds Jimbo was makin', he was takin' this fight mighty serious. When I got up there, it was over, and there was blood all over, and Jimbo had a big ol' badger in his mouth, shakin' the life out of it. I couldn't tell whose blood was whose. Jimbo finally dropped it then pushed it a couple of times with his nose to make sure it was dead. When he turned to come to me, he was limpin'. That badger had got hold of his right front paw durin' the fight, and it looked like one of Jimbo's toes was ripped right off.

Runnin' Wolf had tied the pack horse back to the picket line and had run up to us as me and Jimbo started back down. Jimbo was hoppin' on three legs, and when we got to the fire, Sun Flower and Raven Wing just moved me out of the way and started doctorin' him. Runnin' Wolf was carryin' that badger back down and said he could use the hide. He also handed me the turquoise piece Butterfly had given Jimbo. I guess the badger had bit his neck as well and just got the collar instead of his neck. I gave the turquoise to Sun Flower for safe keepin'.

Those two had Jimbo's foot bandaged and had cleaned up several other bites in no time at all, and Jimbo seemed to love the attention. Sun Flower took off his collar and checked the grizzly claws and made sure they were still tied on tight. She then just put the collar in her bag instead of back on Jimbo.

The lightnin' was gettin' closer and the thunder louder as we made a final check and made sure everything was secure, and then we could hear a roar comin' at us, and you could see a wall of hail. We got inside the lodge mighty quick, and Jimbo just curled up by the door on the inside again, and the hail hit with a real vengeance. The hail only lasted a few minutes, but then the rain poured down again. Sun Flower got her bag and pulled out Jimbo's collar and started cuttin' a rawhide strip. When she was done, that piece of turquoise was secure right in the middle of the collar, and she moved over to Jimbo so's he wouldn't have to move and put it back on him. Then she went to work and made a moccasin for his hurt paw and laced it on him.

While we waited out the rain, I made sure all the guns were dry and the powder was dry and protected. Runnin' Wolf was cuttin' the prairie chicken feathers for the arrows, and Raven Wing started on dinner.

The rain only lasted a few hours, and a couple hours 'fore dark, it had stopped, and we ventured out. The sky was clearin' to the west, and by sunset, it was mostly clear. Everything was wet and muddy, and the river was a roarin' torrent of muddy water. The air was clean and cool with the fresh smell that comes after a rain. Me and Runnin' Wolf moved the picket line for the stock over to some fresh grass, and when we were done with that, Sun Flower had an outside fire goin'. We sat around it and ate smoked deer and biscuits.

By then the clouds were only a dark line way off to the east and the stars were shinin' overhead, and it was cold enough we could see our breath. We moved some of the packs back out of the teepee and turned in for the night. I could see the light from the night sky through the smoke hole and went to sleep, listenin' to coyotes yippin' all around us.

Next mornin' there was a thin layer of frost on the grass and brush leaves. This was 'bout the third week of June, and I'd never seen frost this time of year before, and I said so. Sun Flower said it could freeze any time of the year in this country. The fire felt mighty good by the time we had it goin', and we had hot coffee and leftover biscuits for breakfast. By the time we got loaded, the sun was up, and it was warmin' up fast. The river was still runnin' high but not like the day before. We started out and just followed it along the west side, watchin' for a good place to cross. By midday, I figured we'd traveled 'bout ten miles and the river was 'bout down to normal level, but this time of year, normal was pretty high, and it was still mighty muddy. So we just stayed on the west side, headin' south.

By midafternoon we came to a place where the river widened out, and we decided to make our crossin' here. The water was only 'bout two feet deep, but it was movin' mighty fast. The horses and mules made it across all right, but Jimbo was still favorin' his sore paw, and the current swept him downstream. By the time he fought his way across, he was a half mile north of us. I galloped Ol' Red along the shore, tryin' to get ahead of him, but by the time I was in a position I could help, he had made it out. He shook, and muddy water went flyin' in every direction.

We were much farther south now than we were when we first hit the Bear River on the way to Rendezvous, so we left the river, headin' east by south toward Black's Fork. The rain had refreshed the land. Where the flowers were wiltin' and the grass turnin' brown a couple of days before, now everything was alive and bright colored. We crossed hill after hill with these big shallow draws between them, and by late afternoon, we made camp in the bottom of one of these draws with a little creek runnin' down through it. There were new blooms comin' out on the flowers, and the grass was turnin' green right before our eyes. There was good grass along both sides of the creek, and it was small enough you could step across it in most places. We just hobbled the stock again so's they could move along the creek to stay on good grass. The women started to set up the teepee, sayin' it needed to dry out 'cause it was still damp when we put it away.

We had been seein' antelope all afternoon, and I figured some fresh meat would be right welcome, so I took Ol' Red and started out. Jimbo's paw was botherin' him after travelin' all day, and he wanted to go, but when I told him to stay, he just lay down and watched me ride out. I rode to the top of the ridge and stopped there, just admirin' the view. By now I would have thought I was used to the views out here, but the distances I could see still amazed me. I could see three separate herds of antelope from where I sat, and they were not even close to one another. I couldn't see any way to get close enough to any of them in this open country, so I just continued on. Goin' up the far side of the next rise, there were some big patches of oak brush, and I jumped a small herd of deer that were too far out to shoot. As I topped this ridge and started to circle back toward camp, a badger scurried through the sage to his hole and turned around and hissed at me from his dirt mound as I rode by. When I got back down in the bottom of the draw and headed back toward camp, a family of foxes came out of their den and watched me ride by, the young ones not even stoppin' their play. I wondered if any of them had ever seen a person before. I rode back into camp without any game but growin' to love this land more all the time.

There was a fire goin' when I got back with a spit set up across it, and there were three rabbits on the spit. I looked at Runnin' Wolf, and he pointed to Raven Wing. She and Sun Flower were carin' for the rabbit hides, and they just smiled at me, and I noticed one of the bows Runnin' Wolf had been workin' on lyin' right there where the women were workin'. Runnin' Wolf was workin' on the badger skin, and I could see now he was makin' a quiver out of it. I sat down and called Jimbo over and unlaced his moccasin, and he went right to work cleanin' his paw with his tongue. When the women finished fleshin' the rabbit skins, they picked up a pouch, asked me to keep the rabbits, turned, and started off down this little creek. I made up a pan of cornbread and could see we would need to hunt a bear 'fore long to refill the grease pouch. The sun was 'bout to set when they came back, and the pouch was bulging with wild onions, camas root, and cattail shoots. The fresh roasted rabbit tasted mighty good, but Jimbo looked like we were tryin' to starve him. He got one rabbit for himself, but it was plain he wanted more.

After we finished eatin', Sun Flower picked up one of our blankets, and the two of us walked up to the top of the ridge. We sat down with her in front of me. I wrapped the blanket around us both, and we watched the stars come out across this endless sky. It was a cool but pleasant evenin', and sittin' there with my arms around her as it got dark was mighty fine. I thought 'bout Ma and Pa and figured they would like this beautiful, brash, intelligent girl as much as I did. As a pack of coyotes started their yippin' on the opposite ridge, she laid her head back against me, and she pulled my arms tighter around her. We just sat like that for the longest time. Then without sayin' a word, she stood, pulled her dress off, and sat back down on my lap, putting her arms around my neck and kissing me. We made love in that cool night air until we were both cold and tired and walked back down to camp. The teepee was warm and comfortin' with just some coals still glowin' in the little fire pit inside. Runnin' Wolf and Raven Wing were asleep as we crawled under our bedroll. The night was calm, and I slept sound with Sun Flower in my arms all night.

When I woke and just lay there, listenin' as always, I could hear something movin' through our things outside the teepee and very quietly moved my hand to my Hawken. Sun Flower laid her hand over mine and squeezed it and whispered it was Runnin' Wolf. I couldn't believe he got up and went out without me wakin' up. I thought then I couldn't let myself sleep that sound, for this land had too many dangers. But then, with all of us together, I knew we were safer. Just like now, I was asleep, but Sun Flower was aware of everything all around us.

When I went out, it was light. The sun wasn't up yet, but it wouldn't be long. As I took in the world 'round us, I could see a cow and calf moose 'bout a half mile down this little creek, and as I watched them, the calf dropped to its knees and started to suckle. Then from out of sight, up the creek, I heard the familiar slap of a beaver tail hittin' the water and wondered what had spooked it. Then I saw a pair of coyotes come from behind a little rise in that direction and run up the hill over the top of the ridge. This land was wild and harsh but beautiful beyond describin'. It was full of life, and at the same time, death could come mighty quick and easy.

I was lookin' at the lay of the Bear River Mountains just south of us and figured we were only 'bout a day and half from the dugout. And I had the feelin' I was goin' home. Runnin' Wolf was starin' at those same mountains and came over to me and, pointin' up at one high rugged peak, said his village should be on the other side of that peak in the valley of Rock Creek on the south side of these mountains. I could see in his eyes he wanted to get back there, but then he told me he figured his home was now with Raven Wing and me and Sun Flower, but he had to return and make sure Shinin' Star was all right. He said he had to tell her that her mournin' time was over and she needed to find another man for her to care for. He told me Grub was right. She was a beautiful girl, and there were always lots of men that wanted her. But since he was now the man of the family, it was for him to say whom she would go with. Then he smiled at me and said, "She will tell me who to choose, and I will do as she asks. I want only for her to be happy and cared for."

Raven Wing was gettin' the coffee on and some biscuits in the pan, but she heard what Runnin' Wolf had said. She stopped and walked over to us and stepped right up in front of Runnin' Wolf and put her arms around him, and lookin' in his eyes, she said, "My heart is good to have such a man as you. Only one moon ago, I would have been afraid to be with a Ute warrior, but now I know the heart of a man comes from the man, not his people. I choose to be with you, Runnin' Wolf, because of the man you are, and with Grizzly Killer, a white man with the heart of the people." Then she asked him, "Does your sister know how much you care for her?"

Runnin' Wolf just smiled at her and nodded and then held her tight, and I walked down the creek and started bringin' in the stock.

When I got the stock in, Sun Flower was mixin' a poultice of moss and a couple of other plants I didn't know, and when she was satisfied with it, she called Jimbo. He went right over, and she smeared this green poultice on his paw and packed it in where his toe was missin'. Then she pulled his moccasin on and laced it up so's he couldn't lick it off.

We ate and got cleaned up and loaded the horses and mules. One of the pack horses was feelin' a bit frisky this mornin', and when I tightened down the diamond hitch over the load, he went berserk, buckin'. I didn't have the hitch tied off yet, and he threw the whole load off. By the time I got him settled down, we had to start all over again with his pack, but this time, I had him snubbed right up tight to a cottonwood, and he couldn't move his head at all until after I had the pack tied right down on him tight. But after that, he fell right in line and never gave us any more trouble.

We were still headed mostly east by a little south, and by midday, we were into familiar country. This was country I had hunted some last fall. There were more trees and grass now and less sage. We were gettin' above the cedars and pinions and were now into more quakies and pines. The streams everywhere in this lower country were lined with cottonwoods, but they stopped growin' up higher on the mountains. The grass was still mighty green and thick here on the north slope of the Bear River Mountains unlike the sage country we had crossed to get here. We rode past several smaller streams all through the afternoon, and there was beaver sign aplenty. There was still a lot of trappin' that could be done in this country. By the time we were lookin' for a place to camp, I figured we were only three or maybe four hours from the dugout. We should be there by midmornin'.

This area was sort of a borderland and could be used by several different Injun tribes. The Shoshone and Utes mainly, but also the Arapaho and Cheyenne, would hunt here. The Crow, Blackfeet, and even the Sioux would come through here on raids. 'Cause of this, I was bein' a little more careful of campsites and fires. We found a little trickle of a stream between two hills that would hide a fire and didn't start it till 'bout dusk so the smoke couldn't be seen. The grass was good, so we kept the stock on the picket line right close by. We slept under the stars and were headed out the next mornin' by the time the sun was just peekin' over the eastern horizon.

We were now in country I knew well, and we made good time. Jimbo's paw wasn't botherin' him as much now, and he was back to scoutin' out in front of us. Just as we were headed up the western side of the ridge that was just three or four miles west of the dugout, Jimbo came padding back down the trail. His hackles were up, and he was growlin'. We stopped, and all got down. With Sun Flower and Raven Wing holdin' all the stock, me and Runnin' Wolf crawled up to the top of the ridge, and what we saw was mighty troublesome.

Chapter XIX

Arapahos

ACROSS THE BIG MEADOW, right where the dugout sat, there was a column of smoke twistin' its way to the sky. I could see several horses out on the meadow grass, but we were too far away to tell just what was goin' on or who they were. We backed off the ridge where we couldn't be seen and then talked over who it might be. Sun Flower and Raven Wing did not think any Shoshone would bother the lodge of Grizzly Killer, and Runnin' Wolf said he didn't think the Utes would be in this area this time of the year. He thought they would be raidin' the Goshutes way out to the west for slaves to trade to the Spanish. I said it could be a group of trappers, but no trapper's had left Rendezvous before us that were headed this way.

Everyone knew we had to find out, and I knew a good place only a couple of miles to the southwest from here where we could hide the horses. We turned and headed there. I took several different trails, tryin' to mix up our tracks, and stayed to rocky ground when I could, but I knew any Injun could follow them.

This was a narrow little draw with thick timber at the bottom but once you work your way through the timber for maybe a hundred yards, it opened up into scattered quakies, with tall grass under them. The draw was steep sided, with a trail leadin' right up and out the top, but it was steep and rough. We ran a good picket line and pulled all the packs. I wanted Sun Flower and Raven Wing to stay here with them, but they convinced me they might be needed and they could help. Runnin' Wolf gave the badger quiver with the new arrows in it to Raven Wing, and she got her bow ready. Sun Flower got the squirrel gun from its scabbard, and she checked the prime. Runnin' Wolf got his bow ready and put his quiver over his shoulder and then checked the prime on his long rifle. I checked Pa's ol' rifle and put it back in its scabbard and again double-checked the prime on the Hawken. I checked Pa's horse pistol and reached over and placed it on Sun Flower's saddle. She just nodded at me. We all knew this could be a mighty serious thing we were doin'.

I led out, takin' the steep, rough trail out the top of the draw. Once out of the draw, I started in a circle, takin' the same route I used to circle the dugout when I was checkin' for tracks in the early spring. When we got on the ridge way up above the dugout, we started down, stayin' in the thick timber. When we were maybe a mile above, we stopped and tied the horses. I just let Ol' Red's reins hang free. I knew he would stay right there with the horses. Stayin' right in the timber, we started down toward the dugout. I was headed for a little clearin' 'bout a quarter mile above it where we would have a good view of the area.

The sun was just past center sky, and it was mighty warm for bein' this high up. When we crossed a little seep, Runnin' Wolf stopped me, and he put streaks of mud on his face, and so did the women. With my beard, I didn't think I needed it, but Sun Flower put a little just under my eyes and across my forehead. We just took our time gettin' into this clearin', makin' sure we couldn't be seen. I had the women stay back in the timber just a little bit, and me and Runnin' Wolf crawled out to where we could see. There was a fire goin' in the outside fire pit, and 'bout halfway between that and the stream, there were three men staked to the ground. They were naked and not movin' at all. They had darker skin than mine, so I figured they were Injuns. There were eight horses out in the meadow and one brave out with them. I could see two other braves by the fire but didn't know how many might be in the dugout. I looked at Runnin' Wolf, and he whispered Arapaho dogs. He then said the three staked to the ground were most likely Shoshone and three of the horses would be theirs, so he figured there were five Arapahos.

I really wanted to know how many were down there, and we were just watchin' when two more came out of the dugout. One that looked like he was their bushway walked over to one of the men staked out and pissed in his face. He sputtered and choked awake. We watched another of the Arapaho get a stick and walk over to a pine and scrape up some pitch, then he went to the fire and lit it. When it was burnin' good, he held it over the Shoshone that they had woke up and let the burnin' pitch drip all over him. That pitch just kept burnin' once it landed on him, and the Arapahos laughed and laughed. Runnin' Wolf motioned for us to get back into the timber.

We slowly crawled back to where the women were waitin'. He told them what he had seen and added he did not think any of the three would be alive by dark. He said even if we didn't want to save the three now, the Arapaho knew of this place. We could never stay here if any of them lived. I asked Raven Wing if she could go through the willows and the stream and get close enough to the one watchin' the horses to put an arrow in him. She nodded and said she would get it done. I told Runnin' Wolf to take Sun Flower and Jimbo and circle 'round behind the smokehouse and, usin' it for cover, get into good rifle range. Then I told them I was goin' to get Red and just ride into their camp. Sun Flower looked worried, but she did not question me. I told them I would make the sign of peace with my left hand and for them to shoot when I brought it down. I told Raven Wing to shoot when she had to, but if she could wait, to shoot the same instant she heard the rifles. Sun Flower reached out and touched my hand but never said a word as I headed back to get Ol' Red.

I had far enough to go that I figured everyone would be in position when I got back. I climbed up on Red and went right down to the stream. I figured the noise of the water would hide the sound of my approach, and there were enough willows to hide me most all the way. I set Pa's ol' rifle across my knees, and with the Hawken in hand, I rode right into camp. Those Arapahos didn't see me till I was close enough to shoot, and they were stumblin' all over, tryin' to get their weapons. They hesitated when they saw I was makin' the peace sign, and that was what I was hopin' for. I dropped my left hand to the Hawken's barrel, and when I did, I heard the roar of two rifles and then my Hawken just a split second behind. The one still standin' was pullin' his bow back, and I could see I wasn't goin' to get another shot off, and I dived off Ol' Red just as his arrow nearly parted my hair. Then I heard the scream and the viciousness of Jimbo's attack. Runnin' Wolf was runnin' right past me and out to the meadow. I jumped to my feet and followed him. It was only a hundred yards or so, and in just a few seconds, I could see Raven Wing and Runnin' Wolf were together, and there was a body in the grass with three arrows stickin' out of it. I turned and ran back to find Jimbo still had hold of the Injun he had attacked. But I didn't think he could be alive. There was blood everywhere. The one Sun Flower had shot with the squirrel gun was still movin' just a bit, and Sun Flower walked over to him, pulled out her knife, and scalped him while he was still alive. The one Jimbo had hold of tried to move, and Jimbo started shakin' him again just like he did with that badger. I told Jimbo to stop and stay. If that Injun was still alive, he wouldn't be for long.

Sun Flower had tears in her eyes as she was cuttin' the three Shoshone's loose, and as Raven Wing came into camp, she went right to work doctorin' them. I noticed then these were all young men, I figured just thirteen or fourteen years old. Runnin' Wolf asked her if she knew them, and she just nodded. The one they had dripped the burnin' pitch on was in a considerable amount of pain. That pitch had just kept burnin' right through his skin and into his flesh. It appeared the other two had broken ribs from bein' kicked, and one had a huge lump on his head from a war club, I figured. His eyes didn't look right either, and he hadn't made a sound. Raven Wing said she needed bear grease for the burns. The horses were still tied up way above the dugout on the ridge. I told Sun Flower to come with me and bring the horses in while I went and got the rest of them 'cause the only bear grease was in the packs.

She climbed up behind me on Ol' Red, and we headed out. I asked her who these Shoshones were, and she said they were from another village, that they were friends from the village her mother and father had gone to visit instead of goin' to Rendezvous. She said the name of the one that could talk a little was Red Hawk, that he said they were sent here to find us to let us know her mother and father were fine, that Spotted Elk had arrived, and they were ready for the Blackfeet and met them miles away from the village. He told her that Spotted Elk set up an ambush and surprised the Blackfeet, and many scalps were taken with only two Shoshones hurt, but they would live and that Spotted Elk was a great warrior. He said that he and his friends wanted to meet Grizzly Killer and asked if they could bring word to the daughters of Bear Heart and White Feather, that they had followed the Seeds-Kee-Dee and ran into the Arapaho just a few miles after they turned up Smith's Fork. He said the Arapaho caught them at the lodge of Grizzly Killer, but we weren't there to help.

When we got to the horses, Sun Flower got on her roan, and I handed her the reins of the chestnut and Raven Wing's dun, and she headed back. I took Red in as straight a line as possible to the pack horses. I got to them through the thick timber at the bottom of the draw. It was goin' to take me an hour to load everything, so I just made sure the picket line was still tight and loaded the pack with the cookin' supplies and headed back with just the one horse. I went in the open and straight across the big meadow, and it didn't take long to cover the five or six miles back to the dugout.

When I rode in, I stripped the pack off the horse, and as I put him into the pole corral, Raven Wing already had the grease pouch and was coverin' this young man's burns. They had Red Hawk moved over, sittin' up against the dugout, but the other two hadn't been moved. I walked over to Red Hawk and said in what little Shoshone I had learned, "My name is Zach Connors. They call me Grizzly Killer, and I am pleased to meet such a brave Shoshone warrior." His eyes lit up, and he was smilin' from ear to ear.

Sun Flower was tryin' to make the one that had the head injury comfortable, but his eyes were just starin' out into the distance, and I didn't think he even knew she was there. I walked over, and she said his name was Sees Far and he was their cousin. Raven Wing spoke 'bout the burned one. She said, "This one is Buffalo Heart, and he is the younger brother of a friend of ours." She touched Buffalo Heart's arm, and he opened his eyes. When he was lookin' at me, she said, "Buffalo Heart, this man is Grizzly Killer."

He tried to smile and made a slight nod, and I told him what I told Red Hawk, that I was mighty pleased to meet such brave warriors.

Runnin' Wolf had been draggin' the dead out into the meadow. In this summer heat, it wasn't gonna take long for 'em to get smellin' mighty ripe. I saw they had all been scalped, and Sun Flower said the scalps were for these young men to take back and show they were now warriors. Raven Wing then said they would tell them the scalps were ours, and Sun Flower just said it wouldn't matter. The scalps would show they had been in battle and now they were warriors.

I needed to get back and bring in the rest of the horses and supplies. So I just climbed back in the saddle and headed out.

It took me a couple of hours to get there load up and get back. When I rode in, Runnin' Wolf had all the horses from the meadow in the corral, and he came over and helped me unload and put the rest in the corral. There were now eighteen horses and mules in that little corral, and it was crowded.

Runnin' Wolf told me that Red Hawk said there were many more Arapahos all painted for war when they first saw them, maybe as many as forty, but only these five came after them, and he figured these five were to meet up with the rest after they got these three's horses and scalps. If they didn't meet them, he figured the rest would come lookin' for 'em. He said, "We should load these five Arapahos up and haul them way down the river, almost to the Seeds-Kee-Dee, so's they would find them right off and not come up this far lookin'." I said we would leave at first light. I figured it would take 'bout two long days to get there and two to get back.

Sun Flower and Raven Wing were startin' dinner and were cuttin' up the wild onions and camas bulbs and such in the pot. Red Hawk was now up and walkin' a little bit, and he had moved over to Buffalo Heart and sat down by him. Buffalo Heart's eyes were open now, and it peered to me. Red Hawk was tryin' to comfort him some. Sees Far was still just starin' out at something none of us could see, and it looked like he was now strugglin' to breathe. Sun Flower walked up to my side, took hold my hand, and said she feared for her cousin. I just nodded.

The stew was made with what was left of the smoked deer, so we were down to just the dried elk jerky. We needed to make meat.

I got one of the grizzly skins out and laid it out by the fire and asked Raven Wing to see if Buffalo Heart felt like he could move to the skin, where he would be more comfortable, and he nodded. I put a saddle under the skin so he could lay with his head on it, and with me holdin' one arm and Runnin' Wolf the other, we got him moved onto the skin. Raven Wing helped him eat, and Sun Flower tried to get Sees Far to swallow a bit, but he was not able. After we ate, Sun Flower just sat down by her cousin and held his hand.

The sun was 'bout to set, and I saddled up Red again, and we headed up the trail along the stream. I told Jimbo to stay, and he just sat down on his haunches and watched me ride out. I hadn't gone far when I saw some deer grazin' their way toward the river. I left Red there in the trail and got to a place hidden by willows that I figured the deer would pass and just waited. It was almost too dark to see when they got into range, and I fired. With the pan flash, I couldn't see if I hit. I had to walk back and forth in the tall grass to find if I had hit or not and then tripped over the downed deer. I gutted it in a hurry and then got Ol' Red. This deer was just a yearlin' buck, but it would last for a couple of days.

When I rode back into camp, Sun Flower and Raven Wing were cryin', and Runnin' Wolf was wrappin' a blanket around Sees Far. He had died while I was gone. I hurried and skinned this little buck and cut it in quarters and hung the quarters in the smokehouse, doin' it all by the light of the fire. I took a shovel full of coals from the fire and put them in the fire pit in the bottom of the smokehouse and piled branches from the berry bushes I had stockpiled right by the door on the coals and closed the door up tight.

I didn't know how the Shoshone buried their dead, but I knew Sees Far had to be buried soon in the summer heat. I walked over to the fire and sat down with the rest of them and told them of a hill 'bout a half mile from the dugout that overlooked the stream and this huge meadow, that the mornin' sun hits it first thing, and it would be a place I would like to be my final restin' place. Sun Flower just leaned in to me, and Red Hawk said he was sure the family of Sees Far would be pleased to have him honored by bein' buried overseein' the land of Grizzly Killer.

Runnin' Wolf had told them of our plan to take the dead Arapahos back to the Seeds-Kee-Dee and why. We talked a little 'bout the Arapaho raidin' party and where they might be headed. Runnin' Wolf figured they would follow the Seeds-Kee-Dee, either north to find a Snake village or south and then east through the land of the White River Utes back to their own lands. He figured it would be south 'cause the Utes and Arapahos had been enemies since the times of our grandfathers' grandfather. Raven Wing asked how long we would be gone, and I told her no more than four days. I said we would bury Sees Far at first light and then leave. Red Hawk went over to the pile of weapons Runnin' Wolf had gathered from the Arapaho and went through them. He found Sees Far's bow and knife and started speakin' in Shoshone faster than I could make out. Sun Flower told me, "He says these weapons are Sees Far's, and he will need them to make the journey." Then Buffalo Heart said something, and Red Hawk nodded. Raven Wing spoke softly and said he would need his horse for the journey too.

Before light the next mornin', me and Runnin' Wolf left with the two spades and rode to the top of the hill I had spoken of and dug a grave. We went back and tied the travois onto a pack horse that had been carryin' it, and we laid Sees Far on it. Red Hawk was tryin' to get a lead rope on Sees Far's horse, and Runnin' Wolf went over to help him. Raven Wing came and asked if I would help Buffalo Heart on his horse. I went over to him to tell him no, that it was not a good idea for him to move, but when I saw the look on his face, I just nodded and asked Runnin' Wolf to put my saddle on Buffalo Heart's mount. It took both me and Runnin' Wolf to get him in the saddle, and he just sat there, breathin' real heavy. It was light now, but the sun hadn't hit the valley floor. By the look of the bruises, I figured most of his ribs were busted, and several of the burns were seepin' a clear liquid. We helped Red Hawk too, but he wasn't hurtin' nearly as bad as Buffalo Heart.

The sun was fully over the horizon when we laid Sees Far into the grave. Red Hawk laid his bow and knife alongside him. Then Red Hawk led Sees Far's horse alongside the grave and wrapped the lead rope around his hand and stabbed the horse in the neck and held him while he bled out. The horse went to his knees then lay on his side and, a minute or two after, laid his head on the ground and didn't move again. They didn't want him covered with dirt, so we covered the grave and horse with rocks. It took much longer than I figured. It took a considerable number of rocks to cover the horse so wolves and coyotes couldn't get to it.

It was midday before me and Runnin' Wolf headed out with the Arapahos. I wanted Jimbo to stay with the women, but Sun Flower insisted he go with us to scout ahead in case the other Arapahos were still out there. Jimbo was still wearin' his moccasin, but he wasn't limpin' at all now. We made better time than I figured we would. Without draggin' that travois, the pack horses could move right along. But we had over a hundred miles to travel just one way.

By nightfall we were what I figured was fifty or sixty miles out on the flat land, and other than the river we were followin', it was hot and dry. The flies were becomin' a nuisance, and it wasn't a pleasant thing takin' the gruesome loads off the horses for the night. We moved a ways downwind of them to set up our camp. Jimbo's paw was doin' much better 'cause he caught a rabbit for his dinner. Me and Runnin' Wolf just settled for some jerky. Durin' the night, a pack of coyotes came down and was fightin' over the dead Injuns, and I sent Jimbo to run 'em off. Even four or five coyotes would run from him, and if he gave chase, he could catch them in no time, but he just ran them off and came back.

Loadin' those five bodies the next mornin' was even worse than unloadin' them had been, and I sure hoped we'd make it far enough before nightfall. We covered ground mighty fast on these flats and could strike a gentle lope at times. We were never far from the river, so water for the horses and Ol' Red wasn't a problem. By the time the sun was just past center sky, we had passed where both Ham's Fork and Smith's Fork ran into Black's Fork and could see the green waterway of the Seeds-Kee-Dee. We were still miles away, but we slowed to a walk, watchin' for any sign of trouble. We had been roughly followin' the tracks that the three Shoshone boys had left, with the Arapahos' tracks over the top of them, and when we were what I figured was six or seven miles from the Seeds-Kee-Dee, the tracks separated, showin' this was where the Arapahos started to follow them. We left the bodies right there. I was mighty glad to get rid of such a gruesome load.

Our tracks would lead the Arapaho raidin' party right back to the dugout, dependin' on wind and rain, but it didn't rain much in this country this time of year. Runnin' Wolf figured these five wouldn't be missed for several days or more and that our tracks would be gone by then. We decided to go on down to the Seeds-Kee-Dee and see if we could tell which way the Arapahos were headin'. We cut the trail of many horses 'bout a mile west of the river that headed south, and we followed it for a couple of miles and stopped when we saw a big dust cloud comin' toward us from the west. We hadn't been makin' any dust as we were just walkin' the horses, and neither of us figured we had been seen, as this group was still several miles away. But they were headed right for us, and there were too many of 'em to fight.

Chapter XX

Homecomin'

THERE LOOKED TO BE some breaks 'tween us and the river, so we headed there for cover. We got to the edge of the break and found a wash that came off the flats, and we rode down it. We holed up and tied off the pack horses mighty fast. I got both rifles and checked the pans and saw Runnin' Wolf doin' the same with his rifle, and then he slipped his quiver over his shoulder and got his bow. We climbed back up the wash on foot, and lookin' through the brush where we couldn't be seen, we watched that dust cloud gettin' closer.

They were runnin' full out, and the dust made it hard to see, but when they were only 'bout a half mile out, I could see the lead horses didn't have riders. 'Bout that time, I heard Runnin' Wolf start to laugh, and he said it was just wild horses comin' to the river for water. We watched, and as they got to the break, they slowed and, in a single line, went down through another wash maybe three hundred yards south of us and went on to the river to drink.

It was late afternoon now, but I figured we had three of four more hours of light, and I didn't want to be away from the women any longer than we had to. So I suggested we head back now and ride till dark. We stopped on a bend in Black's Fork just as it was gettin' dark. We were all tired. Ol' Red and the horses needed water and grass, and even Jimbo just curled up and didn't go huntin'. There wasn't much grass here, just a little right on the riverbank. We hobbled the horses so's they could move along the bank, findin' what graze there was. We didn't build a fire 'cause it could be seen too far away on these flats, so we made do with just a piece of jerky again, and I threw a piece to Jimbo as well.

Next mornin' we were up just as the eastern sky was turnin' gray and found the horses had scattered for quite a ways along the riverbank. Jimbo had already gone out lookin' for his breakfast, so I just walked out to Ol' Red and jumped up on his bare back and gathered all the horses. We just ate another piece of jerky after we were in the saddle and figured we'd stop for coffee and a meal once we got off this dry, flat land and started to get into some trees again.

'Bout midmornin' we saw a herd of antelope that was grazin' in the sage near the top of a rise on the northern side of the river. I left all the horses with Runnin' Wolf and backtracked a mile or so then crossed the river and got to the north side of that rise. I left Red at the bottom of the rise and crawled up through the brush. I made sure the Hawken was ready and, very slowly, keepin' my head below the brush, looked over the top. I was a little farther east than I figured I would be, but I figured I could make the shot even if they were over a hundred yards away. They hadn't seen me yet, but just as I was ready to fire, one buck lifted his head, lookin' right at me. I squeezed off the shot just as they all started to run, but after just a couple of bounds, the one I had shot at fell. I threw this little prairie goat behind my saddle and headed straight down to the river. Runnin' Wolf and Jimbo were waitin' for me once I got across. It took just a few minutes to cut it in half so we could split the load onto two of the pack horses, and we headed out.

By midday we were gettin' into higher country with more grass and brush, and when we came to a thick stand of cottonwoods, we stopped to rest and eat. There was good grass, and we built a small fire up under the trees so's the smoke would break up, goin' up through their branches. While Runnin' Wolf was puttin' some antelope on a couple of sticks to roast, I made coffee. And for the first time since we left the dugout, we had fresh meat and hot coffee. We let Ol' Red and the horses graze for a little over an hour and got back on the trail. We struck a gentle lope, and the miles passed by mighty quick.

By late afternoon, I figured we were only 'bout twenty-five miles out, and if the horses could hold to even a fast walk, we could make it in by dark or shortly after. The last of the light was fadin' from the western horizon when we could see the fire at the dugout, and Jimbo went on ahead to let 'em know we were comin' in.

Sun Flower, Raven Wing, and Red Hawk were on their feet, waitin' for us, as we walked the horses right over to the corral. I noticed first the teepee set up, and I could smell the sweetness of chokecherry smoke comin' from the smokehouse, and there were two deer hides staked out that the women had been workin'. As I climbed off Ol' Red, Sun Flower came runnin' over and threw her arms 'round me and just held on. She then whispered to me she had been afraid for us.

We got the stock taken care of and put the antelope in the smokehouse with the two deer. We just rolled the antelope hide up till mornin'. I was tired and hungry, and I knew Runnin' Wolf was the same. Jimbo just curled up by the fire and didn't move. I noticed then his sore paw was stickin' through the bottom of his moccasin. He had worn the bottom right off it. As I took the worn-out moccasin off and checked on his paw, Raven Wing was dishin' us out some stew they had made with fresh deer, and Sun Flower was pourin' coffee. Buffalo Heart was lyin' on the grizzly skin, but he was smilin' and looked better than when we left.

After we ate, we sat 'round the fire and told of our journey, with Raven Wing tellin' these young men what we were sayin'. They all got a good laugh when I told them of us runnin' and hidin' from a herd of wild horses. I asked 'bout the deer, and Red Hawk said Shoshone women were good hunters. Sun Flower told us she went up the river with her gun and waited for the deer to come to the water. She said the gun made her feel like a warrior that could take care of herself. Raven Wing said Sun Flower hit the second one while it was runnin', that she was gettin' real good with her gun. We were all smilin' and happy, sittin' around that fire, tellin' our stories, and for now not thinkin' 'bout Sees Far or the Arapahos.

I asked 'bout the teepee, and Sun Flower said the air wasn't good in the tree lodge, as she called the dugout, and I figured it was made of trees, so her name was fittin'. I noticed then the sides of the teepee were rolled up 'bout a foot high all the way 'round it, and she said that was to let cool air in for the summer. I was tired and ready for sleep, and our beds were already rolled out in the teepee, so I said good night and went in. It was only a minute later when Sun Flower came in, and it felt mighty fine holdin' her again. Next thing I remember was openin' my eyes and seein' it was already light. I could see out under the rolled-up lodge cover, and Red Hawk was up with a fire goin'.

Me and Sun Flower got up and were greeted with a big smile from Red Hawk, and Buffalo Heart was up on one elbow. Sun Flower and Red Hawk talked for a minute, then she spoke with Buffalo Heart. When she turned to me, she said Red Hawk said his side still hurt but not like before, and Buffalo Heart felt better too. This was only the fourth day since they had been attacked and tortured by the Arapahos, but they were both strong young men and were healin' mighty fast. The burns on Buffalo Heart were deep and would take many more days to heal up. Raven Wing had mixed up another poultice for the burns, and Sun Flower said it would keep the skin from becomin' angry and hot. Me and Red Hawk helped Buffalo Heart up, and you could tell he hurt and was mighty sore. He started to walk 'round some and then headed for the bushes.

While Sun Flower and Raven Wing got breakfast started, I went in the dugout, and it was musty and stale inside. I had to admit the teepee was much more pleasant. But I figured the dugout would make a great tack room for the saddles and packs and storeroom for the supplies. With the flour, cornmeal, and sugar bein' in barrels now, the mice and pack rats couldn't get to it. I got some coals from the fire and put them in the smokehouse again and added some more chokecherry branches. It looked like another day or so and this meat would be smoked enough to keep. This time of year, makin' meat was a constant thing 'cause it didn't keep well in the heat of summer.

We ate and, over coffee, made plans for the next couple of days. We were 'bout out of grease, and gettin' a bear was needed. Red Hawk told Raven Wing they needed to get back and let Sees Far's family know what had happened, and they would leave just as soon as Buffalo Heart could travel. Runnin' Wolf said as soon as they could travel, we needed to leave to go to his village and see that his sister was all right. We made plans for me and Runnin' Wolf to scout some of the smaller creeks runnin' into Black's Fork for bear signs and, if we found signs, set up some bait for tonight. Sun Flower said she needed to get the deer hides and now antelope hide tanned. I could tell Runnin' Wolf wanted to get on the trail over the mountains, but he wasn't willin' to hurry Buffalo Heart either.

Me and Runnin' Wolf saddled up and started up the trail I had rode so many times throughout the winter. Jimbo didn't look happy when I told him to stay, but I wanted him with the women. I knew he would warn them of trouble and protect them as well. The creek where Pa was buried emptied into Black's Fork 'bout ten miles above the dugout. But there were three that ran into it before that one, two of them on the east and one on the west. Me and Pa had seen many black bears like the ones we had back home while we were trappin' last fall and hadn't had any trouble takin' one when we needed it. I didn't want to run into any more grizzlies. In the last nine months, I had killed two, and Pa killed the one that killed him, so I knew there were plenty of them around. There were trappers at Rendezvous that said they had never seen one, and I didn't want to see another. We passed the first creek and the second, but the third went off to the west and opened up into a wide basin with several beaver ponds up higher. We started up that one and had only gone 'bout a mile up when we saw bear tracks in the trail.

When we got up into the basin, there was a lot of bear signs. A rotten log had been ripped apart, and there were bear tracks in the damp ground around it. A little farther along, we found where a quakie was used to scratch on, and there was still damp mud on the bark. The bear was usin' this area, maybe lookin' for a beaver that was out of the pond. There were quakies down all around these ponds from the beaver. As we continued on, a beaver slapped his tail on the next pond, and then all was quiet. When we were above the next pond, we saw several marmots scurryin' around some rocks. Runnin' Wolf took his bow, and really takin' his time, he got two of them.

We took them back down where the bear sign was freshest and cut them open and spread their guts 'round the log that had been ripped apart and left their carcasses right there where the sun would beat down on them all day. We figured to come back just 'fore dark and get set up and wait for that bear to make his nightly rounds. We followed that same trail back down the creek, and when we were 'bout a mile from Black's Fork, Ol' Red just stopped and snorted. Runnin' Wolf's chestnut reared, spun in the trail, and took off 'fore Runnin' Wolf could control him. I could feel every muscle in Red was tense. Then no more than twenty yards from me, in the brush alongside the trail, a big bear stood up on his hind legs. Red snorted again but didn't move. I brought the Hawken to my shoulder and fired all in one motion, and the bear dropped down and charged. Ol' Red jumped, and I went right out of the saddle. I landed flat on my back and had my knife in hand at the same time. At that instant, I thought of Pa and how this was what happened to him. I knew this wasn't a grizzly, but at that moment, it looked mighty big. Then right next to me, a rifle roared, and the bear fell right at my feet. I looked up in time to see Runnin' Wolf lower his rifle and get a big ol' grin on his face. This had been quite a homecomin', this first week back at the dugout.

Runnin' Wolf asked me if I was plannin' on fightin' that bear lyin' down with only my knife, and I said, "Naw, I was just takin' a bit of a rest 'fore I started to skin 'em." The chestnut was havin' no part of that bear on him, so Ol' Red had to carry the whole thing. It was mighty big for a black bear, maybe 350 pounds. I wanted to wait till we got back to skin him, but he was so heavy we skinned and gutted him out and then tied him over my saddle. I walked out, leadin' Red. Runnin' Wolf just headed for the dugout, and I was maybe halfway back when here he came back with Sun Flower's roan saddled for me.

We got back to the dugout and got that bear taken care of, gettin' all the fat we could get. It was 'bout the end of June or first of July, and he didn't have near the fat on him they had in the fall. But it would do us for quite a spell. Raven Wing used some of it in the poultice for Buffalo Heart's burns. He was up and walkin' around now. You could tell he was hurtin', but he tried not to let it show.

The next day, 'bout midmornin', a gusty wind came up, and by midday it was cloudin' up. We moved everything in the dugout and teepee, and Sun Flower untied the bottom of the lodge coverin' and let it down to the ground. By midafternoon we could see lightnin' and hear the thunder, and half an hour later, the rain came. It rained hard for maybe half an hour then just sprinkled for a couple more hours, and it was like the mountains came to life. The fresh smell of the rain and shine it put on the meadow grass was quite a change. The color of the wildflowers became brighter. From start to finish, this storm lasted maybe four hours, and it was like it just refreshed the world around us. These mountain rains are cold, not like the ones back in Kentucky, where the rain this time of year can be warm. These Rocky Mountain rains are downright cold.

Sun Flower and Raven Wing sliced big chunks off that bear and got them to roastin' on a spit over the fire while we lashed together a jerky rack. We cut the rest of the bear into strips and placed them on the rack and got a fire goin' under it to start to dry the jerky. When the bear on the spit was lookin' 'bout done, they mixed up a pan of biscuits and set the pan on some coals by the side of the fire. These pan biscuits were something different for all these Injun people, but they all liked them, and they had become a big part of most of our meals. Each week it seemed they were findin' more flowers and plants that they were cookin' with, and the stews were mighty good. I did think at times of Ma's vegetable garden back home and how good a tomato or turnip greens would taste. Then I thought of the henhouse and a basket full of fresh eggs. I hadn't had an egg for breakfast since me and Pa left home.

The Cherokee I grew up with back home grew gardens, but these Injuns in the West just used whatever they found in nature and was always lookin' for something to pick or dig up. They didn't stay in any one place long enough to plant a garden, for they were always movin' to find game and firewood and away from the smell of a village. They moved their villages every few weeks or even more often than that.

I had seen fish in the river, but I hadn't figured out a way to catch them. But the next day, Red Hawk cut a bunch of small willow branches and made a basket trap out of it. It took him most of the day, and after he was done, I'd never seen anythin' like it. I was 'bout three feet long and a foot square and just squared on one end, but the other end was like a funnel goin' into it with a hole at the end of the funnel, which was just smaller than his fist. He put several small pieces of the scrapin's from that bear hide on a stick and then waded out into the river. He set the trap down in a good hole where the water had washed up under a bank and placed a rock on top to hold it down and then put the stick with the bear fat scrapin's inside the trap and just walked up out of the river and over to the fire to dry off. In a couple of hours, he checked the trap and had two trout in it. He moved it to another spot and did the same thing. By dinnertime he had eight trout, and they tasted mighty good. As I was enjoyin' this trout, I started thinkin' how much I still had to learn 'bout livin' in these Shinin' Mountains.

Two days later, Buffalo Heart said he could ride, and they needed to get back so Sees Far's family could mourn him. So we gave them smoked meat and jerky. Runnin' Wolf tied the scalps onto their bows, and I got lead ropes on all five of the Arapahos horses. Red Hawk started talkin', and Raven Wing told us he said the horses were not theirs, that we killed the enemy and they were our prize. I had Raven Wing tell him that we had more horses than we needed and we were gonna be travelin' far and we were makin' a gift of the horses to Red Hawk and Buffalo Heart, that they were warriors now and would need the extra mounts, that they should ride straight north for a couple of days then cut east to the Seeds-Kee-Dee to miss the enemy that might be lookin' for their dead. Red Hawk took the lead rope from me, and with pride on his face, he thanked me. Then he spoke to Raven Wing for a few minutes, and they headed out.

Sun Flower came over to me and put her arms 'round me and hugged me for the longest time. When I asked her what that was 'bout, she said she was happy to have a man like me. I picked her up and held her with a questionin' look, and she said, "Red Hawk said that Grizzly Killer and Runnin' Wolf have even stronger medicine than what the people are saying. He said you are both great warriors and great hunters. That your hearts are good and you are better friends. Then he said they will make sure all Shoshone people know that the sisters of Spotted Elk are well and lucky to have such men, and they look forward to the time when we will meet again."

Then Runnin' Wolf said, "I never expected to be considered a friend of the Snake people. But my heart is glad that I am. It is better to have friends than enemies."

Every afternoon now, clouds would build over the mountains, and we could hear the thunder rollin' down toward us. We didn't get the rain for the last two days, but it wasn't far above us.

We made plans for our travel over the mountains into the heart of Ute country. The women needed two more days to finish tannin' the hides they had started. And I needed to dig out the cache and store what we wouldn't be takin' with us. Runnin' Wolf expected us to be back here in a moon or a little more. The trappin' season wouldn't get started till the beaver had winter fur, and last year that was 'round mid-September. We talked 'bout makin' another teepee and havin' some new buffalo robes for winter, and that would take travelin' northeast into buffalo country. And that meant we could meet Cheyenne, Sioux, and Arapaho at any time out on the buffalo range. It would take 'bout a dozen hides for a new lodge, and we needed some skirting for winter for the old one. So we figured we'd have maybe a month to get twenty or so of the big beasts. And that would give us enough meat for the winter at the same time. It would also give the makin's for some tough and warm moccasins.

The next two days were mighty busy gettin' ready to go. We separated what supplies we would travel with and cached everything else. We dragged deadfall over the cache and made it so it couldn't be seen. That next afternoon, we got another good rain, but again it only lasted a couple of hours. Lookin' up at the peaks of these Bear River Mountains and seein' how far they go above the timberline made we wonder if you could touch the sky from up there, and we were goin' right over the top of 'em.

Chapter XXI

One Tough Mule

NEXT MORNIN' we got all the horses and mules loaded. We had loaded what we figured was enough flour, sugar, coffee, bakin' powder, and salt to last the four of us 'bout a month and a half. That would put us back here 'round the middle of August, just when most of the berries would be ripenin'. I figured we were gonna be mighty busy this fall, gettin' ready for winter, just like me and Pa were last year. But for now, from what Runnin' Wolf had told me, we were lookin' at a week or so on the trail up over the mountains and into the land of the Utes.

We were gonna follow the Bear River up then go over the top and follow the Duchesne River down to what Runnin' Wolf said was Rock Creek and then follow it till we found his village. I had been over this country 'tween Black's Fork and the Bear River before and figured I knew the shortest route, so I led out, and we were on the trail again. Jimbo's paw didn't seem to be botherin' him anymore, and he just moved on out ahead like he always did. We didn't need all these pack animals, but we couldn't leave them behind, so we just divided the load 'tween them all so they were loaded light and wouldn't tire near as fast as they did comin' back from Rendezvous. We were makin' pretty good time, even draggin' the travois with the teepee on it. The afternoon rains came again, and we were wet and cold by the time they were over. I sure wished we had some tent canvas to make some ponchos. But when the sun came out, we dried off right quick.

Travelin' the way we were, by late afternoon we were lookin' down on the canyon of the Bear River, and that night we camped under a stand of quakies right near the east side of the river. We weren't carryin' much meat with us, just jerky and one smoked haunch. We figured on makin' meat as we traveled. So while I took care of the stock, Runnin' Wolf headed off downstream, and it wasn't long till I heard the faint report of his rifle. Half hour later, he was back in camp with a yearlin' doe, and we had fresh deer, biscuits, and coffee. We weren't takin' time to cure the meat, so we cut off what we could eat in the next day or so and salted the hide and rolled it up and left the rest for the wolves and coyotes.

It cooled right off when the sun went down in this high country, but with a small fire built under the branches of the trees, it was a pleasant evenin'. As the stars started to come out, coyotes started their yippin', and a couple of night birds were callin' to each other along the river. We rolled out our bedrolls under the branches of some pines so if rained, we'd have some protection. This time of year, unless the weather got bad, we wouldn't put up the teepee. I hoped when we got buffalo, we could get enough hides, and we could just carry a coverin' for a lean-to rather than drag the teepee around on a trip like this. Runnin' Wolf said his people only used teepees in the winter, and this time of year, they made brush wickiups 'cause they were cooler.

The next mornin' we were on the trail early and were movin' through country that me and Runnin' Wolf had been through before. By early afternoon, we had come to the place where we had fought the Snake warriors and moved on without sayin' a word 'bout it. The climb now was gettin' rough and steep, and we were now in country I hadn't been in before. We weren't makin' near as good of time either. We could smell brimstone comin' down through the trees and came to a place where up on the hill west of the river, which now was more of a creek, there was sulfur just comin' out of the ground. The hillside was white, and the smell got mighty strong as we passed by. We were maybe only a mile or two past the sulfur when the afternoon thunder storms came at us. By now we were gettin' up pretty high, and the thunder and lightnin' got mighty fearsome. We stopped in a thick stand of pines and tied all the stock and sat right under the pine branches for an hour till the worst of it was over. It was just down to a light sprinkle when we moved out.

When we stopped for the day, the timberline wasn't far above us. We were on the edge of a small meadow that had a shallow pond out in the middle of it. There was a huge jagged peak just to the southeast, and all the mountains and ridge tops were up above timberline. The trees only grow up so far in the Rocky Mountains they say the air is too thin for the trees to grow that high up. Back home the trees grow right up over the mountaintops, if you can call them mountains. The people back home did, but they'd never seen the Rockies with all these peaks reachin' for the sky.

We picketed the stock in the meadow where they had plenty of grass and water. We made our camp under the pines just on the western edge of the meadow and made our beds in soft pine needles under the towerin' pines again, where we will be protected from any weather. We saw a small herd of elk way up on a hillside late in the afternoon but hadn't seen any game for the last couple of hours. Sun Flower went out in the meadow along the pond and came back with several flower roots and some camas bulbs, and she boiled them with some jerky.

It was downright cold the next mornin', and I didn't want to leave the warmth of Sun Flower's body that was pressed right up against me. And I lay there, enjoyin' that warmth for longer than usual. Just before dawn, I could hear the howl of several wolves, but they were a long ways off. While I was enjoyin' the calm of dawn and the feel of Sun Flower next to me, I heard Raven Wing get up and get a fire started. This was 'bout the first of July, and you could see your breath, and there wasn't a cloud in the sky. After good, strong coffee and a biscuit, we loaded up and continued on.

This was the highest I'd ever been in the mountains, and the view was breathtakin'. We continued up still, climbin' higher. The trail was nothin' more than a small game trail most of the time, and we weren't makin' very good time. By midday we'd topped out on a pass, and right below us was a lake. We stopped and let the stock rest and ate. I don't know how to describe what we were lookin' at. The peak that was southeast of us last night was right in front of us. We were sittin' right at timberline. The trees right by us were small and stunted, just a few feet higher on the mountain there was no trees growing at all. That peak in front of us went up in sheer rock walls for another couple of thousand feet. There was solid pines goin' east for as far as you could see, with bare rock peaks comin' up out of the pines just as far. You could see lakes in every swale or basin. Runnin' Wolf told us that four different rivers started from right here, all goin' a different direction. He told us that in just a few miles, we would come to another lake where the Duchesne River starts and we would follow it, goin' southeast.

I took Ol' Red, and with Jimbo out in front as usual, I rode to a ridge top just west of us where I could see another river that was headin' northwest and still more peaks way up above timberline. Everywhere you looked from up here, there were high mountains and lakes. I knew these Bear River Mountains were big and high, but from up here, they look to go on forever.

I got back, and we headed south again, havin' to go around this lake that was right below us and pickin' our way through the rocks and timber. It was cloudin' up, and within an hour, the thunder was echoin' through these peaks, and there was so much lightnin' in the air you could feel it pullin' at your hair. We stopped again in a thick stand of pines just as the hail hit. The hail lasted maybe five minutes, then it started to snow. Now I'd never been in a snowstorm in July before, and it was cold, bone-chillin' cold. We all huddled together and finally decided to start a fire. We built a small fire at the base of a big ol' pine after scapin' the needles away and just sat there, huddled 'round it for a couple of hours while the thunder shook the ground and the snow turned the world white.

The sky cleared just as fast as it clouded up, and the sun came back out. The new snow was gone in just a little while, but there were still big patches of snow from last winter on the north sides of the peaks and in most shady areas. It stays cold up this high most of the time. We continued on to the base of a big round bald mountain, and just east of it, there was another lake much bigger than the first one and almost round. From where we sat, we could see the reflection of the sky and this huge jagged peak to our east on its surface and every so often the ripples from a fish hittin' the top of the water. Runnin' Wolf said that was where we were goin', so we worked our way down through the timber and around the south side of the lake. Runnin' out of the lake to the east was a good-sized creek, and Runnin' Wolf said that was the start of the Duchesne River and we would be followin' it down for the next two or three days.

There was still enough daylight left for a couple more hours of travel, so we started workin' our way down. There really was no trail to follow, just the river, and the goin' was slow, havin' to move in and out and 'round the pines. There were no quakies growin' up this high. We jumped an ol' sow bear with two cubs and watched as they ran across a small clearin' just ahead of us. By the time it was time to find a campin' spot, I figured we'd only gone 'bout a mile and half from the lake.

We came to a spot where the stream ran up by a big jagged rock and there was enough of a clearin' with grass for the stock, so we stopped. There was a cool wind blowin', and as the sun got closer to that western horizon, the wind went from cool to cold. Sun Flower and Raven Wing set up the teepee while me and Runnin' Wolf took care of the stock. Jimbo went out scoutin' 'round, and I figured he was after some of the squirrels that were in abundance up in this timber, but in a little while, he came back with a big fat marmot and seemed happy as could be.

It always amazed me how fast these two sisters could put up and again take down this big ol' heavy teepee. By the time we had the stock watered and hobbled, the women had the teepee up, a fire goin', and dinner cookin'. It was dusk by then, and steppin' inside that teepee with the fire in it sure felt good. Jimbo came inside and curled up by the door. Jimbo's paw didn't seem to bother him at all now, but he left a different paw print now with that one missin' toe. Bed always feels mighty good after a long day in the saddle, but tonight, with it bein' this cold and the teepee so warm, I was 'bout asleep 'fore I got under the robes.

Sometime in the night, Jimbo pushed his nose in my face and growled. I was awake instantly and had my Hawken in hand, then I heard the horses stompin' the ground and Ol' Red snort. I pulled on my moccasins and followed Jimbo out into the cold night, with Runnin' Wolf right behind me. There wasn't a moon, and I couldn't see anything out in the dark forest. I couldn't see Jimbo and didn't know where he went. Ol' Red brayed awfully loud, and Jimbo attacked. There was quite a fight for a minute, and I heard Red charge. That mule was screamin' and kickin' and carryin' on like some demon right out of hell. Then I noticed Jimbo was standin' right by us again. Now we could tell by the sound that it was a bear they were fightin', and it was gettin' farther away. I heard Ol' Red's hooves thud into flesh a couple of times, and a couple of minutes later, he came walkin' right up to us like nothin' had happened. I ran my hands over that mule, feelin' for any wounds, and felt a row of welts raised up on his lower neck, but there wasn't any blood. Come daylight, we'd have a good look. Jimbo seemed all right, but in this darkness, we could only feel for blood. Sun Flower and Raven Wing had the fire built up inside the teepee, and once inside, we could see Jimbo had some scratches on his right shoulder, but they weren't deep enough to need sewin'.

Next mornin' there was frost on the grass, and the very edge of the creek had ice formin' in the calm water. Red was standin' 'tween the horses and other mules and the forest where the bear had gone. I walked up to him and rubbed his nose, and he nuzzled right into my hand. The welts on his neck were from a swipe of the bear claws, but they didn't break the skin, and I couldn't see another mark on him. His front hooves did have some coarse black hair in them, and I'd bet that bear was almighty sore this mornin'. I pulled a good-size clump of the bear's hair from the bottom of Red's hoof, and Runnin' Wolf laughed and said, "That's one tough mule."

We ate and loaded up. There was still a little frost on the shady side of the teepee when they untied it and let it slide down the lodge poles, and because we rolled it up damp, we'd set it up again tonight to dry it out good. It was still cold as we headed out, but the sun was warmin' things up fast. By midmornin' it was right pleasant again. The river cut down through a gorge that split a big high ridge, and we left the river to climb that ridge. When we got to the top, we were lookin' down into this big basin, and I counted eight different lakes, with the river cuttin' a path right down 'tween them. I picked out a route, and we headed down toward the largest of the lakes. These high mountain lakes were crystal clear and really something to see. We worked our way around this lake and followed the creek that was runnin' out of it right on down to the river. Once we hit the river again, we continued followin' it south.

By midday we were across that basin and started down the canyon of this river General Ashley and his men had called the Duchesne. There were creeks runnin' into it every so often from both sides, and it was growin' in size with each one. We were gettin' down low enough now. The timber was thinnin' some, and quakies were growin' along the river and creeks now. And we were seein' game again. There were bighorn sheep way up above us on the ridges, and there were deer all along the river that would just watch us pass by. The afternoon storms came over, but we just got a little rain. The main storm with all the thunder and lightnin' was way up on the mountain above us now. The lower down the canyon we came, the dryer the land became, and now there were big barren hillsides with just brush and grass and not many, if any, trees.

We came to a big canyon leadin' off to the west where a good-sized stream ran into the Duchesne, makin' the river much bigger, and Runnin' Wolf said that was Wolf Creek. We camped in the cottonwoods along the river just south of where Wolf Creek joined the Duchesne. There was a big high ridge just west of us, and the sun was behind it early, but it stayed light for a long time.

While they all were settin' up camp, I rode up Wolf creek a ways and shot a nice buck and brought it back. I got the hide off it, and Sun Flower cut off a couple of good-sized chunks and got them on a spit to roast. Raven Wing asked if we could stay here for a day or two and dry the meat and tan the hides or start to. Runnin' Wolf told her we would stop tomorrow for as long as they needed in his village, that we would be there before this time tomorrow. She got a bit of a worried look, and he smiled at her, walked over, and told her that the woman of Runnin' Wolf would be welcomed in the village of Stands Tall. He told us Stands Tall was the chief of his village, that he was a fair and wise leader. That the village had done well with Stands Tall as their chief. He told us he was a big man, nearly as tall as Grizzly Killer. I cut several good chunks off the deer and salted them down real good so they would last a couple of days and rolled them in the hide.

It was a long, pleasant evenin', and I was lookin' forward to seein' more of this country on the south slope of these Bear River Mountains. Runnin' Wolf said the Utes called these the Uintah Mountains. All the mountain ranges me and Pa had crossed comin' west and even the Blue Ridge back home were runnin' north and south, but these Uintah mountains of the Utes ran east and west. The women set up the teepee to dry it out but rolled up the cover a few inches and tied it to let in the cool night air.

Just at that time, Jimbo came into camp from down the river, and he smelled like he'd died a month ago. He came right up to us, and we all scattered. I yelled at him to get away, and that confused him. I could tell he had no idea what he'd done wrong, but the way he smelled, he must have found a mighty ripe carcass of some animal and rolled in it. His smell just made your stomach turn. I took him by the collar and led him out in the river, and I started scrubbin' him with sand. Now that water was almighty cold, and the more I scrubbed, the three of them on dry ground laughed. Jimbo wasn't likin' any part of this either, but somehow I figured he knew what he'd done to deserve this. I sure wished I had some of the lye soap Ma used to make. My teeth was chatterin' from the cold water, and then Sun Flower pulled off her dress and, naked as can be, came out in the river to help me. Right then I wished I'd had enough sense to take off my buckskins 'cause now they were soaked through, even my shirt. I watched her walk out to us with a smile in water up past her knees. I still couldn't get used to the fact that to her, bein' naked in front of others was just as natural as any other part of her life.

We got that ol' mutt scrubbed as best we could, and she helped me out of my wet buckskins as we stood by the fire. Runnin' Wolf and Raven Wing had built up the fire and then took a walk down along the river. Sun Flower got us a blanket off the bedroll, and I wrapped it 'round me and got my buckskins laid out by the fire to dry. Jimbo was shakin' and dryin' himself off by rollin' in the grass. He didn't smell good, but now we could stand to be 'round him. I was still cold and just went in and got under the robes with Sun Flower right behind me. As she slid her naked body right down on top of me, I was gettin' warm mighty fast.

The next mornin', as we headed out, we moved a little ways off the river up on benchland where there were few trees and just scattered sage and brush. This canyon was now opened up into a valley a mile wide, and the river had turned to the east. We were makin' right good time now, travelin' in this open valley, and when we stopped at midday, I figured we'd come farther than we had all the day before. The land was changin' again as we continued down the river valley. The river was lined with cottonwoods, but the hills were covered with cedar and pinion pine. There was ledge rock on the ridges, goin' up both sides of the river, and after our midday stop, we traveled only another few miles and come to another river flowin' in from the north. Runnin' Wolf was smilin' when he said this was Rock Creek. We turned up this creek and traveled only a couple more miles, when we could see smoke from a village maybe another six or seven miles up the creek.

Chapter XXII

Shining Star

ROCK CREEK RAN down through a beautiful green valley that was a couple of miles wide, and as we headed up the river, we were lookin' right up at the peaks towerin' above the timberline of these high Uintah Mountains. I was keepin' Jimbo in right close to us now as we were gettin' closer to the village, and we were 'bout a half mile out, when two riders approached us. They were boys maybe twelve years old and tryin' to act like men. But when they saw Runnin' Wolf, they got mighty excited. Runnin' Wolf went forward and greeted them, and they were talkin' a lot faster than I was able to follow. I was gettin' better at the Ute tongue all the time. I knew a lot more Ute than Shoshone at this point, but I was only able to pick up a little of what was bein' said. I looked at Raven Wing, and she said she couldn't understand most of it either. But she said it seemed they thought Runnin' Wolf was dead. And there had been trouble in the village.

Runnin' Wolf turned and came back to us as one of the boys turned and, just as fast as his horse would go, headed for the village while the other rode back to us with Runnin' Wolf.

Runnin' Wolf had a very troubled look as he got to us, and he said, "This is Gray Horse. He is my mother's sister's son. He tells me Shining Star has been taken just two days ago, and there is no one in the village to go after her. We will go talk to Stands Tall now."

As we rode into the village, Sun Flower rode right up by my side, and Raven Wing was on my other side, with Runnin' Wolf leadin' and Jimbo right 'tween Runnin' Wolf and me. There was a crowd of women and children waitin' as we rode into a groupin' of short round wickiups. There was a lot of talk and pointin' as we rode in, with most of the attention on Jimbo and our Shoshone women. In the center, a shaded arbor had been built of poles in the ground with the top covered with branches with the leaves all on, providin' a dappled shade from the sun. An old man was sittin' under the arbor, waitin' for us, and as we stopped and got out of the saddles, he stood up. He was the tallest Injun I'd ever seen. He was every bit as tall as me. He looked very old, but he stood tall and proud with a shine in his dark eyes that made you know his mind was still sharp. Runnin' Wolf called him Grandfather. Stands Tall looked at each of us and motioned for us all to sit. Runnin' Wolf then told him our names, and when he said mine was Grizzly Killer, the crowd behind started to talk, and Stands Tall said they had been told that the great warrior Grizzly Killer had captured and killed Runnin' Wolf. Runnin' Wolf looked at me, makin' sure I understood what was said, and I nodded. This talk was slow enough for both me and the women to follow along.

Runnin' Wolf then had Raven Wing come and sit by his side and told his chief that I was the great warrior Grizzly Killer and that I was his brother, that I had saved his life, not taken it, and that we as brothers had taken these beautiful Shoshone sisters as our women. Raven Wing was now sitting by his side, and he said she was now as much Ute as Shoshone. He said there was no better friends in all of our lands than this white man called Grizzly Killer and the women Raven Wing and Sun Flower. Then he called Jimbo. He told Stands Tall that Jimbo was a friend to any friend of Grizzly Killer but a mighty warrior to all his enemies. That Jimbo was the Great Medicine Dog, and his medicine was as strong as Grizzly Killer's.

He then told a brief story of what had happened and us havin' to kill some of the Shoshones and then of makin' friends with them, of gettin' Raven Wing and Sun Flower from the Frenchmen, and goin' to Rendezvous. I could tell he was in a hurry, but he had to make everyone know that even though they thought me and the women were their enemies, we were their friends.

When he was finished, he asked where Shinin' Star and all the men were. Stands Tall got a troubled look on his face and said Many Talks took many of the young warriors on a raid for horses and slaves to the west desert and was not expected back till fall. He said that Gray Cloud took more and went to hunt buffalo, so there were only six to provide for camp, and they were on the mountain, huntin' elk and deer, and would be back in two more suns. He said, "Six suns ago, the Sahpeech war chief Black Hand came to give you, Runnin' Wolf, horses for Shinin' Star's hand in marriage. But he learned that we thought you were dead, so he said there was no man in her family now to care for her, that he will now be her man." He went on that Shinin' Star had rejected Black Hand, and he got very angry. When the village awakened yesterday, Shinin' Star and Black Hand were gone. Since there were no warriors here, no one went after them.

Runnin' Wolf looked devastated, and I could see a fury buildin' up inside him. He said there were two great warriors here now, and that if Grizzly Killer would ride with him, we would leave now. He looked at me, and I nodded. He then asked Stands Tall if he would look after and protect our women while we were gone, that bein' Shoshone, they were nervous bein' in a Ute village. He told him Raven Wing spoke some Ute and Sun Flower just a little. He said they both had weapons and could help hunt and protect the village if needed. Stands

Tall nodded and said they would be honored guests and the village would protect them as their own.

Runnin' Wolf made sure Raven Wing understood everything and told her to set up their lodge near the chief's wickiup. Sun Flower never said a word. She just smiled and nodded, lettin' me know she understood what we must do. I asked if there was anything of Shinin' Star's in the village and was shown to her wickiup. Black Hand had not taken along any of her belongin's. I had Jimbo go inside and smell everything and then took her bedroll and tied it up and put it behind my saddle with my own. I told Runnin' Wolf to pick an extra horse, and I would too so we could change mounts often to make better time. Sun Flower led her roan over to me and told me to take her. She said she was a good strong horse and would serve me well.

With nothin' but a handful of jerky in our saddlebags, we headed back down Rock Creek to the Duchesne River and headed downstream. We were headed downstream but not stayin' close to the river at all so we could keep up a good lope most of time away from the trees along the river. This country was dry benchland with short sage and prickly pear cactus. The Uintah or Bear River Mountains were now twenty or more miles north of us, and off to the east was nothin' but more of this high dry basin. It looked like it went on for more than a hundred miles.

Not much more than a couple of hours after we left, we came off this dry bench where another river ran into the Duchesne from the west. It was now 'bout the first week of July, and the spring runoff was 'bout over, so crossin' these rivers wasn't a problem. We stopped here just long enough to give Ol' Red and the horses a breather. Runnin' Wolf told me then that Black Hand was a Sahpeech Ute[6] and he was very fast to anger, that he had tried to take Shinin' Star as a wife

[6] Sahpeech is Ute for the San Pitch River, Utah.

before, but she had chosen another, and now that her man was killed, he had come back. He told me the Sahpeech lived 'bout four days' travel to the south and west, but travelin' like we were, we should make it in under two days. There was a large mostly dry canyon headin' southwest from here, and Runnin' Wolf said that was the trail that led over the mountains and down into the valley of the Sahpeech. He said he hoped to catch up to them before they got back to his village.

Jimbo was a little ways from us, runnin' 'round, smellin' everything like usual, when he barked and headed southwest. We mounted up, and when we got to where Jimbo had barked, we could see tracks of where Black Hand had stopped with Shinin' Star, and now Jimbo had picked up her scent and was on their trail. There had been no rain here, and the tracks were plain in the dry ground. We changed mounts, givin' Red and the chestnut a break, and hit the trail, tryin' to catch up to Jimbo. We struck an easy ground-eatin' lope, and as the sun set, the western sky became a blaze of orange sight to behold. We traveled well into the dark, and then when the canyon started to get steep and covered with pines, we stopped and changed mounts again. The trail was steep and windin' through the pines. We could only go at a slow walk. It was well after midnight when we topped out and decided we needed to rest Ol' Red and the horses and get a couple of hours of sleep. There was no water here for the stock, so we tied them to trees and lay down under a pine and slept for two or three hours.

It was too dark to see any tracks when we hit the trail again, but Jimbo seemed to know right where to go, so we just followed him into the night. The trail goin' down the other side of this pass was mighty steep and narrow, and I couldn't see the bottom. The goin' was painfully slow here, but we were still goin'. By the time it got light, we were off the steep pass and headin' southwest again 'cross miles of rollin' hills atop this high mountain plateau. There were pines on the north sides of most of the hills and in the draws where the water would run. We crossed another small river that was runnin' east and stopped to let Ol' Red and the horses drink and graze for a while. Jimbo caught a cottontail rabbit, and while he ate it, me and Runnin' Wolf had a piece of jerky. I figured we had come near a hundred miles from Runnin' Wolf's village in less than eighteen hours. I had never traveled that far that fast before.

By midmornin' we came to a spot where they had stopped and camped. The coals of the fire were still warm, and after studyin' the tracks, Runnin' Wolf said he figured that Shinin' Star was tied up. He said that Black Hand didn't figure he was bein' followed and had slowed down now. He figured we would catch them today. We were close enough to them now, and if he was watchin' his back trail, he would see us comin'. I knew it was a risk, but I suggested we leave Jimbo on the trail, and Runnin' Wolf and I moved way off to the side. If Black Hand saw Jimbo at a distance, he would figure he was just a wolf.

I got Shinin' Star's bed robe and let Jimbo smell it again, and he stayed right on their trail. Runnin' Wolf and I moved a mile or so west of the trail and followed along at a good, fast lope. It appeared the trail was headin' down this big wide draw still headin' southwest, and we were up on the western rim in timber. We were movin' as fast as we could through the trees, when Runnin' Wolf saw a thin column of smoke comin' from the bottom of the draw, maybe a mile ahead and below us. We tied the horses and worked our way into a position where we could see into his camp. We were maybe a half mile above them. He had his horses hobbled on the grass along the small stream that ran down through this draw, and it looked like he planned on stayin' there at least for a while. Just then, without makin' a sound, Jimbo came right up to us. We picked out a route we could use to get down to them without bein' seen and headed down.

We were just a couple of hundred yards from them, when Runnin' Wolf stopped and whispered to me that he was gonna just walk into Black Hand's camp and try to talk to him, that he didn't want to have to kill him if there was any other way.

At 'bout fifty yards out, we hadn't been seen yet, and Black Hand was yellin' at Shinin' Star that if she didn't cook for him, she wouldn't eat. She told him, as long as he held her captive, she would never eat again. He slapped her, and she fell to the ground, and then he set a rabbit on a stick over the fire. Jimbo started his low growl, and Runnin' Wolf motioned for me to hold him and stay. He set his rifle down and walked right on in.

He was only 'bout twenty yards from them when they saw him, and both Black Hand and Shinin' Star just stared for a minute. Then Shinin' Star got up and started for him, yellin' his name, and Black Hand knocked her down again and pulled his knife. Just from the look of Black Hand, I figured Runnin' Wolf wouldn't be a match for him in a fight. He was a mighty fearsome-lookin' man. He was built wide and powerful and just had a look of meanness in him.

Runnin' Wolf walked right in and asked him what right he had to take his sister against her will and then treat her like a slave. This took Black Hand off guard, and I could see the anger building in his face. He said, "She has no man, and she is now my woman and I have the right to treat her as I please."

Runnin' Wolf had now raised his voice and told Black Hand that Shinin' Star did have a man, that he was the great white warrior Grizzly Killer, and he was here now to take his woman back. I was not sure who was more surprised at that—Black Hand, Shinin' Star, or Me. He told Black Hand to take his horses and go in peace but not to return to the land of the Uintahs. Black Hand told Runnin' Wolf he was lyin', that Shinin' Star had no man but him, and he was not leavin' now or ever without his woman.

I told Jimbo to stay and stood up and walked in, and as I got closer, I noticed two things right off. Grub Taylor had been right with what was said 'bout Shinin' Star when we were at Rendezvous. She was a mighty beautiful woman, and Black Hand was surprised and furious all at the same time. I ignored Black Hand and walked right up to Shinin' Star and put my arms around her and, in the best Ute I could, asked her if she was all right. She was stunned and just looked at me. Black Hand came at me, yellin' to get away from his woman. He still had his knife in hand, but he wasn't ready to use it just yet. When he was close enough and without sayin' a word, I swung my fist and caught him square in the face. He landed flat on his back, but this was one tough, strong man, and he was back on his feet mighty fast. His nose was flattened, and both his lips smashed. He was a bloody mess. I told him to leave now or die. Just as he started toward me, Jimbo came up to my side and growled. Black Hand stopped, and Runnin' Wolf told him he couldn't win, that we were takin' Shinin' Star back with us. He told us we were cowards not to fight him fairly and that he would follow us till we were all dead. I believed he would from the look in his eyes, so I pulled my knife and told Runnin' Wolf to hold Jimbo.

He came at me, tryin' to catch me off guard like I had caught him, but I was expectin' that. I sidestepped his lunge with the knife and kicked the side of his knee with all I had, and he went down. He rolled and got up, but I could tell he was hurt. He came at me again, not movin' near as fast, but this time, he had figured my move and caught me on the shoulder with his blade, and I could tell it was a deep cut. He spun 'round to finish the job, but I hadn't moved and was waitin' for him. I drove my knife deep into his belly, and with all my strength, I lifted up and opened him up clear to his ribs. He had a look of surprise as he fell to his knees and, tryin' to hold in his guts with both hands, fell to the ground and died.

I was shakin' all over. I had killed a few Injuns before but not like this, not in a hand-to-hand fight. This fight was violent and bloody and lasted less than a minute, and a man was dead. Shinin' Star ran to her brother, and Jimbo ran to me. I half staggered over to a fallen log and sat down. Runnin' Wolf and Shinin' Star came over to me, and Shinin' Star started doctorin' my shoulder.

Half hour later, I was still shakin' a little from the intense fight, but Shinin' Star had the bleedin' stopped. The cut was deep enough it needed to be sewed up, and I had a needle and some sinew in my possibles bag. I got it out and asked Runnin' Wolf to sew it up for me. Shinin' Star took the needle from Runnin' Wolf, looked at it for a minute, and smiled. She then frowned, and I nodded. She was careful, but it did hurt. I tried not to let it show, but it hurt.

Runnin' Wolf said, "We should get as far from here as we could before nightfall, and we will take Black Hand with us and find a spot to bury him where he will not be found."

Black Hand had ten horses that he had trailed all the way to pay for Shinin' Star, and we had to take them all with us. We rolled Black Hand's body up in his robe and tied it on and headed back the way we had come. Ol' Red and our three horses were up on the rim of this draw in the timber, so we worked our way up to them, and it was midafternoon by the time we started back, and within a couple of hours, we crossed a deep little wash that would make a good grave. We followed it 'bout mile off the trail and put Black Hand's body in it and sluffed the bank down on top of it. Shinin' Star was mighty quiet durin' this whole time.

The three of us were leadin' eleven horses now, but they were used to the trail, and we moved right along. We were back up on the big plateau, and when we got to the small river where we had let the stock graze before, it was just a couple of hours before sundown. All of us and the stock needed a good night's rest, so we stopped for the night. We hobbled all the horses but, as usual, just let Ol' Red loose. There was plenty of grass for 'em to graze through the night. Runnin' Wolf said he was goin' huntin', and Shinin' Star went down to the river and bathed. I was gatherin' firewood when Shinin' Star got out of the river, but I couldn't help lookin'. A beautiful naked girl with water glistenin' on her skin was a sight I would never be able to turn away from.

I had a fire goin', and the western sky was painted with such colors as you wouldn't believe, when Runnin' Wolf came back with a deer cross the back of his horse. As he got it to the ground, Shinin' Star, still not sayin' much, just walked over and started skinnin' that deer. She got the skin off one haunch, cut three big chunks of meat off, and got them roastin' on sticks over the fire. Then she went back and finished the skinnin'. We ate that fresh roasted deer and drank the cold stream water while Jimbo ate three cottontail rabbits. Then sittin' by the fire as it got dark, the tenseness of the fight and two days and nights in the saddle all started to hit me, and I needed sleep. I got my bedroll and handed Shinin' Star hers, and as I unrolled mine and lay down, the last thing I remember was some coyotes yippin' in the distance, and then I was asleep.

It was a chilly night up this high, and we just had one blanket each. I felt the warmth of Sun Flower's body next to me and put my arms 'round her and pulled her naked body right up against me and slept. When I opened my eyes, the sky was already gray along the eastern horizon, and the warmth of Sun Flower in the chill of this mountain air sure felt good. Then I realized where I was, and Sun Flower wasn't here, and this naked girl in my arms was Shinin' Star. I tried to move without wakin' her, but as soon as I moved, she opened her eyes and smiled at me. I didn't know what to do, but I did know I wasn't goin' to betray Sun Flower, so I just threw the blanket off me and got up. It was cold, so I put my blanket over Shinin' Star and got a fire goin'. Runnin' Wolf was still under his blanket, but I could see the smile on his face, so I threw a piece of firewood at him. He said every great warrior needed more than one woman, some even had three or four, so I still had more to go.

I felt I needed to talk to Shinin' Star, but I just didn't know enough of the Ute tongue, and right now, I wasn't so sure how helpful Runnin' Wolf would be. So we ate more roasted deer and saddled up. We wasn't pushin' near as hard as before, but we set a steady pace. Climbin' up over that pass was even more fearsome in the daylight. At least at night you couldn't see how far it was to the bottom, and the trail even looked steeper and narrower than it did durin' the night. It was slow goin', but we made it up over the top without any trouble.

From the top you could see the full length of the Uintah Mountains. They looked to be nearly a hundred miles north of us and went to the east as far as the eye could see. You could still see snow hangin' on the sides of the peaks. We started off the top of this pass and worked our way down the trail through the timber and started down this long canyon back toward the Duchesne River. We got to where the river comin' from the west met the Duchesne just as the stars were comin' out and stopped for the night. Jimbo went out lookin' for his dinner, and we put more of the deer to roastin'. I sure wished we would have brought the little coffee pot and some coffee.

After we ate, I got my bedroll and laid it out off to the side of the fire, and Shinin' Star got hers and followed me. I shook my head no and told Runnin' Wolf to tell her I already had a woman. She looked hurt and spoke. Runnin' Wolf told me she asked if I did not like her. I smiled at her and said I liked her very much, that she was a beautiful woman, but that I already have a woman. When Runnin' Wolf had told her what I said, she looked at me with a puzzled look and said, with Runnin' Wolf tellin' me in English, "If you only have one woman, now you have two." Then she said that I had fought and killed for her and that Runnin' Wolf gave her to me and she would be my second woman. Then she just smiled and put her blanket next to mine.

I had no idea what to do to make her understand, and I sat down by Runnin' Wolf to get him to explain it to her. But to Runnin' Wolf's way of thinkin', I'd lost my mind. He said men took more than one woman, that the women helped each other and it was easier for them, that even Chargin' Bull, the Snake chief, had two women, and he did not understand why I didn't want two women. Then he asked me if I didn't like his sister. I told him again I liked her, but I felt like it would be betrayin'

Sun Flower. He looked puzzled and asked why. I could tell my white-man beliefs made no sense to these people, just as their beliefs made no sense to me, so I just crawled into my bedroll, wonderin' how I was supposed to explain all this to Sun Flower. When I opened my eyes and listened for the natural sounds the next mornin', Shinin' Star was lyin' there next to me, but this time, she still had her doe skin dress on.

Travelin' easy like we were, I figured it would take us 'bout four hours to get back to their village on Rock Creek. I was both exited to see Sun Flower and worried 'bout what Runnin' Wolf and Shinin' Star would say. They were both actin' like Shinin' Star was gonna be my woman too.

Chapter XXIII

Two Wives

IT WAS LATE MORNIN' when we saw the village, and we were met by those same two boys as when we first rode in a few days ago. They were mighty excited and headed right for the village with the news. I could see our teepee standin' high above the wickiups, and 'fore long, I could see Sun Flower and Raven Wing standin' in front of it. A couple of the braves came out to us, and Runnin' Wolf asked if they would take the horses out to the herd for him.

By now there was a crowd of women 'round Shinin' Star, and they were talkin' way too fast for me to pick up much of it. I just rode through them all and right to Sun Flower, jumped down, and picked her up in my arms. Her smile and the look in her eyes made my day. Runnin' Wolf was tryin' to get through everyone that was askin' all sorts of questions when Raven Wing just pushed through them all and threw her arms 'round him. Shinin' Star saw that and went right over to him to meet the Shoshone woman her younger brother had chosen.

I was surprised at the amount of the Ute tongue Raven Wing had picked up. She was talkin' to Shinin' Star, and

Runnin' Wolf was just smilin'. Raven Wing really had a gift for learnin' different tongues. Sun Flower, it seemed, was pickin' up a lot that was bein' said, and she had a strange look on her face. I couldn't understand what was bein' said, and I started to get worried again.

Another tall man that looked like he was important said there would be a feast tonight to celebrate the return of Runnin' Wolf and Shinin' Star. Sun Flower told me that was Two Feathers, the son of Stands Tall. She said he and the other hunters had brought in much meat.

Runnin' Wolf then brought Shinin' Star over to us and introduced Shinin' Star to Sun Flower. Shinin' Star started talkin' and asked Sun Flower if she understood. Sun Flower nodded, and I got even more worried. Shinin' Star told her that I had saved her from Black Hand and that Black Hand was a very powerful warrior and I had killed him with only a small wound on my shoulder, that she was very pleased to meet the woman of such a great warrior. She said that Runnin' Wolf had given her to me, but I did not want her 'cause I already had a woman. Shinin' Star told her she was very lucky to have such a great warrior with such powerful medicine.

Sun Flower grabbed my arm, looked up at me, and smiled and then told Shinin' Star that the one above had truly blessed her to bring such a man to her.

We went up and sat under the arbor again, with Stands Tall, Two Feathers, and five other men I had not met. Shinin' Star was there, and the rest of the village was standin' around our circle. Stands Tall asked Runnin' Wolf to tell what had happened, and Runnin' Wolf told of the chase, catchin' up to them, and how the fight started and Black Hand was killed. He told them what we did with Black Hand's body.

I was able to understand most of what was said, but not all. Stands Tall was silent for a few minutes, and then he spoke slowly and deliberately. He said it was a serious thing to kill another of our people, that he was proud of Runnin' Wolf for tryin' to get Black Hand to give up Shinin' Star and leave without a fight. But it had been Black Hand's choice to fight like it had been his choice to take Shinin' Star against her will. He then looked at me and said Black Hand was one of the greatest warriors of the Utes. He had fought many battles and had always won, that it would take a great warrior with powerful medicine to kill Black Hand. He went on that they had heard by a runner that Runnin' Wolf had been killed by the great white warrior Grizzly Killer and that Grizzly Killer had taken his power from the great bears he had killed. He told us his heart was glad that the runner was wrong and that I was a brother to Runnin' Wolf and our people, that the medicine of the great bear was in me. He said that Shinin' Star would make me a good second wife, and their hearts were glad that she would now have a man to provide for her. I felt the color drainin' from my face, and I started to shake inside. I wasn't afraid of any man, and I knew I couldn't let it show, but these women scared the hell out of me.

I needed to be alone for a while, and I saddled Ol' Red and, along with Jimbo, rode up Rock Creek. This was a beautiful wide valley filled with sage, the green of grass, and wildflowers of every color. There were cedar and pinion on the slopes down low, changin' to quakies and pines the higher up I rode. I could see the valley was narrowin' down into a steep-sided canyon just up ahead. After 'bout an hour, I stopped, and while Ol' Red munched on the grass along the creek, me and Jimbo played and wrestled around. Life seemed a lot simpler last winter when it was just me, Jimbo, and Ol' Red. But I really didn't want to spend another winter alone either.

I lay down in the grass, just watchin' some fluffy white clouds passin' overhead, thinkin' 'bout all that had happened, when Jimbo jumped up and headed downstream. Just a few minutes later, I saw Sun Flower on her roan, followin' Jimbo right to me. She climbed down and walked over and sat down next to me. Without sayin' a word, she took my hand in hers. She knew I was troubled, but she couldn't figure why. I didn't know how to explain my feelin's to her so she might understand.

I knew most men would jump at the chance to have two beautiful women, and I had to admit there were some mighty appealin' thoughts 'bout it. But I still felt I would be betrayin' Sun Flower, and the thought of that was overwhelmin' me. I thought back to Pa's last words when he said "Never do anything that won't make yourself proud." I asked Sun Flower why they wanted me to take Shinin' Star when I already had her and I didn't want anyone but her.

She was lookin' right at me with those big beautiful dark eyes and said, "My heart is happy to have you want only me. But there are many reasons that a man takes another wife. His power grows bigger the more wives he can care for. Sometimes he is obligated if his brother dies, then his brother's wife will become his to take care of. Sometimes a man's first wife gets old or hurt, or there is too much to do, so the man takes another wife to help his first. And sometimes a man falls in love with another woman. Runnin' Wolf and Stands Tall wants you to have Shinin' Star for more than one reason. Runnin' Wolf loves his sister very much, and he knows you will always take care of her. He knows you are a good man and will never treat her bad, and she is a beautiful woman that will always make you happy too. He wants the best for both of you. Stands Tall knows there are no men in the village that Shinin' Star wants, and by the way she looks at you, everyone can see she wants you."

Bein' 'round the Cherokee as much as I was growin' up, I knew the Injun ways and beliefs were different than ours. And I knew that was one of the things that caused so much trouble 'tween the Injuns and whites. I was now livin' in a land with tens of thousands of Injuns and only a few hundred white men scattered over thousands of miles and no white women. I was livin' like the Injuns and with them, and they didn't understand the difference in our beliefs. I held her tight, lyin' there in the grass along this crystal clear mountain stream they called Rock Creek, and wondered what Pa would have said 'bout all this.

I asked her then, "What does Sun Flower want me to do?"

She sat there in the grass and pondered on that for quite a while. Then she said, "It would be a good thing for us to have another woman. We will have more importance with both the Utes and Shoshones. We will need much help preparing for winter, tanning the hides, making another lodge, gathering enough berries and nuts for the pemmican. We will need a lot of help living at the log lodge. What if we have a baby? What if we have trouble? Shinin' Star would be a big help to all of us, and what 'bout Shinin' Star? Who is going to hunt and care for her? Runnin' Wolf is her family, and she should be with us because she is our family too."

I told her, "Shinin' Star bein' with us is different than her bein' my second wife, and what do you feel 'bout that?"

She said, "Women have always shared their men, just like when visitors come to a Shoshone village, the men will share their wives with them. I will share you with Shinin' Star, and I will make sure you always want me as your first wife."

She then slid her dress up over her shoulders, and she helped me out of my buckskins, and we made love lyin' there in the grass, under the bright blue sky as the afternoon storm clouds were buildin' over the high peaks just north of us. I held her tight up against me for the longest time and told her she would always be my love. I would never understand the Injun way of thinkin' any more than they would understand mine. I thought then my life would be much simpler if I just took Sun Flower right then and we rode away. But Runnin' Wolf and Raven Wing had become my family too. I'd grown to love them like the brother and sister that I never had, and I couldn't just run out on them any more than I could leave Sun Flower. I was mighty troubled. It seemed everyone just expected me to take Shinin' Star as another wife.

We rode back to the village as slow as I could make Ol' Red walk. Jimbo kept Runnin' back to us, seein' why we were takin' so long, but I was tryin' to put off facin' what was expected of me in the village. When we rode in and up to the teepee, Runnin' Wolf and Raven Wing were there. Raven Wing told Sun Flower they needed to go help, and the two of them left.

I walked down to the creek to ponder on all this some more, and as I sat there on a rock, watchin' the water rush on by, I started thinkin' 'bout just what had brought me here. I thought of Ma and Pa and back home, of the two explorers that had stopped in Pottersville three or four years back that had been with Captains Lewis and Clark in the Corps of Discovery. It was the stories they told us of these great western mountains and of all the different Injun peoples, of all the different animals, the giant bears, and the little antelope, of the countless numbers of buffalo on the endless plains that got Pa wantin' to see all this, of how after Ma had got sick and we buried her, Pa just lost interest in the farm and we decided to come west. I remembered Pa seein' the post in Saint Louis 'bout General Ashley hirin' men to take supplies to his Rendezvous and how excited we had been to get hired on. I thought 'bout the first buffalo herd we saw and that there must have been ten thousand of them. I thought of just how much I had changed since we left home.

It seemed like a lifetime ago that I was gettin' up and doin' chores on the farm, yet it was less than two years ago. I'd grown to love this western wilderness and figured I would stay here forever. I had only known Sun Flower for a few weeks now, but I had a mighty strong love for her, and Runnin' Wolf had become a true and trusted friend. Sun Flower told me I should be proud that Shinin' Star wanted me.

It was late afternoon on a warm July day, and there was a cool light breeze blowin' down the creek as I walked back from the creek to the teepee. The village was buzzin' with activity, and there were whole elk haunches roastin' over several different fires.

I was standin' by the side of the teepee when I saw Sun Flower walkin' toward me. There were several women with her, includin' Stands Tall's young wife, Dove. I had learned his older wife had passed away last winter. Sun Flower was dressed in the new dress she had worn at Rendezvous, with the red sash and red headband that I didn't even know they had brought with them. Then I saw Raven Wing dressed the same. Me and Runnin' Wolf just watched, smilin' as they walked toward us. I thought then there couldn't be two more beautiful sisters. Then behind them all came Shinin' Star. She was dressed in a pure-white dress that was decorated with colored quills and fringe cut long around the bottom and a row of fringe across her breasts that ran over the shoulders and across her back. She had her cheeks brushed with a light reddish tint, and in her hair were tied strips of white weasel fur and blue ribbons cut from trade cloth that Sun Flower must have given her. I thought again of Grub Taylor and what he would think right now of the beauty of these three walkin' up to us. It was a sight to remember.

We made our way over to the brush arbor, and I found my grizzly robe was spread out for me to sit on. I looked at Sun Flower, and she just smiled, so I figured the women had supplied that. Runnin' Wolf had left us, but in just a few minutes, he came back with a wolf hide across his shoulders tied in front of his neck by the front legs. He was wearin' a headband with two eagle feathers in it and otter fur hangin' down from his temples. I forgot to bring some twists of tobacco and ran back to the teepee and got it and was back in just a couple of minutes.

Stands Tall was just sittin' down on a very colorful rug that had been weaved from what looked to be dyed wool when I returned, and the chief motioned for me to sit. As I sat down on the grizzly robe, Sun Flower and Shinin' Star came up and sat down, one on each side of me. Runnin' Wolf sat down, and Raven Wing sat next to him. Then Two Feathers and the other five men finished the semicircle under this brush arbor. The rest of the village was just behind us. Two boys started a fire just out from the arbor but directly in front of us, and a drum started to beat. A row of young dancers in the most colorful costumes I'd ever seen started followin' one another, dancin' in a line 'round the fire. Then women brought us strips of roasted elk and wild onion and sego lily root that had been wrapped in leaves and roasted in the coals.

After everyone had eaten, Stands Tall picked up a roll of soft tanned skin and unrolled a pipe, and I handed him the pouch that I had several twists of tobacco in. He smiled and nodded and filled his pipe. Runnin' Wolf then stood and got a burnin' stick from the fire and held it for the chief while he lit the pipe. After the pipe was passed around, much the same as the Shoshones had done but without the talk, a small bundle of sage was lit and passed 'round, with each wavin' the smoke over themselves. I did not understand the reason but followed along and would ask Runnin' Wolf 'bout it later.

When this ritual had ended, Stands Tall spoke. His speech was slow and deliberate, and I could understand most of it. "We will dance tonight to celebrate the return of Runnin' Wolf, whom we thought had gone to the land beyond, and Shinin' Star, who was taken against her will, and to honor our white brother Grizzly Killer for bringing Running Wolf and Shining Star back to us." He went on, "Even though the Snake people have been our enemies, Raven Wing and Sun Flower are now our sisters, and they should live long and raise many sons and daughters." He looked right at Shinin' Star and then said, "My heart is glad she had found such a great warrior to fill the emptiness she has felt inside." Then with a smile, he said, "Let us dance."

The fire was built up, and the drums started a rhythm again, and there was chanting and dancin' well into the night. There was never a question asked if I chose Shinin' Star or if I wanted another wife. It seemed to be just a fact that now I had two wives. Two months ago, I had never been with a woman, and now I had two that was dependin' on me and expecting me to be a husband to both. All I knew 'bout bein' a husband at all was just from watchin' Pa, and again I hoped I'd learned well enough.

It was just two or three hours before dawn when the last of the dancin' was finished and everyone was back in their wickiups. I had no idea what to expect 'bout goin' to bed with Sun Flower and Shinin' Star.

Chapter XXIV

The Attack

JUST 'BOUT THE TIME I figured out Sun Flower was leavin' me alone with Shinin' Star, Jimbo came up to me and started his low, throaty growl, and it was plain he wanted me to follow him. Shinin' Star had a puzzled look on her face, and I asked her to get Runnin' Wolf. She could sense the urgency in my voice, and in just a minute, Runnin' Wolf and Raven Wing were there. I told Raven Wing to get Sun Flower and all their weapons. I asked Runnin' Wolf to have Shinin' Star alert Stands Tall that there might be danger and to get Two Feathers. While they were doin' that, I got my Hawken and Pa's old rifle along with Runnin' Wolf's long rifle, with his bow and quiver and our possibles bags. When I got back to the arbor, Sun Flower was there with her squirrel gun, and Raven Wing had her bow. Two Feathers came up with his bow and a questionin' look.

Runnin' Wolf told him the dog sensed danger and his medicine was strong. The moon was almost full, and the night was light. The fire had burned down to just coals when me, Runnin' Wolf, and Two Feathers followed Jimbo out into the night. We followed him north, maybe a half mile, and as we started up on a little rise, he stopped and dropped down to his belly. Two Feathers and Runnin' Wolf crawled to the top of the rise, and in just a couple of minutes, they were back. Runnin' Wolf said we had to get back to the village. There were many horses bein' held by a warrior just over the rise, and he feared the village would be attacked. We followed our same path back to the village at a fast jog.

When we got back, Stands Tall and the other men were at the arbor. It was then explained what we had found. We had to get the women and children to the other side of the river. I felt sure the village was bein' watched, so we needed to move them without bein' seen. Raven Wing and Shinin' Star left us and went inside the first wickiup. Stands Tall said we would let them come into the village and surprise them when they were not expecting it. I saw several women and children on their hands and knees, stayin' in the shadows, movin' toward the river. Raven Wing and Shinin' Star and now a couple of other women were movin' in the shadows to each wickiup, and within a half hour, the village was empty.

Two Feathers thought whoever it was would not attack till dawn, but we couldn't be sure. It could be Navajo, Comanche, Arapaho, or Snakes. Runnin' Wolf said it wouldn't be the Snakes and told them of the Arapahos we had dealt with movin' down the Seeds-Kee-Dee. He said if it was the Arapaho, they had split up because there weren't as many horses as they were movin' down the river.

Shinin' Star did not have a weapon, and Runnin' Wolf told her to make sure the other women and children were well hidden and safe. I was hopin' we couldn't be seen bein' in the shadow of the arbor. Stands Tall and Two Feathers laid out a plan for us to split up, half on each side of the village, and when they attacked, we would have them in a crossfire. We didn't know for sure which way they would come, but the way the village was set with Rock Creek just to the west, the best cover they had to hide their approach was from the northeast. Me and

Sun Flower, Runnin' Wolf and Raven Wing, along with Stands Tall and Two Feathers, were on the northwest side of the village, well hidden in the brush, while the other Ute warriors hid in the brush on the other side just across from us.

We sat there in the brush, silent and motionless. Jimbo was right between Sun Flower and me, and I just watched him. I knew he would know before the rest of us when they were comin'. I figured it had been a couple of hours, and just as the sky started to turn gray along the eastern horizon, Jimbo started his low growl. I put my hand on his head and motioned for him to let the others know. He moved silent as a ghost and was back in just a minute. As the last of the stars faded from the sky, I caught a glimpse of movement out in the brush to the northeast, just like we had figured. I had my powder horn and several balls laid out in front of me and had taken my ramrod out from under the barrel so I could reload faster and made sure Sun Flower was set up the same way.

These warriors were movin' into the village without makin' a sound, and I counted twenty of them. Some had bows with arrows ready, but most were carryin' lances or war clubs. When they were set in front of each wickiup, one shouted out a war cry and flung the hide cover open. I fired, and then almost at the same time, Sun Flower and Runnin' Wolf fired. Then almost instantly, there were arrows flyin' and men on the ground. One warrior was runnin' right for me, and as I brought Pa's rifle up and fired, he threw his lance. His head almost exploded with the impact of that lead ball, and his lance struck the ground barely an inch from me. I could hear Jimbo's vicious growl and saw a warrior go down under him. There were hand-to-hand battles goin' on across the village, and as I finished reloadin', I saw Runnin' Wolf stand up and shoot the last of his arrows. I fired again, and another warrior fell, and just as I pulled out my tomahawk and knife to charge, Sun Flower fired again. I saw one of their warriors flinch from her shot, but before he fell, he pulled back his bow and let his arrow fly.

Raven Wing saw it happen just as I did. It didn't seem possible, but that arrow hit Sun Flower and buried deep between her shoulder and breast. Raven Wing reached her at the same time I did, but she screamed at me to go and kill them all. I charged into the melee, but it was 'bout over. One warrior turned to face me and swung his war club, but I blocked his swing and brought my tomahawk down right on the top of his head. There were seven or eight of them runnin' through the brush to get away from us. This peaceful Ute village had been turned into a bloody and gruesome mess.

I ran back over to Sun Flower. Raven Wing had cut through the shoulder lacing on her dress and had the wound exposed. She was covered with blood, and I ran to the teepee and brought the wool blankets. Sun Flower was pale and was takin' short breaths, tryin' to control the pain. Runnin' Wolf ran to the river to get more help while Two Feathers and a couple of others rode out, followin' the Arapahos to make sure they weren't comin' back. Runnin' Wolf brought an old woman he called Grandmother and Shinin' Star back with him. Grandmother moved Raven Wing out of the way and started givin' orders. Shinin' Star ran to a wickiup and returned with several pouches and a leather roll. She unrolled the leather, and there were several tools in it made of bone and some chips of flint used for cuttin'.

Grandmother was talkin' as she worked, but I could understand none of it. She moved the arrow slightly, and Sun Flower jumped. She had me and Runnin' Wolf hold Sun Flower down, and she got a good grip on the arrow shaft and pulled. The flint arrowhead came out with the shaft and a lot of blood. Sun Flower gasped, and her breathin' became a lot faster. Grandmother poured the powdery contents of one of the pouches over the wound and pressed it into the hole with her hand. I cut several long strips off one of the blankets to use as bandages. When Grandmother slowly moved her hand away, the bleeding was stopped. Shinin' Star and Raven Wing then started to put the bandage over the wound, tyin' it as tight as Sun Flower could stand.

Just then, a wailing started up from the village, and Grandmother, with Runnin' Wolf, hurried in that direction. I was kneelin' beside Sun Flower, coverin' her with a blanket, when Runnin' Wolf came back and said Spotted Horse had just died from a lance through his side. The only other wound was a bad cut on Weasel's back, but they thought he would heal. I told Raven Wing and Shinin' Star we needed to get Sun Flower into the teepee and Raven Wing said no. She said, "Grandmother said if we move her, the bleeding will start again."

I asked Runnin' Wolf if he would get me some long branches that I could make a lean-to with, and in a few minutes, he was back. We lashed together a lean-to, and I covered it with Sun Flower's buffalo robe to keep the sun off her. She was sleepin' now, and Jimbo was curled up right next to her. Raven Wing and Shinin' Star was lyin' there by her, and I went and got Ol' Red and the chestnut.

Me and Runnin' Wolf spent the next couple of hours draggin' the dead Arapaho warriors to a wash 'bout five miles from the village. I didn't understand the takin' of scalps, but it was part of the Injun way of life. When we were done, there were twelve Arapaho scalps that we brought back.

We were all tired, but Stands Tall was an old man and didn't look good. He was sittin' by himself when we returned. As me and Runnin' Wolf walked up to give the scalps to him, he tried to stand but started to fall, and I caught him. I felt blood on his sleeve and sat him back down. Runnin' Wolf ran to get Dove, his wife, who was helpin' the wives of Spotted Horse prepare his body for burial. I was helpin' the chief out of his buckskin shirt when Dove and Grandmother came hurryin' back with Runnin' Wolf. We carefully got his shirt off and saw he had a broken arrow shaft stickin' out of his upper arm. We got Stands Tall laid down, and the women went to work on gettin' the arrow out of his arm. It hadn't hit the bone, and you could see the point pushin' against the skin on the other side, so Grandmother picked up a rock and hit the broken shaft, pushin' it through the skin and out the back of his arm. She then poured some of the powder she'd used on Sun Flower on the wounds and wrapped a piece of soft leather around it. He smiled and thanked her and said he would be fine.

Sun Flower was mighty pale and was covered with now-dried blood. Raven Wing was lyin' by her side and had fallen asleep while Shinin' Star was sittin' on the other side of her, holdin' her hand. I went and got our cookin' pot and built a small fire by the lean-to. I filled the pot with water and set it on the fire to warm. Then I got the coffee pot and started a pot of coffee. When the water was warm, I took a piece of the blanket with the hot water and started to very gently clean the dried blood off Sun Flower, but Shinin' Star took the cloth from me and continued. Sun Flower opened her eyes and tried to smile, but she was weak and in pain. I was ready to pour a cup of coffee, when Grandmother came by, and when she saw my cup, she took it from me and dipped it in the warm water and poured the contents of another pouch in the water and stirred it with a stick. Raven Wing was up now, helpin' Shinin' Star, and they were cuttin' the rest of the lacing off Sun Flower's dress. It was soaked with blood, and they were takin' it off her. Grandmother said something and handed Shinin' Star the cup. Raven Wing lifted Sun Flower's head just enough for Shinin' Star to get the cup to her lips, and with Raven Wing tellin' Sun Flower to drink, she managed to take in a few sips. Grandmother said something else and walked away. Raven Wing looked at me and said she needed to drink all this.

I thought back to the day I buried Pa and how helpless I'd felt not bein' able to help him. I had the same helpless feelin' now. But now I wasn't alone, and Grandmother was a healer and she knew what to do. I walked a little away from the village and asked God to save Sun Flower. I couldn't remember the last time I had prayed, and I hoped God remembered me. I felt a little better when I walked back to the others.

It was evenin' when the boys came runnin' into the village, shoutin' that Two Feathers and the others where comin' back. A few minutes later, they came ridin' in. Two Feathers went right to his father as the rest of us gathered around. I could see the concern on Two Feathers's face when he saw the bandaged arm and paleness of Stands Tall's face, but Stands Tall stood up and greeted his son. I could understand enough of what was said to know they followed the Arapaho warriors a long ways, and Two Feathers was sure they wouldn't be back. Runnin' Wolf told me they had followed them 'bout halfway to the Seeds-Kee-Dee, and two of them had been wounded and were bleeding.

There was meat roastin' on fires all around the village, and the smell made me realize none of us had eaten all day. Raven Wing had meat boilin' in the pot, and she made up a pan of biscuits. Shinin' Star and Jimbo had not left Sun Flower's side all day. Shinin' Star smiled as I walked up. She was still wearin' the white dress from last night and had the ribbons and white fur in her hair. She also had dark circles under her eyes from no sleep. Raven Wing got a cup of broth from the pot, and Shinin' Star put more of the ground powder that Grandmother had left her in the broth and woke Sun Flower to get her to drink it. It took a little while for her to wake up, and with Raven Wing holdin' her head again, she was able to drink most of the cup. I kissed her check, and she smiled at me then drifted off to sleep again. Raven Wing told me the powder would help her with pain and sleep.

After we ate, I got the grizzly robe and other blankets to make a bed for me next to Sun Flower. But Raven Wing and Shinin' Star took them and were makin' up a bed, when Stands Tall, with Two Feathers helpin' him, walked up to us, followed by most of the village. Stands Tall said in his slow and deliberate speech that everyone in the village owed their life to Grizzly Killer and his Great Medicine Dog. I called Jimbo, and he slowly came out from under the lean-to and stood by me. Dove came forward with the whole shoulder of a deer and laid it on the ground in front of Jimbo, and when he picked it up and wagged his, tail the whole village cheered. Two Feathers asked if the children could touch the big dog, and Jimbo acted like he loved the attention of the line of children walkin' by and rubbin' his head, then Weasel came, and even through the pain of the cut down his back, he dropped to his knees and rubbed Jimbo's ears. He said, "The dog saved us all, but me he saved twice. The Arapaho that he killed was the one that cut my back open, and he would now be in the land beyond if the dog would not have attacked when he did."

Stands Tall asked Shinin' Star how Sun Flower was doin', and she answered, "Resting but not good." He then looked at me and told me that both Sun Flower and Raven Wing fought as great warriors to save the village. He said, "Grandmother is a great healer and has treated wounds for longer than most of us have lived. Everything that we can do for her will be done, and if we need anything, just ask. Gray Horse will be close by to serve you for anything you might need."

Just before we all turned in for the night, Grandmother brought another pouch of herbs and gave Shinin' Star instructions to boil them in water and make Sun Flower drink the tea every little while. We slept with me lyin' next to Sun Flower on one side and Shinin' Star next to her on the other and the grizzly robe over us all. Shinin' Star would wake me 'bout every two hours, and while I would gently hold Sun Flower's head, Shinin' Star would get her to swallow as much of the tea as she could. The tea looked like it had several different tree barks in it, including the white bark of quakies, different flower petals, and powders that had been ground fine that I had no idea what they might be.

Come mornin', Sun Flower opened her eyes and smiled at me. But she was still mighty pale. Shinin' Star moved to get up to brew some more of the tea, and Sun Flower held her hand and wanted her to stay. So I got the tea brewin' in the small coffee pot. When I moved to the fire, Shinin' Star put her ear down by Sun Flower's mouth, and I could see Sun Flower was tellin' her somethin. Shinin' Star smiled at her and kissed her on the forehead. Just as the tea was startin' to boil, Grandmother came by. She felt Sun Flower's head and neck, and then with Shinin' Star's help, they took the bandage off.

The wound was a fearsome-lookin' thing. The skin was almost white around it, but it was lined with red. It looked like it was startin' to close up but was oozin' a clear liquid from the part that was still open. Grandmother gently probed around it with her fingers. It made Sun Flower jump, and I could tell it hurt. Then she got right close and smelled it, then she asked for one of the cups. She poured several different powders in the cup and then just enough water to make a paste. When she had it all mixed up, she used her finger and spread the paste over the wound. I cut a clean strip off the cut-up blanket, and Shinin' Star and Raven Wing bandaged the wound again.

I was almighty worried. Sun Flower's color was kind of a slate gray, and her skin was always cold. Before Grandmother left, I had Runnin' Wolf ask her 'bout the color and feel of Sun Flower's skin, and she said it was from the loss of blood. She said the more Sun Flower could drink, the faster she would make more blood, but if she was too weak to make more blood, she would die. I must have figured all along that Sun Flower dyin' was possible, but I hadn't let myself think of it, but now it was said right out loud, I was mighty scared.

The next two days were spent without me or Shinin' Star leavin' Sun Flower's side. We would help her drink the tea Grandmother provided and help Grandmother change the poultice twice a day. The weather was very warm and sunny durin' the day, and we would roll the heavy robe off her, but at night, it would get right cool, and we would pull the grizzly robe up over us all.

The third mornin' when we woke, I noticed her cheeks had a little pink in them, and her hand felt warmer. When she looked at me, those beautiful dark eyes had some of the sparkle back in them. She drank a whole cup of the tea and, a little while later, a cup of broth. After that, she had to get up to go to the bushes. She was a small woman and had lost a lot of weight. When I picked her up, she felt like a child in my arms. When Grandmother came by to change the poultice, even she had a smile on her face when she saw Sun Flower sittin' upright by the fire. Raven Wing and Shinin' Star took down the lean-to and made the bed up in the teepee while Sun Flower was sittin' by the fire.

She gained a little more strength each day and, within another three days, was walkin' without support and spendin' most of the days outside the teepee. The camp was runnin' low on meat again, and Two Feathers came and asked if Runnin' Wolf and I would go on a hunt with him. The other braves would stay with the village, and they would go out when we returned. Sun Flower told me to go, that Shinin' Star and Raven Wing were there if she needed help with anything.

Ol' Red and Jimbo seemed as willin' to go as I did. We each took two pack horses and headed up the mountain to the west of Rock Creek. The game was plentiful, and it was easy to see why the Utes picked this area to spend the summers. There were currents and chokecherries along the creek and what they called buffalo berries that I was not familiar with. We'd seen wild raspberries and strawberries, and there were sego lilies on the dry hills and camas growin' in the marshy areas. This was truly a bountiful land.

By the time we made camp, we were up near timberline on the banks of a clear alpine lake. There was a large herd of elk grazin' 'bout a mile from us on the other side. Jimbo came in with a snowshoe rabbit that was brown this time of the year, which he ate for his dinner while we ate jerky from a cold camp so's not to spook the elk.

By noon the next day, we had five elk down and were gettin' the pack horses loaded. It was early evenin' when we rode back into camp, and the women all started in on the meat, and before dark, it was all on racks to dry or over fires roastin'. I sat down next to Sun Flower by the fire in front of the teepee, and Runnin' Wolf took care of Ol' Red and the horses. Shinin'

Star brought me and Sun Flower a bowl of stew then got one for herself and sat next to me, and the three of us ate.

Sun Flower was tuckered out, and I helped her lie down while Shinin' Star was helpin' get Runnin' Wolf and Raven Wing something to eat and get everything cleaned up. I called Jimbo, and we went for a walk down along the creek. It was just gettin' dark, with the moon risin' to the east. 'Bout a quarter mile above the village, the creek made a bend and widened out. There was a large flat rock that went out over the water, and I slipped off my moccasins, sat on the rock, and let my feet dangle in the cold water. In just a few minutes, Jimbo let me know someone was comin', and I picked up the Hawken and waited.

Chapter XXV

Luckiest Man in the Mountains

IN JUST A MINUTE, Shinin' Star came into sight. Jimbo ran up to her, and she dropped to her knees and rubbed his head and ears, then he led her right to me. She'd seen my bare feet and smiled then stepped out on the rock sat next to me with her feet in the water. She took my hand and leaned her head on my shoulder but never said a word. We sat there in silence with just the sound of the water for quite some time, then she stepped off the rock and into knee-deep water. She lifted her dress up over her head and just stood there in front me, naked. She was a mighty beautiful woman. Then with a wicked little smile, she dropped down into the water and splashed that cold mountain stream water all over me. I jumped off the rock into the stream, put my arms 'round her, and just held her tight. We made love on that flat rock till we were both shiverin'. Then I built a small fire, and we warmed each other and made love again.

It was past midnight when we walked back to the teepee. As I stepped inside and saw Sun Flower, I had a feelin' of guilt something awful. She moved the robe down for me to lie down, and as I did, Shinin' Star got in beside me. Now I was lyin' 'tween two beautiful women, and they both just snuggled up to me and went to sleep. I lay there for the longest time, wonderin' 'bout this. I wondered what Ma and Pa would think. I even wondered what Emma Potter would think. Then I wondered what Grub Taylor would think. After a while, I decided I didn't care what anyone would think. I have the love of two beautiful women, and I figured I was 'bout the luckiest man in the mountains.

Next mornin' as we were all eatin' biscuits and drinkin' coffee, I figured it was time to make our plans for the next month or so. Sun Flower was still weak, and I knew it would still be another week or so 'fore she would be able to ride all day. They all agreed we needed another lodge, and it would take many buffalo for the lodge, winter robes, and warm clothes.

I figured it was now 'bout the end of July, and it would be the first of August 'fore we were on the trail again. We would have to trail all the horses to have enough to carry the buffalo and all our supplies. Runnin' Wolf said it would take six or seven suns to reach the land of the buffalo, and we would need to be very watchful for the Arapaho and Cheyenne, for we would be huntin' in their country.

That afternoon, Sun Flower asked to go ridin', so I saddled Ol' Red and her roan. I asked Shinin' Star if she wanted to go, and she smiled at Sun Flower and said she had work to do. As I helped Sun Flower into the saddle, Shinin' Star brought a blanket and tied it to the back of the saddle and said it was in case she got cold.

Sun Flower led off, and we followed Rock Creek up to the clearin' were we had made love and talked a few weeks ago. She rode on through and kept followin' the creek. When the canyon narrowed, the goin' got a lot tougher, and I was worried she was pushin' too hard and said so. She smiled at me and said she wanted to show me she was stronger than I figured. Another couple of miles, and we came to where a very steep rocky draw cut into the side of the canyon on our right, and I told her she had proved her strength, and this was far enough.

I climbed out of the saddle and walked over to help her out of the saddle, but she tried by herself. Her right arm would not hold her, and she fell on her backside. The look on her face told me she didn't know whether to laugh or cry. I picked her up and held her in my arms. She put her head on my shoulder and started to cry. She said she didn't want to disappoint me by bein' a weak woman. At that, I burst out laughin' and set her down. I got the blanket and spread it out on the side of the creek, and we sat on it. She asked me why I laughed at her. I told her I thought it was funny that she would think I would ever be disappointed in her. I told her she was the bravest, strongest, most beautiful woman I had ever known, and I could never think she was weak or be disappointed in her. She smiled and leaned into me. I held her tight to me, and she said she would ride every day so she would be strong when we left. We watched a mountain lion sneak across a ledge of rock across the creek from us, and several deer came down to the stream to drink. A pair of golden eagles was circlin' high above the cliffs against a dark-blue sky. We just sat there and watched the water tumble over the rocks and then made love under the afternoon sun.

It was late afternoon when we headed back, and there were deer all along the creek. In an Injun village, meat is always needed, so when a nice buck stepped out of the trees, I shot it, and after guttin' him and tyin' him behind my saddle, we went on back to camp. It was just 'fore dusk when we rode in, and Shinin' Star and Raven Wing had that buck skinned in just a few minutes. They cut out the loin, and in a matter of minutes, the deer was gone to others that needed the meat. They had the hide staked out before dark.

Sun Flower thought she was stronger than she was. It had only been 'bout three weeks since that arrow had almost killed her, and she still needed more time. She didn't feel like eatin', but we all insisted she had a little. She was asleep as soon as she lay down.

She was determined to build her strength, and we went ridin' every day. Most of the time, Shinin' Star would go with us, and we spent the time gettin' to know one another better. Sun Flower and Shinin' Star became as much like sisters as Sun Flower and Raven Wing, and we became a right close family.

Over the past three weeks, Gray Horse had spent a lot of time with Jimbo, and the two had become fast friends. I could see a sadness in his face when we told everyone we would be leavin' in just a few more days. We spent the last days in the Ute village, mendin' our packs and makin' sure all our belongin's were in good order. I braided several rawhide ropes that we could use for lead ropes or to tie packs with. The women had tanned several elk and deer hides while we had been there and were spendin' a lot of time on some deer skins that Raven Wing and Shinin' Star said was to replace the dress Sun Flower ruined in the battle.

We decided that with nineteen horses now to trail, we would drive most of them and only have the ones carryin' our supplies on lead ropes. I did not want Sun Flower holdin' a lead rope with her shoulder still weak from the arrow wound. Those last few days passed in a hurry, and I could see both excitement and sadness in Runnin' Wolf on the mornin' it was time to leave. Gray Horse and several of the young boys cut our horses from the herd, and the whole village was there to wish us well. Raven Wing spoke the Ute tongue now just as well as the Utes, and Sun Flower wasn't far behind her. I could tell what was bein' said, but they still laughed at me when I tried to speak it. We spoke to Two Feathers at length that mornin', makin' sure he knew where we would be spendin' the winter. I figured the dugout on Black's Fork was just 'bout straight north of Rock Creek on the north slope of these Uintah Mountains. Stands Tall and Dove came to us and told Runnin' Wolf that his father would be proud of the warrior he had become. He told me that all the Ute people would know of me and I would be a welcome friend in all of the Utah lands.

With Gray Horse and several of the Ute herd boys helpin' to get the horses started, we headed up east, and it wasn't long before we were on the canyon rim, lookin' back down at the village far below. We headed east across miles of treeless benchland Runnin' Wolf called Towanta Flat. Then we dropped down into another valley that looked to be miles wide and crossed what he called the Yellowstone River. We continued east, stayin' in the foothills of the mountains. Most of this country was dry benchland with sage and scattered brush. Along the streams that ran south out of the mountains, there were thick cottonwoods and heavy brush. There were berries of every kind with some even startin' to turn ripe. Within the next two or three weeks, we would be in berry-pickin' season again.

When we stopped just after midday, we were on the banks of another river Runnin' Wolf called the Uintah. While the horses drank and grazed for a while, the women walked along the river and brought back a couple of armfuls of wild onion, camas, and other roots. I had been keepin' a close eye on Sun Flower, but she seemed to be holdin' up just fine. This country was pretty easy travelin', and although we were movin' steady, we weren't pushin' real hard. Draggin' the lodge poles on a travois kept our speed down. But in this country, we would still cover fifty or sixty miles in a long day, and this time of the year, the days were long.

By early evenin', we came to a creek that Runnin' Wolf said Ely, Grub, and the other Ashley men called Ashley Creek, and we camped there for the night. The last twenty or so miles before we dropped into Ashley Creek had been mighty dry desert, but Runnin' Wolf said we would head northeast now over the mountain till we hit the Seeds-Kee-Dee then keep northeast till we were out on the buffalo range.

I sent Jimbo out on a wide circle just to make sure we were alone, and he came back with a jackrabbit in his mouth, so I knew all was clear. We had seen many prairie dogs and a few antelope across this desert area, and as the sun set, there were coyotes yippin' all around us. Sun Flower had held up well today, but this long day of travel had worn her out. She fell asleep sittin' by the fire, and I carried her to the bedroll, and she just smiled at me as I covered her up.

We started out the next mornin' and had traveled maybe two hours when I spotted some riders off to the east, and they were headed right for us. There was a rock outcroppin' 'bout a half mile ahead, and we headed there. Runnin' Wolf got on the rocks to watch while me and the women got a line on all the horses and tied them right tight. When I got up to Runnin' Wolf, he was standin' up and wavin' his hands at the riders, then he said, "They're Utes."

I was standin' next to Runnin' Wolf as they approached. There were six of them, and all but one stopped out 'bout a hundred yards. The one that kept comin' was comin' slow and careful. When he was 'bout fifty yards out, he shouted, and Runnin' Wolf answered back, tellin' him his name. Then he and the others came on in. He seemed leery of me and asked Runnin' Wolf, "Who is the white man?" He was lookin' right at my grizzly claw necklace, and when Runnin' Wolf said I was the one called Grizzly Killer, they all looked surprised. He said his name was Rabbit and they had been told Grizzly Killer was an enemy to the people.

I spoke then, and I really hoped I didn't make a mistake with the words. I told him I was a brother to Runnin' Wolf and a friend to all the people, that only those that tried to hurt me or my family and friends were my enemies. Rabbit then said they had heard I traveled with a killer dog that was bigger than a wolf. I whistled, and they all jumped when Jimbo came out of the brush behind them and came and stood 'tween me and Runnin' Wolf. I told him to sit, and he sat down on his haunches, and they all could see the grizzly claws on his collar.

Rabbit told us the Arapaho had hit their village and took four young women and killed many, that they were lookin' for a huntin' party of theirs that was in this area and were goin' after the Arapaho to get the girls back. He told us the Arapaho had turned north again, followin' the Seeds-Kee-Dee. He said they needed the huntin' party's six warriors. Runnin' Wolf told them of the Arapaho's attackin' his village, of the twelve we had killed, and of them killin' Spotted Horse and woundin' Weasel and Sun Flower. He told them we were travelin' with our women, or we would go and help them. Rabbit said he saw more riders with us, and at that, Runnin' Wolf called the women out. Raven Wing walked right up to Runnin' Wolf, and Shinin' Star and Sun Flower walked up, one on each side of me, and all six men just stared. Runnin' Wolf told them that Sun Flower was still healin' from her wound of battle and that she had killed the Arapaho that had shot her with an arrow, that we too were headed north to the buffalo grounds.

Rabbit told us it was an honor to meet us and wished us well. He warned us to be on the watch for the Arapahos, that there were still more than twenty of them. He said when they left their trail, they were on the east side of the river, goin' north, not east, to their lands. Runnin' Wolf told them of the five we had killed a month ago, saving the Snake boys, that he figured they were goin' back to see what had happened to them. Rabbit said they had lost over twenty warriors then for four girls and a few horses. "We will teach them to stay out of Utah lands."

They rode on, goin' northeast, while we got the horses ready for the trail. Runnin' Wolf said, "If they are east of the river, we will stay on the west until we get on the plains north of the mountains. It will take longer but will be safer."

We headed north and started the climb over the mountains, and our travel slowed with the steepness of the mountains. The land was covered with sage and just small patches of brush and quakies till we got up on top of these steep breaks. It was well into the afternoon, and the stock needed to rest. We found a small spring with good water and grass all along the edges and decided to make camp. It was early, but it had been a hard pull to get up here.

Runnin' Wolf and Raven Wing took their bows and left camp and, within an hour, were back to get a horse to carry in a deer they had shot. The women made a stew with the onions and roots they had picked along Ashley Creek, and fresh deer, then a pan full of biscuits, and we spent a right pleasant afternoon and evenin'.

It was two or three hours 'fore light when Jimbo started his low growl and the horses were gettin' mighty restless. I rolled out from under the robes and told the women to get their weapons and crawl into the trees away from camp. I signaled Jimbo to make a wide loop, and Me and Runnin' Wolf moved out into the night in opposite directions.

Chapter XXVI

The Rescue

THE MOON HAD SET, and the night was mighty dark. I could still hear the horses stompin' the ground and carryin' on. I had moved a couple of hundred yards out and was just waitin' low on the ground, listenin', when I heard movement right behind me. I spun and rolled, bringin' the muzzle of the Hawken up just as Jimbo jumped and tore into a large black bear. They were less than ten feet from me, but it was so dark I couldn't see to shoot without a chance of hittin' Jimbo. Jimbo was a two-hundred-pound mighty strong dog, but he was no match for a three- or four-hundred-pound bear. Jimbo backed off, and the bear must have forgotten 'bout me. He was more concerned with Jimbo, and Jimbo seemed to be leadin' him away from me.

Runnin' Wolf ran up by my side. We could hear Jimbo growlin' and tauntin' the bear, but we couldn't see a thing in the shadows and brush. Once the women could hear the fight and knew it was a bear stalkin' us and not an enemy, they built up the fire. We could hear Jimbo and that bear gettin' farther away, and after maybe ten minutes, we heard the bear runnin', with Jimbo barkin' right behind him. The bear must have figured this wasn't goin' to be the easy meal he was expectin'.

In just a bit, Jimbo came back. He was limpin' a little on his left front leg, and we walked back to camp and the light of the fire. It looked like that bear had swatted him a good one, and he had a couple of deep claw scratches on his upper leg. We stopped the bleedin' and wrapped his leg good and tight. None of us felt like sleepin' now, so we made a big pot of coffee and waited for it to get light.

We were packed and ready for the trail by the time it was light enough to see, and I had to wonder where that ol' bear had gone and if we would see him again. We headed north, and by midmornin', we came out on a point where we could see down into the canyon of the Seeds-Kee-Dee. It was a sight to behold. We must have been a mile above the river, lookin' almost straight down. The canyon sides were covered with cedar and pinion down low, turnin' to ponderosa pine up where we were. There were red rock outcroppin's all along both sides of the canyon, and the ground was a dark red in color. Even at this distance, you could see the white water of the river as it cascaded its way down this deep gorge.

We made good time travelin' most of the day. We stopped at midday to rest the horses and eat, and by midafternoon, we had crossed the mountaintop and were lookin' down off a rim into a valley with a creek runnin' from the west and into the river. The trail off this rim was steep and narrow, and the goin' was slow. Jimbo was not out in front anymore, and I could see he was favorin' that leg. It took a couple more hours to get down to the creek, and we decided this was a good place to camp.

Raven Wing made a poultice from moss and some other plants, and the women put it on Jimbo's cuts and rebandaged his leg. Runnin' Wolf went up the creek a ways and shot another young doe while I was carin' for the horses, and we gave Jimbo a whole front leg and shoulder to chew on all evenin'.

The next day we crossed Henry's Fork and was in country I knew again. We were only 'bout twenty or thirty miles from where that first rendezvous was held. We moved farther west off the river, three or four miles, and were movin' slow to keep the dust down. We crossed Smith's Fork and then followed it for many miles, stayin' west of the Seeds-Kee-Dee. We camped that night in a thick stand of cottonwoods just a little south of where Ham's Fork ran into Smith's Fork. We made sure the fire was down to just coals by nightfall so its light couldn't be seen in the dark.

The next day we continued north, stayin' well west of the Seeds-Kee-Dee. Jimbo was movin' a lot better today, and I took him, leavin' Runnin' Wolf with the women, and we headed northeast till we hit the river. Stayin' down in the draws and coulees, makin' myself as hard to see as I could, I looked the river bottom over real close as I moved along.

There was a wind comin' up from the south, and the clouds were buildin' over the Uintah Mountains earlier than usual this day. I came to a deep wash and followed it right down to the river and followed the river, stayin' right on the bank for maybe a half mile when I saw a well-used campsite under the cottonwoods on the far side. The river was wide and shallow here, and with the campsite lookin' deserted, I crossed to get a better look. There was still a small trail of smoke comin' off the coals of a fire, and as I carefully moved around the camp, there were four sets of smaller moccasin tracks, one with toes stickin' out and blood spots from the toes. The trail they left looked to be seven horses with three of 'em draggin' travois. I could see whoever had been makin' the small moccasin tracks were still on foot when they left. I figured this might well be the stolen Ute girls bein' taken along, with the wounded Arapahos movin' a lot slower than the main raidin' party. I followed their trail for a ways, and as slow as they were movin', I figured we could catch them in no time at all.

I turned around and set a good lope back to the river and on to get Runnin' Wolf. I wasn't much more than an hour catchin' up to them, and when I told them what I had found, there was no question we were goin' to see if we could get the Ute girls back. We hobbled all but four of the horses between two hills where they couldn't be seen very far off and followed my back trail to the river. Sun Flower's arm and shoulder weren't strong enough to hold and shoot the squirrel gun yet, and Shinin' Star didn't know how. I was upset with myself for not showin' her and made my mind up she would know how to shoot 'fore we got back to the dugout. The wind was steady and hard, with the clouds buildin' even heavier over the mountains.

When we got to where they had camped, Runnin' Wolf went over the tracks just as I had earlier, and he figured just like I had. We set a good fast lope, and by early afternoon, we found their horses droppin's were still warm. From then on, we would stop before we crested every hill and would crawl to the top and look through the brush. The fourth time we did that, we saw them just startin' up the next of these rollin' hills. We stayed two or three miles behind them the rest of the day, and they set up their camp by a water hole. We had been seein' antelope and lots of prairie chickens all day long. Runnin' Wolf pointed out some little black dots on a hill maybe three or four miles off, which he said were buffalo. We slowly moved a mile or so to the north of the trail in case they checked behind them when they stopped for the day and made a dry, cold camp. Ol' Red and the horses needed water, but they would have to wait. We picketed them to the ground solid so they couldn't wander, and at dusk, we moved out, leavin' Sun Flower to watch the stock. We went on foot so their horses wouldn't catch wind of ours. The wind was still blowin', and the clouds had moved over, so the night was mighty dark.

Shinin' Star had her knife, and I showed her many times without firin' it how to shoot the horse pistol, but I planned to keep her out of the way. But I wanted her along 'cause she might be needed for the girls. It was mighty dark when we approached their camp, but they had a good fire goin'. There was fresh antelope roastin' on the fire, and the three wounded men were still on the travois' placed around the fire. We were 'bout a hundred yards out and down in the brush, and I sent Jimbo way out around to the other side. I could see three of the girls and two of the warriors. Runnin' Wolf whispered the girls were Utes. I knew we could let none of these warriors escape, or they would bring the main group back to track and kill us all. We spread out and very slowly started to move into good bow range. I was only 'bout thirty yards from their fire when I heard a scream come from the bushes to my right and could hear the sounds of the fourth girl bein' raped. The two by the fire laughed, and then I heard Jimbo. His attack on the two in the bushes with that girl was vicious and swift. As the two by the fire jumped up, I fired, and one fell into the fire and didn't move. Runnin' Wolf's shot came a split second later, and the other one's left leg just flew out from under him. Jimbo was fightin' those in the bushes, and I jumped up and ran to the noise.

The light was mighty poor. The first warrior that I had shot fell in the fire and had smothered more than half of the flames. I had been lookin' right at the light of the fire. But as my eyes adjusted to the darkness out in the brush, I could see the girl on the ground froze with fear. One of the Arapahos was missin' half of his neck, and his upper body was covered with blood. Jimbo had the other's arm in his mouth, and it was broke bent at a right angle. I could see white bone stickin' out of Jimbo's mouth, and he was shakin' his head, growlin', movin' backward, and tryin' to rip the arm off. When I said "Stop," he let go, and the Injun moaned but never moved. I told Jimbo to stay and walked back to the fire. The smell of burnin' hair and flesh was strong, and Runnin' Wolf was draggin' the one in the fire out. I grabbed his other leg and told Shinin' Star and Raven Wing the girl in the brush needed them.

The other three girls were all huddled together, holdin' one another, and after we got that Arapaho out of the fire, Runnin' Wolf went to talk to them. Just then, I heard a terrible scream and headed back toward the bushes, when the young Ute girl, Shinin' Star, and Raven Wing came walkin' toward me. Shinin' Star walked up to the fire and threw a bloody mess into it. I saw then it was the complete manhood of the warrior that was still alive. Raven Wing pulled back her bow and put an arrow into each of the wounded men while Shinin' Star cut the manhood off the other one that was still alive. He had lost so much blood from his leg wound I was not sure he even knew what she did. Then she held it up for the girls to see and said see they were men no more and would travel in the world beyond as not men. Runnin' Wolf took all their scalps while I got their horses.

The one that was bein' raped when Jimbo attacked was not able to talk. She was scared and tremblin' all over. I picked her up and held her and just whispered to her and rocked her back and forth. She didn't look to be more than twelve years old, and in a few minutes, I could feel her body start to relax a little. I put her on a horse and got on behind her where I could continue holdin' her, and that left a horse apiece for the six others to ride. We took our time and walked the horses back to where we left Sun Flower and our stock.

Not knowin' how far away the rest of the Arapaho raiding party was and the stock needin' water, we mounted up and rode through the night back to the Seeds-Kee-Dee. We got in the river and went upstream for a couple of miles to hide our tracks just as it was gettin' light. We made camp on the west side, in a thick stand of cottonwoods and willows. Anyone comin' up on us would have to be mighty close to see us. This young girl with me, whom the others called Little Mouse, had fallen asleep off and on durin' the night, and when I got off Ol' Red, she just fell into my arms. I laid her down in the grass, and Sun Flower and Raven Wing came right over to care for her. They took her down to the river and bathed her, and when they came back, she lay right down and was asleep in minutes. Shinin' Star was with the others, two of which were cryin' from the relief of bein' with friends. I had everyone rest for a couple of hours while me and Jimbo watched, and then Runnin' Wolf took watch while I lay down for a while.

'Bout four hours later, we moved out again and, in not more than a couple of hours, were back with the rest of our horses. We had a good-sized herd now, and I wasn't sure we should keep this many. The clouds were lowerin', and it looked like rain, but so far, I hadn't felt a drop.

Well, this was a fix we were in. We had to figure what to do next. We were right on the edge of the buffalo country, and we had seen a few yesterday, so do we take these girls huntin' with us, or do we lose another week or two takin' them back? Runnin' Wolf said the Arapaho would send warriors back when the ones we killed didn't return, and with the arrows, they would know it was Utes who killed them. They would be lookin' for them to the south. He figured we should do our huntin' farther north and then go back to the dugout and then take the girls back. Shinin' Star told the girls that and why as Runnin' Wolf was speakin' English. One started to cry again, but they all nodded that they understood.

Sun Flower asked if we could just go a little way back to the river today. She said sitting on the horse any more would be hard on Little Mouse. We moved out at a slow walk, headin' northeast, and hit the river in 'bout three hours. It was late afternoon, and we all needed rest and food. Runnin' Wolf started hobblin' the horses, and Ol' Red, Jimbo, and me headed up the river to look around. I could plainly see the Wind River Mountains and knew we were gettin' closer to the home of Sun Flower and Raven Wing. I jumped a few deer from the brush along the river and shot a little buck that was too curious for his own good and headed back to camp. The girls had a big stack of very dry firewood gathered, and they had an almost smokeless fire goin' when I got back. When Sun Flower got out the pot and pan, it was plain these girls had never seen metal pots or pans before. There were still wild onions and roots left from our camp on Ashley Creek, and they all went right to work peelin' them and puttin' them in the pot, and then they started on that deer. It wasn't long 'fore that deer was skinned and pieces were cut up and in the pot.

Jimbo had scared Little Mouse so bad when he attacked the men on her. She was still real jumpy 'round him. Sun Flower was the youngest of us at eighteen, and Little Mouse was stayin' by her like a shadow. The deer hide was staked out, and the young girls went right to work scrapin' it with stones. Raven Wing brought the rib bone I had made with a knife lashed to it over and showed them how to use it, and they were amazed at how much easier it was.

Sun Flower sat Little Mouse down and called Jimbo, and as he approached, she tensed up. He lay down and put his head by her feet. Then Sun Flower told her he was her friend, that he saved her, and he would protect her, not hurt her. Little Mouse looked at me, and I nodded. She then very slowly reached out and patted his head. He wagged his tail and inched a little closer, and she smiled for the first time since we found them.

These four girls ate like they had been starved for days. They had never seen a biscuit or tasted coffee before, and Sun Flower put enough sugar in the coffee for them to think it was quite a treat. These girls had nothin' at all. I didn't want to put up the teepee in case we needed to make a fast escape, so we just got the bedrolls and robes out, and all slept close to one another. It rained lightly durin' the night for a little while, but we stayed warm and dry.

The next day we crossed the river and headed east. The clouds were still low and threatenin', but the wind had died right off. We traveled maybe twenty-five miles by early afternoon and came up over a rise and looked out over a wide, shallow valley with maybe a thousand or more of those shaggy big beasts in it. Some were lyin' down, and some were up grazin'. We stopped and backed right off. Just a couple of miles back, we had crossed a small creek that had good grass and a few cottonwoods all along it, so we went back to it, and while the women and girls set up camp, me, Jimbo, and

Runnin' Wolf went scoutin', makin' sure we were in a safe spot. I rode upstream, and Runnin' Wolf rode down, while Jimbo made a big wide circle.

A couple of hours later, we were all back, and neither me nor Runnin' Wolf had seen anything but buffalo tracks. We spent a relaxin' afternoon makin' plans for the hunt and decided to circle way out around them come mornin' and see just what was on the far side. I hoped we could find pockets with just a few buffalo we could take without stampedin' the whole herd.

Real early the next day, me and Runnin' Wolf left, with Jimbo stayin' to watch camp. He wasn't happy 'bout stayin' behind, but he did stay. We rode south what I figured was 'bout three miles and then east. Each time we came to a rise, we approached on hands and knees. We came up on a dozen or so young bulls that were out of sight of any others and dropped two of them. After guttin' them, we moved on, and by noon we had six down.

I had Runnin' Wolf hightail it back to camp while I started the skinnin', and within a couple of hours, he was back with the women, the girls, and a dozen extra horses. Skinnin' those big beasts was a lot of work. I used Ol' Red and a rope to pull most of the hides off, but it was still a lot of hard work. I was amazed at how these four girls, all twelve and thirteen years old, worked. They laughed and played while workin', and it made the chore downright pleasant. They were all eatin' pieces of raw liver, and Sun Flower cut open the gall bladder of one and dipped a piece of liver in it and put it up to my lips. I shook my head, but she kept on till I tried it. I was amazed it was pretty good.

The sun was just settin' when we got back to camp. It was still mostly cloudy, but the sun was comin' through a few holes in the clouds by the western horizon, and the colors of that sunset reminded me of a paintin' me and Pa had seen over a bar in St. Louis. The women had spent the mornin' makin' dryin' racks and gatherin' firewood, so we all went right to work puttin' the meat on the racks and gettin' the dryin' fires started, then we put hump ribs on sticks, roastin' over the cook fire. Next mornin' we ate slices of boiled tongue before me and Runnin' Wolf went out again.

We spent the next week with each day much the same. That next day we had five down by midday, and I went back after the women and horses. They had all six hides stretched out and staked and were gettin' them scraped when I got there, and we threw more wood on the dryin' fires and headed back to Runnin' Wolf.

By the end of the seventh day, we had twenty-six buffalo down, and I figured that was more meat than we could carry. Once you dry the meat, it loses most of its weight, but it still takes up a mighty lot of room.

We had hunted around the edges and never did scare the main herd off. We stayed there at that camp for another week, workin' those hides and makin' rough packs to carry all that dried meat. We ate liver and heart and tongue and hump ribs every day, and Little Mouse had become just as playful as the others by now. We gave each of the girls a buffalo robe that was brain-tanned right soft by the time we left that camp. Many of the hides would still have to be worked more when we got to the dugout, but we had a great start gettin' ready for winter.

We had a mighty big pack string when we got loaded up and headed southwest back toward the Seeds-Kee-Dee. I figured travelin' slow like we were we would be 'bout four days gettin' to the dugout. Some of these Injun horses had never carried packs before, and we had some trouble when the packs would shift. It took us all day to get to the river.

When we got to the river breaks, we approached mighty slowly. There was a breeze blowin' from the south, not hard, just a subtle little thing, but I thought I caught the smell of woodsmoke just as we got to the first break. We turned back north and traveled another three miles or so before we stopped, and then we made a cold camp in a wash back off the river a ways. It wasn't the nicest camp, but I figured it was the safest.

I didn't feel safe leavin' the women alone, so leavin' Runnin' Wolf with them, me and Jimbo went on a scout. We crossed the river and headed south on the far side with the breeze right in our faces.

I got above the breaks on that west side, and when me and Jimbo were maybe four miles south, I was gettin' the smell of smoke again. I moved farther out off the edge of the break and moved south another mile then got off Red and left him there in the brush. Me and Jimbo moved mighty slow and quiet as we approached the break and could see down into the river bottoms. Just a little farther south, there was an Injun camp. I counted fourteen warriors and no women, so this was a raidin' party. They were too far away for me to tell what tribe they were from, and I wished Runnin' Wolf was here. He was much better than me at tellin' the different tribes.

I knew I was takin' a risk, but I needed to get closer to tell if it was the Arapahos lookin' for their dead or for us or if it was the Utes lookin' for the girls. I figured if it were the Arapahos, they had never seen Jimbo, but the Utes would remember him. So I decided to send Jimbo out into the open where they would see him. But before I did that, I went and got Red. If I needed to run, I wanted him right close by.

Well, Jimbo just trotted right down there like he didn't have a worry at all. He was 'bout a hundred yards from them when they saw him, and a couple of them grabbed their weapons. Then one of them shouted, and the others lowered their bows, and then one of them stepped out and started to walk toward Jimbo. I could now tell it was Rabbit, the Ute we had met on the trail, lookin' for the girls.

I stood up and mounted Red then started down off the top of this break, and when I hit the flood plain, I loped right up to Jimbo and raised my arm in the peace sign, and Rabbit did the same. We talked as the others walked up and joined us, and Rabbit told them all who I was. I told them all four girls were safe and bein' cared for by my and Runnin' Wolf's wives. I told them they were a little ways from here, but we were afraid the main body of Arapaho might come lookin' for the ones we killed. Rabbit and several others held up their weapons, and I could see many scalps tied to them. Rabbit said he thought they would send no more.

Rabbit called out to some of the warriors, and as they came up, he said, "These men are the girls' fathers. Redfoot is the father of Little Mouse, Hawk is the father of Laughing Eyes, Eagle Claw is the father of Morning Dew, and Three Bears is Little Bird's father."

I held out my hand and told them they all had mighty strong and brave young daughters, and they should be proud of them. Then I said, "Let's go get them."

Their camp was loaded in less than ten minutes, and we struck a fast lope right up the flood plain of the river.

I whistled real loud as we approached the wash, and Runnin' Wolf stepped out. In just a minute, the girls came runnin' out of the wash, and their fathers were down and runnin' toward them. It was quite a gatherin'. Little Mouse, draggin' her father by his arm, came over to me. She was tellin' him of me and the dog savin' her, that I was the strongest warrior in the world and Jimbo had the most powerful medicine of any animal that ever lived.

We moved our camp out of the wash and down by the river under the cottonwoods. We gave the girls each a horse, and we gave one pack horse loaded with dried buffalo meat to the four of them, and they each had a new tanned Buffalo robe. Rabbit and Redfoot came over to protest we were givin' too much, that we had already saved their lives, and I simply said we hadn't given them anything they did not earn, that they all worked very hard on the buffalo hunt, and it was only right they received the rewards.

We stayed there and ate buffalo and celebrated the rest of the day and into the night. While we were loadin' up the next mornin', the four girls, their fathers, and Rabbit came over to say their good-byes. The girls were huggin' Sun Flower, Raven Wing, and Shinin' Star while we said our farewells to the men.

Runnin' Wolf told where we would be spendin' the winter and told them, if they got to our side of the mountains, to stop and visit. They would always be welcome. Rabbit came forward and looked me right in the eye. He said, "I never met a white man before, and I had heard bad things about them. I did not know when we first met that what Running Wolf said was true. I know now that everything he said is true and more." He told me I would be a friend forever and if I ever needed help, to call on him.

Just as we were ready to mount up and leave, the four girls ran over and hugged us all again. Little Mouse hung on to me long and hard, and she had tears in her eyes as we left.

Chapter XXVII

Going Home

WE HEADED SOUTHWEST from the Seeds-Kee-Dee and continued on till we hit the place where Ham's Fork ran into Black's Fork. We had made a little better time today. The horses were startin' to get used to the packs and weren't fightin' them near as much. We might even have a good pack train by the time we reach the dugout. We camped in a stand of cottonwoods on a bend in Smith's Fork, just a ways above Ham's Fork. It was a much calmer and quieter camp without the young teenage girls, and I thought we all sort of missed them.

The currents and buffalo berries were ripe along the river, and the women spent the evenin' pickin' berries. I figured we would make it to Black's Fork 'fore the end of the day tomorrow, and it felt like I was goin' home. I figured it must be the end of August by now, and then we would be set for the fall trappin' season. Once we had the packs stripped off the horses, we went through checkin' their hooves and hobblin' them for the night, and when the women came back, they had cattail shoots and camas bulbs and onions and got a stew started. We had used the last of the flour several days ago with all the extra mouths we had been feedin', but we were still eatin' mighty well and were only two or three days from the dugout.

After we ate, Sun Flower and Shinin' Star each took my hands, and we walked down along the river. We came to a bend where the water was calm, and Sun Flower looked right at me and told me I stink. I needed to bathe. The two of them started to undress me, and then they pulled off their dresses and pulled me into that cold water.

I must admit, it had been over three weeks since I had a bath, and I knew it was needed, and bein' with these two was enough to warm that cold water right up. As we washed each other, it made me wonder why the white people weren't as free 'bout life as the Injuns were. They enjoyed sex, and it didn't matter to them who knew it. It was just as natural to them as any other part of their lives. Most of the people back home would think what I was doin' here was terribly wrong. It sure didn't feel wrong, and I was beginnin' to figure the Injuns had a better way of life.

I got my buckskins to put on, and Shinin' Star grabbed them and set them in the river. I now didn't even have a blanket to throw around me. She just started to scrub them with sand, and when I asked her what I was supposed to wear now, she just smiled and pointed at Sun Flower. I turned, and Sun Flower was standin' there, holdin' a brand-new set of buckskins. Shinin' Star came out of the water, and they both helped me into them. They were just as soft as could be and made out of elk skin brain-tanned and worked to a softness I had never felt before. I didn't know what to say. This was the best set I had ever had, and the smile on these two women's faces, well, I just held them both then realized they were still naked. Shinin' Star walked back into the water and finished scrubbin' them old greasy buckskins while Sun Flower finished washin' her hair. Then they both walked back to camp, dryin' in the air before they put their dresses back on.

Back in camp, Runnin' Wolf and Raven Wing were already there, and Runnin' Wolf was wearin' a new set of buckskins as well. He just smiled when he saw me and said, "Looks like they had all been busy."

It was cloudin' up the next mornin' as we headed out, and by the time we reached Black's Fork, it had started to rain. Even a summer rain out here in the Rocky Mountains gets mighty cold, and by the time we stopped, we were all 'bout frozen. While me and Runnin' Wolf took care of the stock, the women put up the teepee and got a fire goin' inside, and we all had to hang our clothes high in the teepee to get them to dry.

Next mornin' everything was mighty wet, but the sky was clearin', and it looked like the sun would be out in another hour or two. We let the packs and teepee dry out for a while 'fore we started to load, and by the time we were on the trail, there was still a cold bite to the air, but it was turnin' into a right nice day.

We made pretty good time as we traveled the now very familiar country of Black's Fork, and by late afternoon, we had come off the sage flats and into the grassy meadow country. When we stopped for the day, I figured we would be home by midday tomorrow. There were ripe berries all along the stream now, and we all spent the evenin' pickin' them. Shinin' Star said we would need another bear or two for the grease, but I didn't think that would be hard to get. We slept out under the stars that night, and it was gettin' right chilly by mornin'. These two women, one on each side of me, sure felt good.

By late mornin' the next day, we could see the hill where we had buried Sees Far, and it was just a few minutes later, we rode into the yard of the dugout. Jimbo was runnin' all over the place, markin' his territory all over again, and even Ol' Red let out a bray that told the whole world he was back. We stripped the packs off all the horses and turned most of the horses loose out in the meadow. The grass was dry, but it was up past their knees. We put the saddle horses in the corral in case we needed them in a hurry and then went to work storin' all our supplies.

The smokehouse wasn't big enough to handle all the dried buffalo we had brought back, so a lot of it went in the dugout. We had saved what looked like miles of buffalo intestines for casings for the pemmican the women planned on makin'. All this and the dried meat all had to be hung up off the ground. The dugout still had a bad musky smell, and I started a fire in the fireplace and blocked the door wide open to help with the smell. I walked to both caches, and neither had been touched. When I came back down from the hill, the teepee was up, and a fire was goin' in the outside fire pit.

That big cookin' pot had become a major part of makin' our meals, and I wished I got another of them at Rendezvous. But right now, I could a smell a stew cookin', and Sun Flower was showin' Shinin' Star how to make the biscuits.

The next mornin' me and Runnin' Wolf went out with the axes and found a couple of dozen new lodge poles and cut them down, limbed each one, and tied them on the horses to drag back to camp. When we got there, the women had several buffalo hides laid out, fittin' them together, makin' a new lodge skin. Me and Runnin' Wolf tied three of the new poles together at the top and stood up the main triangle. Raven Wing came over and enlarged it and said, "This will be a big lodge, so Grizzly Killer won't need to stoop over in it."

It took all of that day and most of the next with all three women sewin' those hides together, and when they got done, they had used fourteen full hides. They made a dye out of charcoal and berry juice, and Shinin' Star spent another two days paintin' a beautiful big grizzly on the side of this new teepee and a wolf on the side of the older one.

There was a spot on the ridge just above the dugout that you could see the dugout, the meadow, and the stream lined with willows, and just as the sun was settin', I walked up there. I just stood there and looked over this spot and remembered last year when me and Pa had first found it, how Pa had said it would make a great place to spend the winter. I thought 'bout all we had done together gettin' ready for winter and then of how it all changed that day, trappin' up on the creek I now thought of as Grizzly Creek when that ol' grizzly had killed Pa. I thought of gettin' ready for winter then by myself and the awful alone and helpless feelin' when I'd lost the mules and horses to the Shoshones and the feelin' of salvation when I heard Ol' Red bray and saw him comin' back across the stream home. I remembered findin' Jimbo in that abandoned Shoshone camp and how his company had made the long, hard winter so much easier.

I looked at Sun Flower and Shinin' Star there by the fire and Runnin' Wolf and Raven Wing still unloadin' packs and storin' the different items. I thought of all that had happened in the time since me and Pa had left home, with all the fights and the killin', with Pa bein' buried here in these mountains. I had also found love, love of this wild, rugged, and yet wonderful land, love of two beautiful women, and the love of good friends.

I sat down there in this little spot, just watchin' the settin' sun turn the sky into the most colorful picture you could imagine, from deep purples to the most brilliant reds, yellows, oranges, and every color in between. I lay back and closed my eyes with the thoughts of the last year still goin' through my mind. Jimbo was lyin' right there by my side, and I felt like I was home and safe. Just then I heard a noise behind me and sat up to look just as a huge grizzly came out of the trees only a few yards from me. As I turned around to bring my rifle to bear, the grizzly stood up on his hind legs, and right before my eyes, he changed into my pa. I staggered back and tripped over Jimbo, who hadn't moved or made a sound. Pa chuckled and said, "Easy boy," and he walked up to me, and we hugged. We sat and talked 'bout the last year, and he told me how proud he and Ma were of me. He told me to take care of my family, that I had much to accomplish in this life and I couldn't do it alone, that I had made both good friends and powerful enemies. He told me I had learned well the lessons of the wilderness, but he had neglected to teach me of the treachery of men. He stood and said he had to get back to Ma and started to walk away. Just before he entered the trees from which he had come, he turned and looked at me and then down toward the dugout and said, “Beware of the one on the spotted horse.” Just as I was askin’ what he meant, he stepped behind the pine and was gone.

I felt Jimbo’s nose and tongue on my cheek and opened my eyes. I looked around and realized I had been dreamin’, but never before had a dream seemed so real. The light was just ’bout gone now. I was lookin’ at the pine the grizzly had come from and where Pa had disappeared. I got up and walked over to that tree, and in the soft ground around the tree were fresh tracks of a huge grizzly. A chill shot down my back, and I thought of the wolf tracks from when Runnin’ Wolf was hurt.

As I walked back down the hill to Sun Flower and Shinin’ Star, I felt a warm feelin’ and somehow I knew deep down in my heart that Pa was still watchin’ over me. I didn’t know what he meant by his warnin’, but I knew I would be watchin’ for anyone ridin’ a spotted horse.

THE END

A look at the next book in the series,

Grizzly Killer: Under The Blood Moon

The second book in the action-packed, best-selling Grizzly Killer series.

In 1828 few white men had seen the Rocky Mountains, those that had were the rugged few we call Mountain Men.

Zach Connors was one of the best, known to the Indians as Grizzly Killer. He was both feared and respected throughout the Rocky's. Along with his dog Jimbo, Running Wolf his Ute partner and their wives they travel to Rendezvous, where they battle the dreaded Blackfeet and Zach fights for both justice and honor.

After, they come face to face with a man eating grizzly, and confront those seeking revenge for the justice he dealt. All the while living their lives among the towering peaks in the wild and unforgiving wilderness of the spectacular Rocky Mountains.

Available from Wolfpack Publishing and Lane R Warenski

About the Author

Lane R Warenski lives in a log home in Duchesne County, Utah, where he has an unrestricted view of the highest peaks in the mighty Uinta Mountains. He was raised being proud of his pioneer heritage and with a deep love and respect of the outdoors. Ever since childhood, following his father, Warenski has hunted, fished, and camped the mountains of the West. Whether it was the daily journals of William Ashley and Jedediah Smith or the fictional stories written by the great storytellers like Louis L'Amour and Terry C. Johnston, throughout his life, Warenski loves reading the history of the first explorers that came west, most of whom never dreamed they were opening this wild and rugged land to the pioneers and settlers that followed.

Find more great titles by Lane R Warenski and Wolfpack Publishing at www.wolfpackpublishing.com/lanerwarenski/

Made in the USA
Coppell, TX
30 June 2020

29640038R00148